The Last Wish of Sasha Cade

The Last Wish of Sasha Cade

Cheyanne Young

Kids Can Press gratefully acknowledges the financial support of the Government
of Ontario, through the Ontario Media Development Corporation.

Published in Canada and the U.S. by Kids Can Press Ltd.
25 Dockside Drive, Toronto, ON M5A 0B5

Kids Can Press is a Corus Entertainment Inc. company

www.kidscanpress.com
www.kcploft.com

The text is set in Minion Pro and Red Velvet.

Edited by Kate Egan
Designed by Emma Dolan
Jacket photos courtesy of elenaleonova/iStock

Printed and bound in Altona, Manitoba, Canada in 6/2018 by Friesens Corp.

CM 18 0 9 8 7 6 5 4 3 2 1
CM PA 18 0 9 8 7 6 5 4 3 2 1

Library and Archives Canada Cataloguing in Publication

Young, Cheyanne, author
    The last wish of Sasha Cade / Cheyanne Young.

ISBN 978-1-5253-0004-2 (hardcover)
ISBN 978-1-5253-0140-7 (softcover)

    I. Title.

PS3625.O9455L37 2018   813'.6   C2017-907279-X

FSC
www.fsc.org
MIX
Paper from
responsible sources
FSC® C016245

For Hallee, my angel.
For Chris, my hero.
And for Nova, who is a very good dog.

Prologue

The cancer would take its time killing Sasha Cade. I think we all knew that, in the beginning. Her lymphoma wouldn't be like what happens to someone's random uncle, where he finds a weird lump in his throat and it's diagnosed as stage four, and bam, a month later he's pushing up daisies. "If we'd only caught it sooner," everyone would say.

Sasha and I knew it wouldn't be like that.

Her cancer would take a slow journey, inflaming her lymph nodes one by one until she could connect the painful dots all over her body like tourist stops on a road map to death. The treatment would cost thousands — tens of thousands — draining Sasha's adoptive parents' savings account. Luckily, they could afford it.

It was clear from the moment Sasha returned from that fateful doctor visit that cancer was the villain in my best friend's tragic life story. As we sat on the brick retaining wall in front of her house a week after the news, Sasha told me not to think of it like that. She didn't want the cancer to be the bad guy here. She didn't want to give it credit for anything, much less ruining her life, because she was still alive and she still had things to accomplish.

That morning, in Mrs. Rakowski's English class, we'd all had to recite our villain narratives. The assignment was meant to challenge our creative thinking. We had to take a known villain, something or someone the general population hated, and write five hundred words from their perspective, convincing the audience that they weren't actually villains at all. Mrs. Rakowski wanted us to make our villains relatable, maybe even characters worthy of pity.

I had chosen Gaston from *Beauty and the Beast*. My fingers shook as I read my narrative aloud in front of the classroom. Gaston was just a hardworking man in want of a loving, intelligent wife. There were too many airheaded floozies in town fawning over him, but he wanted a woman with a brain. A woman like Belle. Was that so wrong of him, to crave someone as delightful as she? Was he *really* so bad?

Sasha winked at me, her surreal blue eyes sparkling with pride as I walked back to my desk, which was right behind hers.

"Told you you'd rock it," she whispered as I slid back into my seat. "You're so much stronger than you think you are."

Sasha had been the first to read her narrative, on pageant moms. The spotlight didn't bother her — she didn't exactly revel in it, but she wasn't bothered. As someone who was pretty much universally loved in school, she was used to people noticing her.

Matt Phillips took small strides to the front of the class. He looked even more nervous than I had felt, his eyes carefully avoiding the middle of the room where Sasha and I sat.

"Cancer, by Matt Phillips," he said, swallowing and then glancing briefly toward Sasha. Her shoulders lifted.

Matt was in a constant battle for valedictorian with Celeste Cho, so it goes without saying that his narrative was incredibly well written. He spoke in first person, as cancer.

Cancer simply wanted to grow and flourish, planting its children as cells and tumors so they could spread and have a happy family. It was just like any other living thing — it *wanted* to live. Just as humans take oxygen and fresh water, just as they eat the flesh of animals to survive, so did the cancer need flesh to thrive. Human flesh.

It didn't mean any harm when it took over a human body, eventually strangling the body's ability to live. In fact, it was sorry it had to come to this.

After all, cancer just wanted to feel the thrill of living, just like we all do.

The class was deadly silent during his reading — even the students busy on their phones had shifted their attention toward him. When he was finished and everybody in the room had chills from head to toe, he looked directly at Sasha, his shoulders slumped, his teeth digging into his bottom lip.

"I'm sorry," he choked out, one hand scratching his neck so hard it might bleed. "I wrote it before … well, you know. Before we knew."

Sasha just smiled, her features as soft and beautiful as before she learned about her sickness. She thanked him for his insightful new perspective on cancer, said she could understand why the disease would choose the fertile cells of her body as the home in which to raise its malignant children.

She just wished the lymphoma had asked her permission first.

Chapter One

Last night had been a good night, one of the best Sasha has had in weeks. Her body is still frail, her cheeks sunken in and her eyes rimmed with dark circles under a nearly bald head, but she'd had a ton of energy. Even though it was a school night (for me, at least), Sasha had declared it Best Friends Movie Night.

The thing about having a best friend dying of cancer? Your parents let you do almost anything you want, including spending days at a time away from home and letting your grades slip from A's to C's. I wouldn't exactly call it a benefit, though. My best friend has to be dying to get these privileges.

We'd spent the night in the Cades' home library, which has become Sasha's temporary bedroom ever since the cancer weakened her body too much for her to walk up stairs. In the corner of the room, on top of the built-in desk, the television plays the DVD menu screen from *Sixteen Candles* on a loop. We must have fallen asleep watching it.

I sit up on the brown leather couch, my body aching to go back to sleep, but Sasha's phone alarm is blaring throughout the small, book-filled room.

"I want to tell Daddy bye before he goes to work," she'd said last night, setting her alarm for six thirty. Her voice was frail and barely more than a gasp of air. "One of these mornings will be my last, and I don't want to miss the chance to see him."

I think my stomach knows before I do. An uneasiness swells up inside of me as I yawn, get up and reach over Sasha's hospital bed to grab her phone. Silencing her alarm, I notice the three dozen text messages that filtered in overnight. There are 124 students at Peyton Colony High School, and every single one of them considers Sasha a friend. But I am her only *best* friend. We are attached at the hip. Left to my own devices, I would probably be more of a loner, spending my time with only Sasha. But she's got a personality that attracts everyone, and because of that, we are often invited to parties, school dances and the popular lunch table.

There has been more than one rumor that we might be lesbians. We ignore them. I have a boyfriend, after all, and Sasha would be way out of my league.

When Sasha's cancer diagnosis hit the school, devastation rocked the entire senior class. Sasha had always been well liked, but after that, she was like royalty. Everyone wanted to sit with us at lunch and take pictures with Sasha as if they were old pals just standing near the lockers between classes. It didn't matter what menial thing was going on, all of her new best friends wanted to document it on Instagram. While I rolled my eyes and wondered where these girls had been the time Sasha broke her leg and I had to carry her books from class to class, Sasha just smiled and treated everyone with kindness.

Once all the chemo and radiation were over and her diagnosis became the big T — *terminal* — all of her newfound friends became just as attached as the freaking tumors. A few weeks ago, when she quit school altogether, she was no doubt the most popular girl in our tiny Texas town. I was happy just hanging out in her shadow, although some of the tragic fame trickled onto me, too. I was the best friend, after all, and everyone wants to know the dying girl.

Now I am in my pajamas, staring her in the face.

And I know it. I just *know.*

I don't need to check for a pulse, or watch her faded Zombie Radio T-shirt to see if it moves with the rise and fall of someone alive and breathing. There is something in her face that tells me. She looks peaceful, at rest.

Dead.

I stand there for a long moment, Sasha's phone in my hand, my feet cold on the wooden floor. I even think about going back to sleep, like that time I saw Dad putting Santa's presents under the tree, forever shattering the illusion that magic was real. Pretend it never happened and maybe it never did.

"Sasha," I whisper, then bite down hard on my lip. A desperate act in futility. *Wake up.*

I even hold my breath in anticipation, stupid as it is.

At the foot of her bed, Sasha's golden lab, Sunny, is also awake. His head rests on top of her foot, and his eyes slide over to mine, holding my gaze for the longest moment. Dogs are intuitive. He's known longer than I have. Probably from the second it happened. He'd fallen asleep on the floor because Sasha was in too much pain to cuddle with him last night, but now he's up here on her bed.

I sit on the edge of her bed and touch her hand with my shaking fingers. It is cold as ice — no, colder. The lump in my throat sinks to my stomach and scorching hot tears of anger flood to my eyes. The back of my throat burns acidic, and — though my heart pounds — I swear I can't breathe.

We all knew this was coming. For months now we've known the lymphoma would kill her. Sasha and I had planned her funeral down to the minute. The six hottest guys in school are her pallbearers and her white, glittery casket is already custom ordered and in stock at Hayes Funeral Home. I've written a beautiful eulogy that references not one but three of our favorite movies. We have known the outcome of this journey for months and knew it would happen soon.

So why do I feel so blindsided?

I pull my feet up on the bed and curl into myself, my hand still on top of Sasha's frigid, lifeless flesh. Sunny lifts up and makes his way across the blankets, settling himself between his human and me. I rest my head on top of his fur and close my eyes. It hurts so bad, so much and for so long.

Movement in the hallway startles me out of my nearly catatonic state. I glance at the phone in my hand to see that only eleven minutes have passed since I woke up on the worst day of my life.

"Mrs. Cade?" That's really all I have to say. There is no misinterpreting the tone of my voice.

The shuffling of her house shoes stops, starts and then stops again. "Raquel?"

All she says is my name, but I know she knows. The world suddenly feels so small. We are two people who loved this dead girl, and at this moment, we are the only two people on earth with this pain.

Mrs. Cade calls for her husband, and I hear her sobs before

they walk into the library. Sunny rests his head on top of Sasha's chest. I hold on to Sasha's hand, somehow still seeking comfort from my best friend. I can't face her parents alone. I don't want to see their faces when they learn for certain what I already know to be true.

Sasha Cade has died, and no matter how much we prepared for it, the pain might kill us, too.

Chapter Two

It was a couple weeks ago, on one of Sasha's bad days. Her parents had just moved in the hospital bed so that she could live out her remaining days at home with family and not in some sterile, chemical-smelling hospital with pitying nurses and doctors who all have frown lines on their upper lips from delivering bad news all day long.

I was eating a bag of pizza-flavored Combos and had just sucked all the filling out of one of them. That memory seems trivial at first, but after I recall it, every little detail comes back almost like it just happened. I can practically feel the empty pizza Combo in my fingers, Sunny sitting at my feet, eagerly hoping I'll drop some on the floor.

Sasha grimaced at my snacking choice. Food was her enemy now that she felt sick all the time and only occasionally sipped on chocolate milk. "I wonder what they'll do with my dead body," she said, looking at the sparkles in her nail polish.

"What?" I nearly choked on my pretzel shell. "They'll bury it, Sash. We've kind of spent the last few weeks planning the whole ordeal."

She shook her head. "No, not that. Like, when Mom and Dad walk in and find me dead in here, surrounded by all these old law books and stuff —" She motioned toward the dark wood bookshelves of Mr. Cade's library. "What happens to my body? Do they just pick it up and dump it in a bag or something?"

No longer hungry, I crumpled up the Combos and gave her a look. "You're really morbid."

She shrugged and tugged the blanket up to her shoulders, the fabric outlining the thin contours of her body. Before, she was curvy and dark skinned and beautiful. Now she was, well, dying.

"Your parents will call 9-1-1, probably," I said, looking toward the high ceiling as I considered it. I'd never found anyone dead before, so it wasn't like I had prior experience. "The paramedics will come and they'll put you on a stretcher and roll you into the ambulance. Then I guess you'll go to the morgue, or something."

"And then you'll get started on making my funeral awesome," she said, her chapped lips stretching into a grin. Her bony finger pointed at me. "Don't let Mom talk you into roses or carnations or some shit, okay? I want wildflowers and sunflowers. Lots of 'em."

"I got you," I said, glancing over at the binder on the nearby table. It had all of our funeral plans laid out with sticky notes and color-coded instructions. Sasha had even written her own obituary for the newspaper, but I hadn't seen it yet. I stiffened my shoulders and pointed my nose up. "I'll say, 'Mrs. Cade, I know your daughter is dead but I'm in charge here. No fucking roses!'"

Sasha choked out a laugh. "See? You're morbid, too."

Now that Sasha is dead and we did wake up to find her

body, I'm not sure if the 9-1-1, call-an-ambulance thing actually happened in that order. I don't know how they plan to move her body.

I don't stick around long enough to find out.

* * *

When I pull into my driveway, it's almost as if everything is normal. I sit in my car, staring at the white bricks of our old ranch-style house, a world apart from the lakefront mansions in Sasha's neighborhood. My hands shake on the steering wheel. Mom's Corolla sits next to my car, meaning she hasn't left for work yet. Dad is gone, like always. Truckers have weird schedules and I never know when I'll see his semi parked on the gravel driveway off to the side of our garage.

If I sit here long enough, the engine idling, radio DJs rambling their morning show routine, I can almost pretend this is any other morning. I'm sitting here because I'm about to back out of the driveway and head to school. I'm just Raquel Clearwater, a senior at Peyton Colony High, and it's the middle of August on a typical Monday.

I blink, and the vision fades away. My heart breaks through that momentary absence of emotion, and I am raw again. I don't know what I expected to happen the day Sasha died. I guess I knew there would be tears, but part of me thought maybe I'd be a little optimistic about it all. Death would mean she wasn't suffering anymore. She could be at peace. I guess I thought it wouldn't hurt this bad.

I cut the engine and grip my keys so hard they dig painfully into my palms. The sun is rising and the school bus screeches to a stop in the distance. People are heading off to work and the planet is spinning just like it always does. Funny how your soul can be ripped in half and yet the world still looks exactly the same.

The front door opens before I get to it, and Mom steps out in a navy pencil skirt and a white blouse that's not very good at hiding the stomach pudge she hates so much.

"Oh, honey," she says, and I walk right into her open arms. She's shorter than I am now, since I got Dad's tall genes and she got Grandma's miniature ones, but her hug is just as comforting as when I was a little girl.

I lean into her embrace, burying my face in her hair, inhaling the scent of her summery bodywash. For the first time since I woke up this morning, something other than sorrow wiggles its way into my soul.

"How did you know?" I whisper.

She pulls back, holding my shoulders. Tears fill her eyes, threatening to ruin her makeup. "Sue just called me. She wanted to make sure you would be taken care of today, so don't worry, honey, I'm not going to work."

I make this half-snort, half-sobbing noise somewhere deep in my throat. Mrs. Cade's daughter is dead and she's worried about *me*. Mom leads me into the living room and allows me to cry on her shoulder for I don't know how long. The ache in my chest is deep, hollow and somehow powered with a fuel that never seems to run dry. I cry and cry, and it doesn't go away. Nothing makes this easier.

Deep down I feel shame for wanting it to be easier. I keep thinking if I cry a little longer, maybe I'll cry myself out and I'll feel better. When my eyelids are so heavy they're nearly swollen shut, I sit up and brush my choppy hair out of my eyes. Mom's work shirt is soaked, the entire shoulder wet and clinging to her skin. I can see the anchor tattoo on her shoulder, visible through the white fabric. Little details like this seem to matter to me. They are all pieces of life that Sasha will never ever get to experience again.

"God, I'm sorry," I mutter, wiping at my eyes. "You want to go and change?"

Mom's hands slide to her knees and she peers at me with red eyes, tear lines of mascara running down her cheeks. "Don't worry about me, Raquel."

Each breath hurts. As much as I tell my brain to stop, it keeps drudging up some random memory of Sasha and me: playing Queens of the Playground at recess, flirting our way into free tokens at the arcade, the time some creepy guy wouldn't stop hitting on me at the Fourth of July parade and she slapped him right across the face. Each new memory brings forth a tidal wave of tears and a pain in my chest that feels as though the Grim Reaper has shoved his staff right into me and is dragging it down, breaking each rib just for the thrill of it.

By noon, Mom feels comfortable enough to leave me alone while she makes lunch, not like I want to eat any of it. But when she sets a bowl of her famous tomato soup in front of me, along with a grilled cheese sandwich, I'm suddenly starving. Eating feels wrong, given that Sasha can't eat anymore, but I can practically hear her sarcastic laugh, telling me to stop being stupid.

Rocki, Rocki, Rocki. Don't be a drama queen — that's my job.

"How are you doing?" Mom asks softly as she dips her spoon into her soup.

I shrug. "I thought I had prepared for dealing with this. I

thought —" The bite of grilled cheese now feels like cardboard in my mouth. "I thought it wouldn't hurt as bad if I planned ahead."

"That's not how death works, honey." Mom's lips form a flat line, then they curve upward. "I remember your first grade field day," she says with a little laugh. "Remember when you and Sasha won the three-legged race? You've pretty much been inseparable since then."

I smile as the knot in my stomach twists in on itself, making one more loop that tugs into place just above my belly button.

After lunch, I tell Mom I need some alone time and she reluctantly stays on the couch while I walk away. I can hear my phone blowing up from my backpack, but I ignore it. By now, surely the whole school knows.

I wander outside, curling my toes over the edge of our pool. My reflection peers up at me, and I sit on the ledge. The concrete is hot from the Texas heat and it burns my butt, even through my leggings. I dunk my feet into the water, soaking my leggings up to the knees. Too late, I bend down and scrunch up the fabric, revealing my pale knees. We didn't spend much time outside this summer, so I am woefully lacking in the tan department.

Sasha had said on more than one occasion that when she was gone, she would try to reach out to me in this spiritual, meta-physical way. "Keep an eye out," she had said. "And I don't mean like a cold draft in the room or some dumb butterfly landing on your shoulder. When I reach out to you from beyond the grave, you're gonna know it's me."

"What, like you'll appear as a ghost?" I said, snorting.

"Maybe," she mused. "But when I visit you, you'll know it. You'll be able to hold on to it."

"Should we have some kind of sign?"

She thought it over for a moment. "No. I'll make it so obvious that you won't need a sign. You'll just know it's me, saying hi to you from the afterlife."

"You have a lot of faith in me," I said.

She grinned. "Maybe I just have faith in my own abilities."

I close my eyes and listen to the gentle swish of the pool water, the soft hum of the creepy pool suction thing as it makes its way across the bottom, cleaning off all the dirt. I take deep breaths and exhale slowly, trying to yoga my way into being peaceful and open to the spiritual realm. If Sasha tries to reach out to me from her afterlife, I want to be able to feel it.

Several moments pass and nothing happens.

I keep my eyes closed, grateful that for once since I woke up today, I'm not crying. I picture Sasha as an angel, her long, dark hair back and flowing in waves around her shoulders. I get all theatrical with it, picturing her smiling at me from atop her heavenly cloud, her bright new angel wings enormous and perfect.

Then my mind wanders into more practical daydreams. Maybe she's not an angel yet because she's stuck in some queue of dead people waiting to get inside the pearly gates of heaven. There's no doubt that's where she's going. Sasha was pure and good and didn't have an evil bone in her body.

The back door swings open, and the sound of flip-flops patters across the concrete. I smell his cologne before he says anything and force my eyes to open for the first time in what feels like hours.

"Zack?"

He sits next to me, kicking off his flip-flops and dunking his feet in the water.

Zack is the very definition of an on-again, off-again

boyfriend. I had a huge crush on him in junior high and even though we had a few classes together, he never seemed to notice me. Finally, freshman year, while standing in the pizza line in the cafeteria, I pulled off the ballsiest move of my life and handed him a note that said I thought he was cute. We've kind of been a thing ever since then.

The breaking up and getting back together drama started way before Sasha got sick, but lately we've been off, off and off. There's no time for a boyfriend when your best friend is dying.

"Hey, babe." He wraps his arm around me, tugs me into his shoulder. He's wearing board shorts and a T-shirt, which, if he were anyone else, would make me wonder if he even went to school today, but Zack dresses like this all the time. His short blond hair and full-body tan make him seem more like a surfer guy than a video game addict — the former is what made me like him all those years ago, and the latter is what he actually is.

I look at him, taking in the concern on his face. It's so much nicer than the scowls and annoyance he showed the last few times I saw him.

"I'm sorry about Sasha."

"Thanks." The word is out of my mouth before I really think it over. Are you supposed to thank someone in this kind of situation?

I'm so sorry to hear that your friend is dead.

Why, thank you for the acknowledgment, good sir.

Ugh.

"So I guess everyone knows?" I ask, looking back at the water. The creepy pool brush is now in the deep end.

"Yeah," he says, kicking at the water with his toes. "The principal made an announcement this morning. 'Sasha

Cade has lost her battle with cancer.' Pretty much everyone was crying all day. Once I heard that, I knew you'd be staying home."

I shake my head. "I don't think I'll go to school for the rest of this week. I'm not in the mood for being pitied by a bunch of idiots who only liked me because I was friends with Sasha."

"Don't be bitter, babe." Zack takes my face in his hands and kisses my forehead. Once, that gesture would have made my heart swoon, but I'm not sure I'll ever feel that way again. About anyone. Or anything. "You should try to look on the bright side."

Since he's holding both sides of my head, I'm kind of forced to look at him. I lift an eyebrow. Then my teeth grit together as anger rockets through me and I shove his hands away. "Where the hell can you find a bright side to my best friend dying?"

My outburst doesn't startle him. He runs his hands through my short hair, making it stick up at the ends. "Well, for starters, you can let your hair grow out again."

He wiggles his eyebrows and I pull away, my chest tight. He can't seem to go one day without mentioning how much he hates my hair. How he fell in love with the girl who had light brown locks going down her back, and that when I shaved it all off, I should have consulted him first. It's been four months since I handed Sasha the razor and told her to make me bald. I don't regret it, not for a second.

She'd lost all of her hair from the chemo, and it was the right thing for me to do. Plus, it was kind of fun. A few years ago, I would have balked at the idea, but once you realize that people all over the world are dying and you're still alive, several inches of hair doesn't mean much.

"You shave your head all the time," I say, flicking my hand over his super short hair. "Why can't I?"

He rolls his eyes. "Because you're a girl. You're supposed to be my princess, not look like you're about to go on the front lines of war."

"I'm not some princess, Zachary. I'm tough. I've delivered five baby calves and I stitched up that lady's Chihuahua, remember?" *And I survived my best friend's death.*

He laughs and pats my back. "Yeah, yeah, okay. You're tough. Still, I'm ready for your hair to be back. And now you can work at the animal clinic again, right?"

I swallow. Zack always made it seem like I was making some epic sacrifice in canceling all my plans for Sasha. When it's done out of love, it's not a sacrifice. The animal clinic, and the small scholarships I've won, will still be there next year. Sasha won't.

"Zack." I take a deep breath. "I appreciate that you came here to see me, but … you're not even acting sad. You just want things to go back to normal, but I'm grieving. Can't you just —" Every breath I take is a fight to hold back tears. Not only am I missing her, I want everyone else to miss her, too. "Aren't you even a little sad?"

"I mean, yeah." He shrugs. I focus on the pool water that reflects in his eyes since he won't actually look at me.

"Why didn't you like her?" My voice feels raw, and each word hurts. "Everyone liked Sasha."

"I liked her," he says too quickly, too defensively. "She didn't like me. She always looked at me like —" He blows out a heavy breath of air, and if I didn't know any better I might have said he's ashamed. "Like I wasn't good enough for you."

The truth in his words hits me hard, and despite being pissed off at my sort-of boyfriend, here I am crying again.

"Babe," he says, drawing out the word with his southern accent. He bumps me with his shoulder. "Don't cry. Sasha wouldn't want you to."

I love how he suddenly thinks he can channel her spirit or something.

"It's just hard." I wish a hug from him was as comforting as one from my mom. "It hurts so much."

"I know, babe, but think of it this way," he says, wrapping a heavy arm around my shoulders. "You're free now."

The splashing of our feet in the pool, the hum of the pool cleaner — every single sound is drowned out by the pounding of my own heart. "What the hell did you just say?"

He holds up his hands, an innocent look on his face. "Rocki, you know what I meant. Your life has been halted lately because of Sasha, but now that she's gone, you're free. Free to be yourself and live your life."

I scramble and stand up fast, water flopping off my feet and onto his dry clothes. "You need to leave."

Zack frowns. "Stop being like this."

I point toward the gate in the fence. My jaw clenches. "Please go."

"Rocki, please."

I shake my head and march into my house, slamming the back door behind me and twisting the dead bolt into place. I head into my room and open my backpack, pulling out the white binder that's been adorned with a glitter pen and decorative duct tape. The time for moping is over. I have a funeral to plan.

Chapter Three

There's only one flower shop that can get the insane volume of wildflowers Sasha wanted for her funeral. Izzy's Flowers is a narrow storefront located at the end of the Peyton Colony Strip, a historic shopping center on the north side of Lake Peyton. The weathered wooden sign above the door has big bubbly lettering and peace signs painted on, a relic from the seventies with no intention of being updated.

Izzy's thin lips fall into a frown when I step into the shop. The fragrance of hundreds of bouquets permeates the air, and a Sublime song plays from some hidden speaker. Izzy, the owner and sole employee — an older hippie wearing a patchwork dress — goes totally still, her hands wrapped around some daisies.

"Oh, child," she says. "It's far too soon. I thought she had more time."

Sasha and I had visited Izzy's Flowers on more than one occasion. This is the only place to get an affordable bouquet of Mother's Day flowers each year, and although Sasha's parents are filthy rich, she always refused to use their money to buy them gifts. Last May, Izzy comped both of our Mother's Day bouquets after we walked in with shaved heads. Sasha called it a benefit of dying young.

I swallow the lump in my throat and approach the front counter, laying the binder down between us and opening it up to the flower page. Izzy helped us choose flowers just a few months ago. On the first visit, Mr. and Mrs. Cade came with us, but Sasha's mom spent the entire time crying and Sasha banned her from any further funeral planning. She said planning your own funeral is something a girl should do with her best friend — that way, her parents wouldn't be burdened with yet another task. Sasha's death had rules like this, things we made up as we went along. Most people don't get an advance warning of their demise, but Sasha did, and she didn't want to waste it.

My voice comes out in a croak. "So … do you have all of these?"

Izzy puts a weathered hand on mine, her messy auburn hair falling in front of her shoulders. "I'm so sorry for your loss, Raquel."

"Thanks." Another raspy croak. I blink quickly to keep the tears at bay and get back to business. I promised to keep it together for Sasha's parents so they don't have to lift a finger. "So, the flowers?"

"I've got 'em," she says, motioning for me to follow her around the counter. I follow the scent of flowers and the faint stench of pot until we get into the back part of the store. Though narrow, it stretches pretty far back, the shelves packed with vases, tools and wire spools.

From a high shelf, she retrieves a binder of her own, all withered and cracking at the corners. She opens it to the first page. "Here's what I was thinking for the casket spray," she says, passing me a hand-sketched, watercolor painting. Long-stemmed sunflowers with white wildflowers fan out, tied together with a white sparkly ribbon. I know the ribbon will be sparkly because she wrote "sparkly ribbon" and drew an arrow to it.

A floaty feeling rises in my stomach and I reach up to cover my mouth. "This is amazing," I murmur, handing back the painting. I wish I could tell Sasha.

Izzy smiles, her eyes a dark blue that makes her seem both wise and a little off her rocker. "She wanted wildflowers everywhere, but they don't do well off the stem." She turns the page and hands me another painting, pointing out the features as she talks. "I was thinking of having long, rectangular planter boxes filled with the flowers in soil. We can paint them white with glitter and line them around the casket, and up and down the rows of chairs at the cemetery."

She peers at me, creases running up her forehead. "What do you think?"

I shake my head, but not from disapproval. It's more like I'm totally in shock. "It's beautiful. But the funeral is in a few days. Can we get this done on time?"

"Well …" She averts her gaze. "Come with me."

We meander through the rest of the shop and into a small storage room at the back of the building. Inside are a dozen of the planter boxes, made and painted, gleaming like they came straight from a fairy castle.

"You made these?" I ask, mouth falling open.

She nods. "Couldn't help myself. I've never had a client plan her own funeral before. I told her it could be done, knowing those suckers don't hold up well, especially in the heat. So yeah, I had to find a way to make it work."

I feel genuine happiness for the first time in the two days that Sasha has been gone. I know she would love this. "Can I pay extra to keep the boxes?"

She waves a hand at me. "No extra. They're yours."

This is working out better than I thought it would. Turns out preparing Sasha's funeral is giving me something to do besides sit around and cry all day. We head back to the front of the store, where I pay for the flowers using Mrs. Cade's credit card. Right now, she's at the funeral home making the final arrangements, the one thing a best friend can't exactly do. My next stop is the photo and print shop to pick up programs and a massive photo of Sasha. On Thursday morning at eleven a.m., we will lay my best friend to rest.

While signing the receipt, I notice a sign — or an index card, rather — that says *Now Hiring*. I point to it. "You're hiring?"

Izzy nods, focused on her work. She picks a few flowers and bunches them together at the stems, then reaches for a white ribbon to tie around them. "Just something part-time. I could use a break every now and then." She quirks an eyebrow. "Are you interested?"

"Yes," I find myself saying before I can think it over. The animal clinic has been my usual after-school job, but they understood when I took some time off to care for Sasha. I love animals and I do plan on going back, but without Sasha, it feels like I'm learning how to be a person all over again. Maybe I need something new for a while. "I'm still in school, so I could only work evenings and weekends," I say.

"That's fine. Perfect, actually." Izzy holds up the simple bouquet, tipping it toward me. "Pink carnations — they stand for remembrance. For you, sweetheart."

"Thank you," I say, taking the flowers and inhaling the sweet scent. "How do I apply?"

"Just come in when you've had time to mourn your friend," she says, taking the index card and tossing it in the trash. "No rush."

* * *

I'm awake before the sun on Thursday morning. Sasha didn't have a viewing — she didn't want one. She said the idea of lying around dead for a few hours in a funeral home sounded like torture. She wanted her funeral to be outside at the cemetery, her casket surrounded by wildflowers and the sounds of nature.

Peyton Colony Memorial Park is as beautiful as it is old, with one edge bordering the massive lake that makes our town a tourist stop and a low-budget vacation spot. There are graves from as far back as the 1800s here, and since the grounds slope slightly downward, every headstone has a view of the water. If only hypothetically.

I wear a dark-pink sundress that stops just above my knees. Sasha picked it out for the occasion. I know she's wearing a matching dress in purple, her favorite color, inside the casket. Not that I will ever see it.

I glance at the stack of funeral programs on my desk. Sasha's grinning school picture from last year is on the front. She'd gone to the salon for a blowout the day before, so her long hair is supermodel-perfect — this was long before the shave. Her high cheekbones and smile make her look like a goddess. I don't know how she managed to nail school photos. Mine are always the worst.

I attempt to deal with my hair, but short, wavy and messy are pretty much the only things it can do. Mom keeps saying I should have a stylist cut it into some kind of actual hairstyle, but I like seeing how it grows out all wacky. Besides, I don't think Sasha will mind.

"How do you like my hair?" I pick up the first program from the stack and look into my best friend's eyes, knowing she can't reply. Even printed on paper, their color is mesmerizing.

My eyes are a hazelish green, like someone dumped a bucket of dirty mop water on top of them. Definitely nothing to write home about. Sasha, on the other hand, had these gorgeous bright blue eyes that contrasted starkly with her dark hair and brown skin. They were the first thing you noticed when you looked at her, two orbs of light set into a face that already glowed. Sasha was single by choice, since nearly every guy she ever met wanted to date her. She was the kind of charismatic person that would be really easy to hate, but no one ever did. People were drawn to her. People wanted to be her best friend, but for some reason, she chose me.

I set the program back on top of the stack.

In the kitchen, Dad's dressed in his funeral best, which is a far cry from his usual wardrobe of faded jeans and a stained T-shirt. He hands me a cup of coffee and Mom forces a plate of pancakes and bacon into my hands.

"You need to eat," she says, watching until I take a bite.

"If you don't mind, I'd like to drive myself," I say after breakfast. My parents exchange a look but Mom nods.

"That's fine. Just be careful."

"I want to get there early and stay late."

"Understandable," Dad says over his coffee mug. Unless the

Texans are playing football on TV, Luke Clearwater is a man of very few words. He has even fewer today.

I'm not sure how I'm supposed to feel as I walk through the cemetery. Sad, obviously. Scared out of my mind because I'll be giving the eulogy? Probably.

Mostly there's this unplaceable feeling deep in my chest that makes my fingers and toes feel light. Like when you're at the top of a roller coaster and it hasn't dropped yet, but you know at any second, your stomach will fly up into your throat, your butt will lift off the seat, and for just a moment, there will be an addicting kind of chaos.

Several rows of folding chairs sit in front of Sasha's casket, which is even more spectacular in the summer sun. The wildflower planters are stunning; every color of the rainbow blooms and stretches toward the sky, making Sasha's casket look like a work of art.

I stand there and watch people arrive. Sasha's parents give me a quick hug but then they're taken away by the duty of greeting guests with pained smiles. Before long, it's obvious that every member of our senior class and many of the juniors have shown up, and they stand around filling every inch of grass. I recognize a few teachers as well, along with our principal and Mrs. Sparks, who was Sasha's kindergarten teacher.

Zack wears a suit that makes him look more handsome than I've ever seen him. His grin tells me he knows how great he looks, his eyes locking on mine as he walks up the rows of chairs. He hugs and kisses me like I never yelled at him to leave my backyard.

"Thanks for coming," I manage to say. He takes a spot next to some of Sasha's distant relatives.

The funeral begins and Pastor Williams reads Bible passages and a poem. I'm sitting up front, right next to Mr. and Mrs. Cade and my parents, but I don't really hear a thing he says. Instead, all I seem to hear are Mrs. Cade's quiet sobs and the crinkle of her package of tissues as she reaches for another one, and yet another.

My typed eulogy gets sweaty from my grip. Public speaking isn't my favorite thing, but weirdly, I'm not nervous anymore.

When Pastor Williams calls me up, I rise and walk to the podium. Zack meets my gaze and gives me a thumbs-up. Then I glance toward Sasha's parents, who watch me with eager, blood-shot eyes.

"Good afternoon," I say, glancing at the casket. "My name is Raquel Clearwater, though you probably already know that."

I open up the paper, spread it out flat on top of the wooden surface. The words blur as tears fill my vision. I draw in a slow and deep breath, glancing back out at the crowd. I see Izzy in a flowy dress, and she smiles.

"I met Sasha in Mrs. Wood's class. My family wasn't doing too well back then, and I had these stupid shoes that came from the dollar store on Fifth Street. It was the first day of first grade and we had to sit in a circle, and some kid saw the dollar store logo on the bottom of my shoes. Everyone laughed and made fun of me. That's when Sasha walked up and declared that she thought they were cool.

"The next day, she came to school wearing the same shoes. Mine were pink and hers were purple." I can't help smiling. "We were six years old and she was already cool as hell. Soon, everyone else wanted the shoes because Sasha had them. The dollar store couldn't keep them in stock anymore because they were flying off the shelves."

There's some soft laughter in the crowd and I focus on the spray of gorgeous sunflowers on top of the casket. "Sasha became my best friend that day, and she has saved me from being an outcast about a thousand more times over the years, in many ways that I won't tell you guys because it'd be mortifying."

More laughter. I glance at Mrs. Cade and she beams at me, the same kind of smile she used to give Sasha all the time. I swallow and glance back at my paper.

"Sasha Cade was kind. She was an old soul with a spark that couldn't be extinguished. She pulled me out of my shell time and time again, and taught me to do what I love without caring what other people think. Once she became your friend, she would move heaven and earth to make sure you had what you needed. I've always known I could never pay her back for how much she's given me over the years. But even if I could somehow do that, she wouldn't have let me."

The next line of my eulogy begins another story from our past, but I skip over it, knowing I'll burst into tears and ruin my speech. I notice Zack is staring at his phone. Annoyed, I scan the crowd. Sasha would have loved this, all these people here just for her. I take a deep breath and skip to the last words on my paper.

"Sasha was a firecracker. I loved her, and I will miss her every day. She's leaving a trail of sunshine in heaven now." Tears spring to my eyes and I rush to the end. "Thank you for coming today."

I look up to the sky, close my eyes and feel the sun warming every cell in my body. I have no freaking clue who I am without Sasha.

But I'll be okay.

Pastor Williams clears his throat and hands me an envelope. In a hushed tone, he says, "Sasha wanted me to give you this, at this moment. You're supposed to read it."

This isn't in the binder.

I take the envelope and turn it over. My heart hammers in my chest. Written in pink Sharpie, in Sasha's perfect cursive, are these words:

> *Sorry to spring this on you, Rocki. I have some final things to say.*
> *Love you always,*
> *Sasha*

Chapter Four

After months of planning every second of this funeral, she would have known that springing a surprise self-eulogy on me last minute, while I'm standing up here with the entire senior class watching me, would have been a shock.

Which means she did it for a reason.

Maybe it's just another way of her pushing me out of my comfort zone, edging me to the cliff of my fears and promising my parachute will open, if I just get the courage to jump. Inwardly, I roll my eyes. *Thanks. Thanks a lot, Sasha.*

I clear my throat, my eyes zooming across the paper in a futile attempt to take it in before I speak the words.

"'So,'" I begin reading, clearing my throat. Sasha wouldn't do anything to embarrass me, I realize after what feels like an eternity. I find a way to step out of my own brain and just read.

"'So, it's my funeral. Let me guess … all one hundred and twenty-four of the seniors are here, right? So glad you made the ultimate sacrifice of your education to come watch me get lowered into the ground.

"'I want to thank Raquel, my bestest friend on earth — I say *on earth* because surely I've made some killer best friends up here in heaven so far. Don't worry, Rocki, no one will replace you. Prince and Shakespeare are just my temporary replacements until you arrive, hopefully old and wrinkly, because life is a gift and I want you to have a long one.

"'So, back to my speech. I trust Rocki is delivering it with as much grace and just the hint of sarcasm that I would have used if I could somehow have been here to give it myself. Ten bucks says Rocki called me a firecracker in what I'm sure was a beautiful eulogy. She never let me read it, but I know she worked hard on it.'"

There's laughter, and I can't help but grin as I wipe away some tears and keep reading. "'Mom and Dad —'" I pause here, trying to read ahead before I say anything aloud, and then I look over at Mr. and Mrs. Cade. Their expressions look as blissful as though their daughter has crawled out of her coffin alive and well for a private conversation. Now I know why she left this note. It's not for me, or even for our peers — it's for her parents. I clear my throat and start again.

"'Mom and Dad, I want to thank you from the bottom of my heart for being the greatest parents a girl could ever have. Thank you for choosing me all those years ago. I know Great-Grandma didn't like that I was mixed race, but you still picked me even with all the family drama. You guys are the best. The absolute best, please know that. Don't ever doubt it, no matter what. I'm sorry I had to go so early. I'm sorry I couldn't give you grandchildren. But please know that my years with you guys as parents meant the world to me.'"

There's a line drawn at the bottom, separating one final note from Sasha. I see the words

Rocki you don't have to read this part aloud.

So I don't. I fold up the paper, let the tears fall freely and step down to where my mom opens her arms and takes me into her embrace.

* * *

The next morning, Friday, I get dressed for school, still not sure if I'm actually going back. I'm not ready to face the world or pretend to have a normal day when nothing will ever be normal again, but the walls of my bedroom are starting to close in on me. And too many missed school days will only mean I have to make up the time, so school feels like something I should do. Something Sasha would want me to do.

Sasha's surprise eulogy rests on my nightstand, the special postscript message now etched into my brain since I've read it a million times.

I know you want a sign, and you're about to get it.
Love you!

Last night, I might have spent an embarrassing amount of time searching the internet for ways to hear from a dead person. All I got was weirdo nonsense, famous TV personalities who claim to be mediums and charge a ton of money, and a whole lot of people saying that kind of thing is impossible.

I push a thick black headband over my eyes and up, lifting the hair out of my face. If Sasha is going to give me a sign from the afterlife, I'm sure she can do it while I'm at school.

The curse of attending a school as small as PCHS is that there's nowhere to hide. You can't exactly blend into a crowd when there's no crowd to begin with. I'm aware of the eyes on me as I make my way through the parking lot and into the school. Part of me even regrets some of the personal things I said at Sasha's funeral. Even though I was saying them for her, everyone in this hallway heard them, too.

I keep my head down and give a polite but tight smile to the few girls who say hello to me. My mom told me to be myself, even if myself was still mourning and wanted to be left alone.

Zack finds me in the hallway after first period. He's wearing a hoodie over a pair of neon-orange board shorts, with flip-flops.

"My beautiful girlfriend is back," he says, falling into step with me as I walk toward the English hallway.

"Hey." It's pretty much the only thing I can be bothered to say right now. Sure, I'm no longer crying, but the pain has cracked open a hole in my heart that's bigger than the Mariana Trench. Suffice it to say that small talk is not on the list of things I am capable of.

In fact, that list is about four things long.

Sleep.

Walk.

Breathe.

Eat.

The rest of the student body and my teachers have all accepted that. Not Zack.

His meaty arm slings around my shoulder, protecting me from the parade of students rushing to their next class. I lean against him, allowing his body to be my shield.

Part of this feels all wrong, like I am dangling Zack from a fishing line with no intention of reeling him in. I cared about him once, and I can probably find those feelings again, if I try hard enough. It's the trying that's giving me a hard time. Zack has no real ambition besides video games and working out. In junior high, that didn't matter. In high school, Sasha thought I could do better.

We reach my class and he stops, pulling me up against the lockers. "I missed you," he says, peering into my eyes. "I missed you *a lot*."

"Did you miss me, or did your boner miss me?" I ask, deadpan, because I know he's letting it touch me on purpose.

He sighs. "It's not my fault you make this happen," he says, nodding downward before putting a hand on my hip. I shuffle back a little, not wanting to be within five hundred feet of a horny teenage guy.

"I have to go." I turn to leave and Zack rushes forward, blocking my path to Mrs. Garza's class.

Something like sincerity crosses his features and he frowns. "Baby, I'm sorry. I don't know how to act, okay?"

My lips press together, and God help me, my ice-cold heart starts to melt a little. "Okay. Sorry I'm being a bitch. I did miss you — I mean I do, I just — Sasha." My shoulders fall. "It's hard."

"I know." Zack reaches up and touches my face. "Come to the movies with me tonight."

"Is that a question or a caveman demand?"

He rolls his eyes. "A question, obviously. Come on, it'll be fun. You can get out of the house and we'll spend time together." He leans in, not even flinching when the warning bell rings. His next class is way across the school so he'll get a tardy even if he leaves now. "Come on, Raquel. Please? We'll go to the drive-in and watch from the back seat."

He wiggles his eyebrows and I exhale so loudly I think everyone in the hallway hears it. He holds up his hands. "Okay, okay, fine. Regular movie theater."

My lips press together, and the risk of getting detention from a tardy on my first day back makes me hasty. "Sure," I say, turning toward my class. "Whatever."

"That means yes?"

I nod, hitching my backpack up on my shoulder. "Yeah. Call me later."

He leans in and quickly kisses me before turning and running down the hallway. Sasha's voice tsks in my mind, and although she's no longer in this class with me, I take a seat in the back and look over at her empty desk. I know what she would say: *Dump him already.*

* * *

When Mom gets home from work, she peeks into my bedroom and makes this weird sound that's a mix between surprise and shock. I turn toward her, mascara wand in hand. "What?"

"You're dressed nicely." She studies me, mama bear unsure about her cub.

"Skinny jeans and a tank top aren't exactly dressed up."

"Matched with those fancy heels and a face full of makeup, I'd say that's dressed up." She points a stack of mail at me, her car keys still clutched in her other hand, purse strap over her shoulder. Checking on me is now her first priority, as if the sadness of losing my best friend will make me disappear into thin air if she doesn't watch me close enough.

I shrug. "Zack and I are seeing a movie tonight."

"That's wonderful." She flashes me a smile and leans against my doorway, flipping through the mail. Her brows pull together and she slips an envelope from the stack. It's shaped like a greeting card, not those narrow envelopes with clear plastic windows that mean bills. "This one's for you," she says, setting it on my desk. "Probably a sympathy card."

I cap my mascara and look over. A strip of cold slices through my chest, and tears spring to my eyes.

"You need a minute?" Mom asks softly.

I nod and yank the card off the desk. As soon as she closes my door, I rip into the envelope. No sympathy card could bring tears to my eyes now — I've had dozens of these cards over the last few days.

But it's Sasha's handwriting on the envelope.

The card inside is a generic blank greeting card, the photo on the cover a fat housecat wearing a purple feather boa around its neck. I nearly rip the thing in my haste to open it and now I'm crying, my makeup probably going all clown-face down my cheeks.

> *Rocki,*
> *I have a secret for you. Please don't be mad. Every-thing will make sense soon enough. Please go to my grave tonight, Friday the 26th, at six. Bring your laptop and make sure the battery is charged, okay? I love you and miss you, bestie!*
> *xx Sasha*

I read the letter several times, and when my phone starts ringing, I almost forget that I'm sitting in my room, that my name is Raquel Clearwater and that a world exists outside of this letter. All I know is there's someplace I have to be tonight — and it's not the movies with Zack.

I answer the call and spend about two seconds debating if I should tell him the truth. Then I just say, "Hello?"

"There's a six fifteen and seven forty-five. Which one do you want to see? I'm gonna buy the tickets online so they're cheaper."

I run my hand down the greeting card, picturing Sasha writing this however long ago. The weird part is the date, which was originally left as a blank space. Someone else, with a different-colored pen and shaky, old-person handwriting, filled in today's date. How long ago did she write this? Who received her instructions to mail it to me after she died?

"I'm sorry, I can't go."

"What? You want to come over instead? Mom's out with her girlfriend so she'll be home late."

"No, Zack, I'm sorry. Something came up. I can't go out at all."

"This is bullshit, Rocki. Do you know how many girls I've turned down lately? All because I knew you'd be back with me eventually?"

"You're an attractive guy. I'm sure it's a lot."

"Fuck yeah, it's a lot. *Jesus*, Rocki. I've got chicks sending me pics on the gaming forums and I've been telling them I've got a girlfriend. Now we finally get some time together and you're blowing me off?"

The old me might have had some choice words to say here,

but arguing with my on-again, off-again boyfriend doesn't thrill me the way it used to.

"Take one of them to the movies," I say as I hang up.

I unzip my backpack and pull out books and school crap, then stuff my laptop and Sasha's card inside. I dig under my desk and unplug the charge cord just in case I need it later. I trade out my sexy date-night heels for a pair of worn-out flats and tell Mom I'm off to the movies.

On the way to the cemetery, I remember driving this same route with Sasha last year when we picked out her burial plot. Her mom thought we were being incredibly morbid, given that Sasha's cancer was diagnosed but not yet terminal. Sasha said better safe than sorry.

Whatever surprises I'd expected to see when I got here, I was wrong. The place looks the same as always, an old cemetery near the back with newer tombstones and mausoleums closer to the main road. I meander through rows and rows of other people's loved ones until I get to Sasha's newly covered plot.

Square pieces of sod cover the mound of freshly packed dirt. Flowers are everywhere, spilling over on top of the neighboring graves.

Sasha's headstone is about four feet tall, made of white granite — the brightest they had — with her name carved in a curly script. Normally they don't install them until a couple of weeks after the person is buried, but Sasha insisted and her parents paid whatever it cost. The date of her death isn't etched in yet, because even money can't buy that kind of knowledge. I put my hand on it and close my eyes, wishing it were a year ago.

I half expect another note here on her grave, but I don't see anything, not even under the flowers. It's exactly six, so I'm not late, but there's nothing here.

I stare at the fresh blades of grass, and an image of Sasha lying inside that casket, six feet below, makes me shudder. It's creepy to think about; she's the person who used to eat all of the chocolate out of the trail mix, steal all the blankets when we shared a bed at sleepovers. She used to be real, physical and here with me.

Now she's ...

A shuffling sound makes me look up and images of Sasha's cancer-covered body lying in a dark box fade from my mind. A short way away, a guy sits on a concrete bench, legs stretched out in front of him while he gazes at the lake. It's as if he's sitting on the Venice boardwalk and not in a cemetery.

I ignore him.

A few minutes pass and my spine tingles. I can feel him watching me from over there, his casual expression so wrong for this atmosphere.

I glance over, trying to be equally casual about it, but I am right — he's watching me. My heart races as I realize the only things I have on me are some car keys and a backpack with my most expensive possession inside. Do people get mugged in cemeteries?

As if sensing my fear, he rises from the bench, all slow and calm, like he knows I have nowhere to run. My car might as well be parked on Mars.

As he approaches, I realize he's about my age, maybe a little older, but he's definitely not someone from school. He wears dark jeans and a plain black T-shirt with running shoes that have seen better days. He reaches into his pocket and I freeze, one hand on the gravestone.

He pulls something white from his pocket. He's near enough now that I can see the stubble on his chin, the way the sunlight casts a shadow under his shaggy black bangs, hiding his eyes until he's right in front of me.

I inhale sharply. He studies me, those otherworldly blue eyes searching my face for something, like maybe he's just as lost as I am. Maybe he's looking for a sign.

Chills cover me from head to toe and more of those damned tears stream out of my eyes. Even as I struggle to breathe, my body can still cry because it acts on its own nowadays.

How is this possible? I can't take my gaze off him, off those crystal blue, ocean blue, impossibly blue eyes.

He unfolds the white thing in his hand, revealing a beat-up greeting card with a fat housecat on the front. "Does this mean anything to you?" he asks, his voice resonating in the most familiar way.

My knees shake so badly I lean on the headstone and cover my mouth with my hand. A week ago when Sasha died, I knew I'd never see her eyes again.

Yet here they are, watching me while I collapse to the ground.

Chapter Five

The stranger's hands are on my shoulders, then my arms, helping me stand back up. As soon as I'm on my feet, I scramble backward, my thigh hitting a nearby headstone. I jump aside and my ankle twists in a section of thick grass. I curse as sharp pain shoots up my leg.

"Whoa," the guy says. He won't stop staring at me with those stupid eyes. "It's okay. I won't hurt you."

I take in the rugged look of his clothing, the calluses on his hands as he holds them up. He isn't that much older than I am, but he's not like the other guys at school. He looks like he's seen some shit. *This is not funny, Sasha.* "Who the hell are you?"

He runs a hand through his hair, takes a step backward. Because I can't look into his eyes, I focus on his lips, all soft lines with the hint of a smirk.

"I'm Elijah." He scratches the back of his neck and I watch his biceps flex. "Elijah, um, Delgado." If he wasn't some kind of weird cemetery stalker, he'd be cute. Really cute.

"You're Raquel, right?"

My nostrils flare. "How do you know that?"

"Well, you're not Sasha. You don't look anything like her, so …" He rubs his shoulder, then lets his pinky slide down the silver chain around his neck. I realize he's just as awkward as I am. Maybe he's not here to murder me or steal my laptop.

I take a deep breath and release my grip on the headstone next to me. Mr. and Mrs. Goodwin both died in the same year just two months apart. How tragic.

"I am Raquel," I say, daring to look into his eyes again. Chills cover my body. I know I asked for a sign from Sasha, but I didn't expect her returning to earth as a hot guy. "How do you know my name?"

He opens the greeting card in his hands and reads. "'At the cemetery, go to the Mary Grove aisle, then fourteen plots to the right. Look for my best friend, Raquel. She'll be the one with the shit haircut but a super charming smile.'" He looks up, folding the card back into a square the size of a business card. "No offense, but your hair," he says, biting on his bottom lip.

I laugh. "That is so like Sasha," I say, reaching up and touching the previously mentioned shit haircut.

"Ah," Elijah says. "There's the charming smile."

We stand here for a minute, the compliment catching me off guard. Although I might already kind of know the answer — as insane as it is — I have to ask. "So … who exactly are you?"

But my words come out at the same time as Elijah says, "Is Sasha on her way?"

A boulder forms in my stomach. He must not notice the horror in my eyes because he gives me a grin just like Sasha's and says, "She probably wants to tell you herself, but I'm her biological brother." He swings a thumb toward his chest. "Same parents. We recently found each other online, but she didn't want to tell people yet." Patting his pocket, he says, "This card is the first time she's asked to meet up."

I swallow as the information falls over me in waves. Sasha has a brother. She knew and she didn't tell me.

"So, is she coming?" He watches me with eager anticipation in his eyes, then he glances back toward the parking lot.

I don't.

I can't.

Sasha, how could you do this to me?

I stare at the new grass covering Sasha's burial plot. "Elijah ..."

His expression darkens, his hands sliding into his pockets. It reminds me of the first time I told Zack I wanted to break up. All I had to say was his name and he knew whatever I said next would be bad news. This is so much worse.

"What is it?" he asks.

I put a trembling hand to my forehead and pinch the bridge of my nose. Out of all the hard things I've done, this is the hardest. The back of my throat burns acidic and I swallow it down.

You got this. You're so much stronger than you think you are.

Sasha's unwavering belief in me was one thing when I was preparing to give a speech in class. It's completely different now. I want so badly to be pissed at her for doing this to me, but I know that's just how she is. Believing that I can do the impossible.

"I'm sorry, but ... Sasha died on Monday." Warm tears roll down my cheeks. "She's, uh, she's behind you. This is her grave."

Elijah turns around, his head dipping to look at the grave and all of the wildflowers surrounding it. I watch his back, see the lines of his shoulder blades hunch as he lowers his head into his hands.

I step forward and put a hand on his shoulder. "She had cancer. Did she tell you that?"

Hands still covering his face, he shakes his head. Then he looks up toward the sky, a tear rolling down his cheek.

He draws in a deep breath, and it seems like he grows a foot taller when he stands to his full height. When he looks at me, I see so many pieces of Sasha in his features. The cheekbones, the concerned curve of his brow. "Sorry to freak out on you," he says, turning his gaze toward the grave. "I had no idea what to expect when I got this card telling me to go to a cemetery. Definitely not this." His bottom lip quivers. "I only just found her. And now she's gone."

My hand on his arm is now sticky with sweat. "It's okay to cry," I say, peering up at him. I can tell he's holding back his emotions, trying to keep it all together. It's the same look I've had all week. "You see that lake over there?" I nod toward the back of the cemetery. "I've probably cried twice that much water in the last week. Sasha was my best friend."

Elijah's lip is trembling. "Tell me about her?"

We head to the nearby bench and I drop my backpack to the ground beside me. "You go first. I had no idea Sasha had a brother. You look just like her."

He wipes at his eyes and slings his arm across the back of the bench. "I didn't know either until I turned eighteen and they released me from the group home. I asked for my paperwork —"

"Group home?"

His tongue flicks across his bottom lip quickly and he nods. "Yeah, uh, it's what they call the place where a ton of underage guys live until they age out."

My throat feels dry. "You weren't adopted?"

He shakes his head like it's not a big deal. "So anyway, I had my paperwork and tried finding my birth parents for a little while." He snorts and gazes out at the lake. "They're both dead. Addicts. But I also learned I had a sister who was three years younger and given up when she was really young. I spent months trying to find her. It was hard because her last name was different."

"Sasha Delgado," I say, trying on the name she had before she was a Cade.

He leans forward, resting his elbows on his knees. "I ended up finding her on a Texas adoption forum. She was looking for our parents, and when she said she was multiracial, I thought it might be her."

"Do you know which races?" I ask, curious. Sasha's obsession with her ancestry had always been a thing. We'd assumed she was probably part African-American, but we could never know for sure. Her parents weren't thrilled at the idea of Sasha searching for her birth parents, so she never did.

At least not that she ever told me.

"Yeah, like three of them," Elijah says. "Our dad was half black, and our mother was from Brazil. She came over here as a little girl."

"Brazil," I say with a smile. It's like a missing puzzle piece of Sasha's heritage has finally slipped into place. "I wonder if that's where she got those beautiful eyes. *Your* eyes," I say, before I can stop myself.

"Ah, the eyes," he says, leaning back on the bench and looking up at the sky. "I've been hearing about my eyes my whole life. Interesting eyes never got me adopted, though."

"I'm sorry." My nails dig into my palms. Why do I keep

saying stupid things? What exactly is the protocol for meeting your dead best friend's brother when you never knew he existed in the first place?

"I wonder why —" I shut up and shake my head.

"The Cades didn't adopt me, too?" he asks, reading my mind. He shrugs. "I was given up after Sasha when I was a toddler. My mom tried giving us both up, but then my dad kept me for a while before he lost his rights and I was put into the system. Maybe the Cades didn't know. Don't make that face," he says, nudging me with his elbow. "I'm okay with it. I'm glad it was her instead of me. She seemed really happy with her family."

"She was. She loved her parents, they're really nice people." *And wealthy people*, I think. *People who gave her a life someone in a group home could never even fathom.*

My heart aches for this boy I've only just met. I want to climb into his past and make it all better again, make the Cades adopt him, too, and give him the same wonderful life that Sasha got to have. I know Sasha must have felt the same way. Maybe this is morbid, but if the Cades had adopted both of the Delgado children, they would still have one kid left to love.

My body moves on its own, and soon I'm hugging him, wrapping my arms around his neck as I pull him close, trying helplessly to heal all of his pain.

It takes him a second, but he hugs me back, his strong arms nearly shoving all the air out of my lungs. I inhale the smell of laundry detergent mixed with the faint scent of motor oil. He kind of smells like our garage when the clothes dryer is on.

"I wish it didn't have to be like this," I whisper. "But I'm glad I got to meet you."

"Same," he says.

When I pull away, we're both crying and it makes us laugh.

"So, tell me about my sister," he says, reaching up to brush away the tears on my face. "And possibly about your interesting haircut."

I laugh harder and somehow that makes me cry more, too. Eventually I pull my shit together and tell him about Sasha. I start from the beginning, from the dollar store shoes incident, to all the times she's saved my ass over the years. I tell him about holidays at the Cades' massive vacation house in Miami, and how Sasha never liked any of my boyfriends but it was only because she wanted the best for me.

The way he looks at me when I tell him about my hair is like he's just figured me all out. I realize all these stories I'm telling him are tinted with my own perspective. He's getting the truth about Sasha, mixed with a piece of me as well. Would Sasha have told them a different way? I run my hands through my hair, smoothing it down even though the breeze messes it up again. I try to talk slower, telling the stories exactly how they were, instead of how I remember them.

We talk until the light posts turn on and the sun starts to dip toward the lake, disappearing beneath the water.

I am euphoric, telling this sort-of-stranger all about Sasha's life and our friendship. Every time I look into his eyes, it's like a part of her is still here, still flashing me a grin while we plan another adventure.

I know I'm talking too much, but now that I've started, it's impossible to stop. Even when I finish telling him something, the look in his eyes makes me want to keep going. So I do.

I tell him about the time when we were fourteen and Sasha

got a new camcorder and we decided to film our own horror movie in her backyard.

"We wrote the script to have three girls get lost in the woods, which was really just Sasha's backyard. But since there were only two of us, we stuffed a pair of pants and a hoodie with towels and set the fake body in a chair. We'd only show glimpses of the third girl, who we named Jennifer, and when she talked, it was really just me talking in a really high voice."

I do the voice and he laughs.

"So I'm holding the camera as we walk through the woods at night, because it's like a first-person camera view horror film, right? And I say something like, 'I'm so scared! We're out in the middle of nowhere, and there's nothing at all, no civilization, nothing,' and right then, her dad comes out of the back door and yells, 'Girls, here's that flashlight y'all wanted!' and we were like 'SHUT UP!'"

I'm laughing so hard at this memory that I lean forward, covering my mouth with my hands. Elijah laughs, too, shaking his head. "I want to see this movie."

I nod and take deep breaths to regain my composure. "Yeah, totally. I have a copy on my computer. Hey, speaking of ..." I heft my backpack onto the bench between us. Crickets chirping in the dark break the silence as I unzip it and pull out my laptop. "My letter told me to bring this. I wonder why?"

His eyes widen. "I completely forgot," he says, reaching into his pocket. "Sasha knows I don't have my own computer and could only email her through the library or sometimes at work, so I wondered why she would give me this."

He holds up a flash drive. The sight of it knocks a sobering knot of reality back into my chest. This whole night wasn't just a fun social call. It's Sasha, speaking from beyond the grave.

I take the flash drive and shove it into my computer. "Let's see what she left for us."

Chapter Six

The moon hangs over the lake, lighting up the water rippling gently with a passing breeze. Decorative lampposts straight from Narnia dot the cemetery at random places, but other than that, we're in the dark. Elijah's black T-shirt and dark hair make his face look like a shadowy phantom next to me, and it's only now I realize how late it is.

I check the time on my phone; we've talked for over four hours. "Technically, the cemetery is closed now," I say, opening my laptop.

"Shit, are we locked in?" He looks behind us, the tendons in his neck straining.

"Nah. There aren't any gates. The sign at the front just says it closes at sundown but it's not like they can lock us in."

"No groundskeeper here to shoo us off?"

I glance at him just as the computer powers up, blasting both of us in the blue-green glow of my wallpaper. I've spent four hours with this guy and I don't know much about him besides his name and relation to my best friend.

"Where do you live?"

"Austin." His lips slide to the side of his mouth. "In the shady part."

"Wow," I say. "That's forty miles away."

I type in my password and my desktop appears.

"Yes, it is," he says all matter-of-fact. "You spend your whole life living just a few miles away from your own flesh and blood and don't even know it."

"Actually, I meant that's kind of *far*." I chew on my lip. I've had my license for two years and haven't driven as far as Austin yet. "Did you drive here?" My car was the only car in the lot when I arrived.

"My motorcycle is somewhere out there," he says, throwing his hand toward the east where it's too dark to see anything. "I came from the highway."

"Motorcycle. That's exactly like Sasha. She would have loved that."

"She did," he says, sliding closer to me on the bench, watching as I double-click to open the folder for the flash drive. "I told her about it and she said she'd love to take a ride on it but — well, we never met up. I might have pushed too hard to meet her at first," he says as tiny lines appear in his forehead. He shakes his head. "I was just excited. I had a sister and I wanted to meet her. But she was always kind of … distant about it."

"That's probably because of the cancer," I say. There's only one file on the flash drive, a video labeled *Hello*. It was saved there on April 3rd. "April? That's almost five months ago."

"That's shortly after we started emailing," Elijah says. He leans even closer and I can smell his soap, or maybe it's his shampoo. Citrusy and clean.

It kills me to think that Sasha had this big secret for so many months. I saw her every day. We talked all the time. She never even hinted about it. How could she have kept something this monumental from her best friend?

Elijah nudges my arm. I look over and flinch, not expecting him to be so close to me. Our legs are practically touching on the bench, and his elbow, resting on the back of it, is just millimeters from my shoulder.

"You okay?" he says, his eyes narrowed in concern as he looks me over. "I'm not trying to push you, but I'm dying to know what's on the video."

If Sasha kept something from me, she had her reasons. Right?

I double-click the video icon and it opens, full screen. Sasha's face appears right in the middle of it. I gasp as a sob lodges in my throat.

"Oh my God," I breathe. Sasha's hair is all stringy, looking like it hasn't been washed in weeks, but really that's just how bedhead on cancer treatment looks. She's wearing makeup, but her eyes are a little swollen. Her Zombie Radio shirt hangs loosely on her thinner frame. This was filmed back when things were still okay. We could hang out and eat junk food and stay up all night. She still got sick a lot, but it wasn't nearly as bad as in her final weeks.

"Hey, Rocki," she says, breaking into a grin. Chills prickle up my spine. Her eyes flicker to the right, my left, and she dips her head a little. "Hey, Elijah."

Now he flinches. She looks over to the left and shrugs. "Or maybe you're over here? Hell, I don't know. You're watching this on Rocki's computer, so I know she's" — she holds up her hands parallel in front of her, like a flight attendant — "right here." She smiles again and this time it reaches her eyes. Tears fill mine. Elijah's arm is around the back of the bench now, and he grabs my shoulder and doesn't let go.

"So," Sasha says, her chest inflating as she sits back a little. I can tell she's on her bed, her computer probably on her lap while she records this. There's a slight bit of golden fur to the right where Sunny is curled up. "By now, you two have met and probably talked, and you're watching this together."

She glances down at her hands, blinks a couple times and then looks back at us. "I guess I owe both of you an apology. Rocki, I'm not going to tell you about Elijah while I'm still alive. I just can't, okay? We met online when I was searching for my birth parents — who my real parents don't want me searching for — and, well, I already know I won't let him meet me when I'm alive." She glances back to the right, directly at Elijah. "I'll explain why in a minute, I swear. But Rocki, you can't know about this until after, okay? I can barely handle the news myself and I don't want to make things complicated. Because frankly, I think you'd encourage me to tell my parents about Elijah, and I can't do that."

I let out a sardonic laugh. "She's right," I say, filling the silence of Sasha's short pause.

She glances at her hands again and then back at us, probably trying to decide what to say next. I look over at Elijah, his eyes reflecting the computer screen. They're watery and blue and beautiful. They flit to me, and we watch each other for the smallest moment. Then Sasha talks again.

"Elijah, my brother, I'm sorry I didn't meet you earlier. I'm sorry I kept my distance and only emailed you." She takes a deep breath. "I'm dying, Elijah. There's going to be people crying at my funeral, people hurt because I'm gone. If I meet you now, you'll be one of those people."

The pain in her eyes while she says these words cracks the dam that's holding back my tears. I blink and they fall down my cheeks, the sensation so familiar it's almost comforting.

"I can't hurt another person, Elijah. I can't have one more person crushed. I've already hurt my parents, my best friend and so many others. I'm sorry. Please understand. Please know that I am so grateful to have found you before I died."

Elijah's grip on my shoulder tightens, his other hand wiping at his eyes. I lean my head against his arm, hoping the gesture comforts him, even just a little bit. On the screen, Sasha continues.

"So here's the deal. Elijah, you'll love Rocki. She's good people. And she's also stuck with you for a while, but something tells me she won't mind ... I mean, you're pretty cute, after all." At this, she leans forward and winks at the screen, *at me,* and my cheeks flush. *God, Sasha! He probably has a girlfriend!* I laugh and sob at the same time, and even Elijah chuckles.

"She doesn't have much of a filter," he mumbles.

Sasha sits back up. "So here's the deal. I've got my best friend and my brother, arguably the two best people on the planet, and I'm speaking to you both from beyond the grave. Why, you might ask?" She lowers her gaze and makes this mischievous smile, and it's like she's staring right into my soul. "This is my last wish: I want Elijah to know me, the *real* me." She grimaces. "Not the cancer-ridden, dying girl that I am now. I want him to know what my life was like, what shaped me into a person. If all of this mess had never happened, we would have still found each other, and I would have told him all these things myself. Instead, Raquel, I'm letting you take the reins. In the next few days and weeks, you'll both hear from me again. I have planned adventures, all of them are things or places or somethings — I'm not going to spoil it now — and each will show you a piece of my soul, a part of who I am. Don't worry about how you'll hear from me — I have some people helping me. They have your addresses and they'll get to you. They've promised to stay anonymous, so don't even try finding them, or you'll ruin the magic, okay?"

Elijah and I share another look. A warmth spreads through my chest at the idea of hearing from Sasha again. Judging by the spark in his eyes, I'd say he feels the same.

On my computer, Sasha continues. "I only have a couple of rules. One: no telling my parents. I'm serious, Rocki. Not a word. Actually, don't tell *anyone*. This is a small town and word travels." She points to the screen with two fingers and narrows her eyes. "I'm serious."

After a beat, she grins. "Rule number two: I want you to do everything together. Rocki can fill in the gaps and tell you more things that I can't. Don't hold anything back, Rocki. You can tell him the embarrassing parts of my life, he's my *brother* after all. He deserves to know."

She looks down and pulls her lips under her teeth. Beside me, Elijah has become so still I'm not sure he's even breathing. I don't want to take my eyes off Sasha for long enough to find out. Several moments pass, nothing but the sound of crickets and buzzing gnats in the cool summer air. I can see her breathing, so I know the video didn't freeze. Finally, she looks up with tears in her eyes.

"I'm a hopeless romantic. A book nerd. I'm outspoken when

someone does something stupid, and I've dragged Rocki on quite a few adventures. Some of them were fun, some were a waste of time. Telling you these things just gives you the facts. It doesn't let you *feel* or truly know me. So this project, it'll be my legacy for you both. One final adventure, from beyond the grave, and you two will live it out for me, okay?"

Sunny looks up at her and she rests a thin hand on top of his head. "I don't know how the afterlife works, but I'll try to be there with you guys every step of the way."

She blinks rapidly and then looks right at me again, her eyes red with tears that I never saw in real life. "This is important to me, Elijah. I can't change the past, but maybe I can change the future. *Your* future. I know I promised to help you and then I died, but don't give up on your dreams, brother. Raquel knows all about college. She can help you finish what we started."

Just when I think she's finished talking, she says, "I'm not even dead yet, and I miss you so much, Rocki. You were the best friend a person could ever have, and I love you so much." Her voice cracks on the last word. She drops her head into her hands and sobs, the racking sound matching my own here in the real world.

Elijah slides his arm tighter around my shoulder, reminding me that he's here. Sasha sits back up, wipes her eyes and tries to smile. This raw moment of weakness feels so foreign coming from Sasha. She was always so strong, so freaking jubilant while we were all losing our minds with worry. I figured she was faking it, and now I know she was. On screen, she tries to smile. "I love you both. And remember: Don't. Tell. Anyone."

She blinks a few times, then reaches toward the camera. And the video ends.

Chapter Seven

It's not a big deal that Zack ignores me all weekend. I have monumental things going on, like the fact that my best friend has a secret biological brother, and that at any moment, I might hear from her again. The mind-blowing factor of these two things is so high it's off the Richter scale. I can barely function all weekend, much less worry about Zack and how pissed he was that I canceled our movie date.

It was worth it.

So worth it.

So why do I get a pang of something like jealousy when I see his Instagram feed filled with pictures of him and other girls at some stupid party on Saturday night?

I should close the app — hell, I should *delete* the app — and go on with my life. I am now a girl with a massive secret. An exciting, life-altering secret.

But because I'm also an idiot, I scroll through the stupid photos, the #partypeeps, #bonfire, #hotgirls photos. Ugh.

Most of the photos could be explained away as your typical party stupidity. It's not like Zack is lip-locked with any of the girls from school; most of them are just arms around shoulders, red plastic cups tipped to their lips, typical party poses meant to make your social media profiles look cool.

But still.

I skim through some of the comments, cringing when Ansley Whittaker says: Damn, last night was insane. You can out-drink all of us.

Beneath it, Zack has replied: you know it babe with a wink-face emoji.

Babe is what he calls me, his on-again, off-again girlfriend. Seeing it used for another girl is the knife that severs our relationship. There's no way Zack and I will ever get back together, not after how careless he's been about Sasha dying. This is a breakup, there's no doubt about it. Probably the tenth time we've ended this relationship. I should be hurting, crying, ripping up the photo of us from sophomore year that's taped to my vanity mirror.

Instead I'm just … free.

It hurts, it does, but there are bigger things in the world. There is a full life ahead of me, one that Sasha wanted me to live without a guy like Zack, who would only hold me back. So instead of crying over my ruined relationship, I spend almost all of Sunday night lying awake in bed, feeling giddy and nervous and other things I can't decipher.

By Monday morning, even Mom thinks something's off, but I dismiss her worries by claiming that I'm still bummed over missing Sasha. It makes me feel awful, using her death as an excuse to conceal secrets and lies from my parents, but Sasha is the one who put me here in the first place.

Don't tell anyone.

Why? I've played the scenario over in my head a million times. *Mr. and Mrs. Cade, Sasha had a biological brother and they reconnected right before she died.* Wouldn't they be happy about this? Surely they would. I just have to trust that Sasha knows what she's doing.

Knew, I remind myself. She *knew* what she was doing. Elijah let me make a copy of the video on my computer, and I've played it more times than I checked Instagram this weekend. Seeing her alive and joyful in the video makes my heart sing. With the promise of more from her in the coming days and weeks, I can almost pretend she's not dead at all. That maybe she's holed up in some hotel room, sending Elijah and me on an adventure while she watches from the sidelines.

Seeing her face never fails to make me smile. I study the computer screen, memorizing the way her eyes sparkle when she smiles, the slight quirk of her eyebrow as she's talking about something that makes her really excited. Why didn't we make more home movies when she was alive? My phone is filled with photos of us: goofy, serious, trying fancy hairstyles on each other, but there are hardly any videos.

My greatest fear is that I'll start to forget the lilt in her voice, the way she crinkled her nose every time she took a sip of coffee because she actually thought it was gross but loved the coffee buzz. The way she'd hold a throw pillow close to her chest, biting her bottom lip while we watched the good part in a romantic movie.

I couldn't live with myself if I forgot those things. Monday after school, I rush through my pre-cal homework, then I power up my computer and watch the video again.

* * *

Zack doesn't talk to me on Monday or Tuesday, and by Wednesday morning, the anxiety that he might find me in the hallways doesn't even bother to manifest anymore. Zack seems like old news now, since I spend every waking second either missing Sasha or checking my email and the mailbox, hoping to get another message from her. I mourn, I obsess.

I eat lunch alone, ignoring my old table in favor of a bench outside the library. When I wasn't dating Zack, Sasha and I used to float around the lunchroom, eating with various friends who were all excited when we came by. The last few months, we stayed at one table, the popular table, where all of Sasha's self-appointed friends (and Zack) accepted us as if we'd always been there. Now that she's gone, those friends haven't asked me to join them all week. Maybe they think things would be awkward now? They'd be right. No worries. I eat my chicken salad alone, eyes on my phone as I refresh my email yet again.

This isn't healthy, and I know it. Part of me doesn't care, and the other part of me — the one smart enough to get into vet school — thinks I should get a hobby.

After school on Wednesday, I call Mom and tell her I'll be a little late, and then I drive over to Izzy's Flowers.

The front room of the flower shop looks like a pink rose monster threw up all over the place. Well … if a rose monster's vomit looks like vases filled with skillfully arranged bouquets.

"Izzy?" I call out, walking through the small footpath between racks and racks of flowers. They're stacked on top of every available surface, lining the floor all the way to the front counter.

"Billy?" Izzy calls out from the maze. "That you?"

"No," I call back, peering through a temporary plastic shelving unit to see Izzy walking up to the counter. "It's, uh, it's me."

Saying my own name would be the next step here, and maybe it's the overwhelming perfume of roses, but my body feels prickly, like thorns full of anxiety are pressing into me. I came here expecting a job, but did Izzy really mean that? Maybe I should buy flowers or something to make it look like I had a reason to come here.

I slip into the small free space on the customer side of the front counter. It's about one floor tile wide, and can't possibly be in accordance with fire codes.

"Raquel," Izzy says, the lines around her lips creasing into a smile. "It's good to see you. I've been wanting to tell you that you gave a beautiful eulogy."

"Thank you," I say, feeling heat rush to my cheeks. I'm not one for loving compliments, and her memory of the funeral only makes my heart jump in anticipation of the next note from Sasha.

"Sorry for the mess," Izzy says. "Billy is half an hour late, *of course.*"

"What are all these flowers for?" I try to glance around, but mostly I focus on making myself as small as possible so I don't knock any of them over.

"Big fancy wedding over in Rosehill," she says. "The bride is a little stuck-up, but of course I'm not allowed to say that." She rolls her eyes. "She wanted more pink roses than anyone in the entire state had in stock, so she ordered from five of us. *Five* florists! Something like ten thousand pink roses in total."

"Wow," I say. "If I had that kind of money, I wouldn't spend it on flowers."

"That's why we work here," Izzy says, giving me a conspiratorial wink. "We take the money from those who have too much."

"We?"

"Well, that's why you're here, right?" Izzy reaches under the counter, her denim dress pooling around her feet, and pulls out a dark purple apron, still in the plastic bag. "You ready to start working?"

I rip open the bag, shake out the new apron and hook it around my neck, tying the strings around my waist. It smells like new clothing, and there's an embroidered Izzy's Flowers logo in the center. Hands on my hips, I say, "How do I look?"

"Like someone still healing from a loss." Her lips tuck into a slight frown. "But there's no better way to heal than to work hard."

Izzy puts a weathered hand on top of mine and then glances behind me, toward the front of the store. "Looks like Billy's finally here," she says, just as the front door opens. "Let's start loading the truck, hmm?"

She grabs a vase of flowers and I follow her lead. Soon, the truck is filled but the store is only a third of the way empty, meaning Billy, a thin Hispanic man with the coolest handlebar mustache, has to make two more trips for the day.

I focus on working quickly and working hard, the desire to impress my new boss growing with each minute that I'm on the clock. While we work, she tells me I'll be getting paid thirteen dollars an hour (woot!) and that I can fill out a tax form before I leave for the day.

She's right about the hard work. It's nine o'clock when we watch Billy drive away with the last load of pink roses, and Izzy flips the *Open* sign on the door to the *Closed* position. Only then, when we have a quiet moment to breathe, do I remember all the things on my mind.

Sasha's dying wish. Elijah. The ever-pressing ball of agony in my stomach that reminds me I'll never see her alive again.

I pull my phone from my back pocket, realizing that I haven't checked it since before I drove here.

I have a few messages from Mom, asking if I'll be home for dinner and then telling me she'll save some leftovers just in case. There's a new email from school, reminding the student body of the blood drive next week. But that's all. I shut off the screen as I slide the phone back in my pocket.

Izzy and I set up a work schedule, which is probably the best schedule ever. She says I can come in whenever I want and we exchange phone numbers so she can text me when we get big orders and she needs my help.

I have a feeling I'll be spending a lot of time at Izzy's Flowers. It's fun, it smells great, and the boss is like one of those spiritual, wise older people in a movie about finding yourself. Now, I need to be found more than anything.

My phone pings as I'm pulling into the driveway, that familiar little chirp that signals the arrival of a new email. I tell myself to chill out.

I park my car and cut off the engine, then slide down the notification bar on my phone.

1 new email from: thefuturesasha@gmail.com

Like the Hoover Dam bursting, an adrenaline rush erupts through my body, making every inch of me feel alive. I open the email and read the message, blinking several times because all those tears that always seem to be lingering on the edge of my eyelids cloud my vision.

Dear Rocki and Elijah,

Hey there, favorites. As I sit here and reflect on who I am as a person, what makes me tick, what makes me feel happy and fulfilled, I almost immediately land on the lake.

For as long as I can remember, my family spent summers, Memorial Days, Thanksgiving weekends — okay, basically every holiday except Christmas — out on Lake Peyton in my parents' kick-ass boat. Sitting on the back of the boat, my feet dangling in the water and Mom floating in front of me, clapping her hands for me to jump into her arms — that's actually my first memory.

There's something magical about floating on the dark blue water, letting the sun warm your skin and the sounds of nature fill your soul. The way the wind blows through your hair, making it hella messy, but still kind of sexy once you get old enough to realize that beach hair is the best — well, that's also magical. I love the lake and I love cruising on the boat. Rocki, please tell Elijah all about that time we went skiing and ran out of gas and had to flag down those drunk college dudes to get my dad from the shore. Tell him the other stories, too, okay?

And here's your adventure. Head out to the marina this Saturday, pack a lunch and take out the boat. The password is 21581, my parents' wedding anniversary, and the boat will already be gassed up, because I've arranged this.

My parents won't know because they don't ever go out on the boat anymore. It'll be just between us, capisce?

Have fun.

I love you and miss you both,
Sasha

Chapter Eight

There's no way in hell I'm going to steal Mr. Cade's boat. That thing is like a second child to him, a two-hundred-thousand-dollar baby that he loves almost as much as he loves his human family. Besides, I'm not even sure *how* to take the thing even if I do stoop so low as to commit grand theft auto (or whatever you call it when it's a boat).

He'd let Sasha and me drive it quite a few times, but that was once we were out of the dock and out in the open lake with nothing around us but water. Steering the thing around all the other boats docked in the marina? Starting it up, making sure all the gauges are correct and the engine isn't going to, like, overheat or something? Not. Happening.

I can't do this. It's the very first thing Sasha's asking me to do for her brother and I'm going to have to back out.

Maybe I'll just meet him there and tell him. He should understand, right?

But sitting on a bench at the marina, simply *describing* what it was like all those summers out on the lake with Sasha's family — that's not going to cut it.

For the millionth time, I wonder why I can't just tell the Cades about Elijah. Surely, they'd understand; they'd probably offer to take us out on the boat themselves. I throw my head back and look at the gray upholstered roof in my car.

Sasha, you're barely gone and I'm already letting you down.

It's been five days since I met Elijah in the cemetery and, not for the first time, I'm kicking myself for not getting his phone number or something. Shouldn't we be able to talk? If anyone could understand the pain I'm in, it would be Elijah.

I'm toweling off my hair when I get an idea so freaking obvious that I curse out loud for not having thought of it sooner. The email was addressed to both of us. That means …

Still standing stark naked in my bedroom, I grab my phone and pull up the email. In the header information, right there in all its pixelated glory, are two email addresses. Mine and elijah0delgado@gmail.com.

Sasha helped me make my email address when I got my first cell phone back in sixth grade. We were idiot kids, and I chose the handle rockibobocki, and I never bothered changing it. Elijah's simple, straightforward email address just fits him. After only one meeting, I know he's the kind of guy who can be trusted. He's serious — he'll totally understand why we can't steal a boat on Saturday. Finally, I have a way to tell him.

I stare at his email address for two days.

Too bad I never get the guts to message him.

* * *

When the final bell rings on Friday, I nearly jump out of my skin. My eighth-period U.S. history class has a substitute teacher, so she'd put on a film for us to watch about the civil war. I've been distracted all week as it is, but a boring film playing too loudly in a darkened classroom was enough to send me into a catatonic state.

I collect my backpack slowly, blinking and swallowing as I try to regain some self-control. Every day since the email, I've been a walking bundle of nerves. The rest of the school is psyched for the weekend, but I couldn't be further from excited. This must be what an anxiety attack feels like, I realize, as I grit my teeth and try to focus on breathing. I don't even go to my locker to drop off my history book, as I need all my energy to make it to my car.

At home, I change into clothes for work. I am numb as I move around my room. Procrastination is no longer my friend.

Poor Elijah has probably been excited for this boat trip for days and I'm an asshole for not breaking the news to him sooner. What have I been afraid of? That he's going to think I'm a lame excuse of a best friend, one who can't even break some rules to honor his sister's death?

Yes, that's exactly it. I need Elijah to like me. The only thing worse than not fulfilling Sasha's last wish would be leaving him feeling like it was all a pathetic waste of time because his tour guide sucked.

Sasha had nothing but blind faith in me, so the least I can do is have some myself. I can make this work without stealing a boat. Before I leave for Izzy's, I sit down in front of my computer, open Sasha's email and click on his username to create a new email.

Hey,
I'm really sorry but we can't steal the Cades' boat ...

Sasha is crazy. I was thinking we could just go visit
the marina or something? I can still tell you stories,
I promise. I just hate to think what would happen if
we got caught.
Raquel

Elijah must be on a computer somewhere, because I get a
reply only three minutes later, while I'm attempting to brush
my scraggly hair into some kind of uniform direction. Heart
thundering, I walk over and click on his message.

Having been in enough legal trouble in my life, there's
no way I'm stealing a boat, either. See attached. ;-)

Before finishing the email, I click on the PDF attachment. It's
a receipt from the marina. My mouth falls open as I read over it.
He's gone and rented a boat for three hours on Saturday. I look
up and check the date at the top of the receipt. He booked it the
day after Sasha's email. He already knew. This whole time of me
freaking out was for nothing because Elijah already had a plan.
I close the PDF and go back to his email.

Hope that's okay? I'll bring lunch, you bring dessert?
See ya,
Elijah

I grin while tiny acrobats do happy dances in my stomach.
Oh, it's more than okay, Elijah. It's perfect.

Chapter Nine

Mom flips on the coffee maker and turns, one hand on her hip while she watches me scarfing down my breakfast. She reaches for a coffee mug and then peers down at me. "You're up early."

"It's ten thirty," I say with a snort as I shovel down another bite. This rumble in my stomach is unmistakably *hunger*. For the first time since Sasha's death, I'm genuinely famished.

Mom grabs a spoon and French vanilla coffee creamer, then pulls out the chair next to me at the kitchen table. "Whatever you put in your Cheerios, I want some."

"Nothing but cereal and milk in here, Mom."

"Could have fooled me," she says. "You have any plans today?"

"Yeah, I'm, uh —" I pull my eyebrows together and stare at my cereal like I just found a hair in it or something. Shit. I've been so thrilled about Elijah renting the boat that I haven't thought up a cover story. It's too soon after Sasha's death to go to parties, or shop all day at the mall, or hang out with other friends. I wouldn't even do any of those things without Sasha, anyway.

I clear my throat, inspired. "I'm thinking of heading to the library. Get caught up on homework and stuff."

"That's wonderful, honey. I have some books to return, so I could go with you."

"No, that's okay," I say a little too quickly. I scoop up another bite of Cheerios and smile. "I'll just take your books back for you. I'll probably be a while … a few hours. Don't want to make you wait."

"Okay, thanks. They're by the couch."

I stand and rinse my bowl out in the sink, forgoing my usual drinking-of-the-milk routine because I don't want to give her the chance to see the lie on my face.

"Have a good day," Mom calls as I leave.

"Don't worry," I say sarcastically. "You know how much I love schoolwork."

Sasha's neighborhood is a stretch of lakefront homes. Just west of it, there's a strip of lakefront restaurants and shopping centers, plus of course the marina. They built a Starbucks three years ago, and our tiny town freaked out at having a big coffee chain.

At the marina, I pull into an empty parking spot next to an older black motorcycle. I'm not entirely sure it's Elijah's, but we'd agreed to meet near the Starbucks, so the chances are good.

A Starbucks truly is the sign of living in modern civilization. Up until Sasha's initial diagnosis, we spent nearly every Sunday morning here, sipping Frappuccinos and watching the sailboats go by.

I park my car and pull a pair of sunglasses from my center console, doing a quick check in the visor mirror to make sure my choppy hair is tucked behind my ears and not sticking out over the tops of the glasses.

Elijah appears on the other side of the Starbucks glass door just after I flip my visor up. He's in a white T-shirt that fits snugly over his chest and arms, revealing a muscular frame I hadn't noticed last time I saw him.

Though it's warm enough to go swimming, I guess we both had the same idea — that swimming together would be weird — because Elijah wears a pair of faded, light blue jeans and those same running shoes. His black hair flies around in the breeze, and that thin silver chain around his neck glints in the sunlight.

I wave at him and reach into my back seat, retrieving a pale green bag from Gigi's Cupcakes.

Elijah meets me at my car, two Frappuccinos in his hands. "Java Chip, right?"

"How'd you know?"

He takes a slow sip from his own coffee, a caramel Frap by the looks of it. "Sasha talked a lot about you in our emails. She said you were both addicted to Java Chip."

"*Addicted* might be an understatement," I say, lifting my straw so I can get a sip of whipped cream. It only just now dawns on me that Elijah probably has no money. "What do I owe you?" I say, reaching for my purse.

"Nothing," he says, his lips still wrapped around his straw. "It's on me."

I hesitate, my hand on my wallet. "My parents give me cash all the time, so it's not a big deal. I can pay you back."

He shakes his head. "I have a job," he says, emphasizing the last word. "If you don't let me buy you a coffee every now and then, busting my ass forty hours a week would be for nothing."

Every now and then. I drop the wallet back in my purse. "Thank you."

I hold up the cupcake bag. "I brought dessert."

"Sweet." He reaches across his motorcycle and grabs a blue backpack from the handlebar. "Lunch is in here. Do you like tacos?"

"Uh, who *doesn't* like tacos?"

"Good deal," he says quickly. I think we're both aware that all of this happy small talk is awkward no matter how we wrap it.

Now that I'm officially spending the day with him on Sasha's first adventure, the pressure to make sure he has a good time is almost overwhelming. We agreed about not stealing a boat — maybe the rest of the day will go smoothly as well.

Still, what if I screw all of this up? I'm the one who knows my way around Sasha's life, so the pressure is on me, not him. "I was thinking I could show you Sasha's boat first," I say, lifting my shoulders. I stammer more words just to keep talking. "You know, so you can see what it looks like. Is that okay?"

He slings his backpack over his shoulders and hooks his thumbs around the straps. "Totally."

To the left of the Starbucks, a sidewalk dips down to the water's edge and then wraps around the back of the restaurants and shops. We pass three wooden docks until we get to the row I've been to a million times. Unlike the public docks, these private slots are guarded by a metal gate with a key code on the door. Each boat owner has their own code, even though it's the same gate. I punch in the Cades' wedding anniversary date and the rusty metal hinges squeak as we enter.

It's a long walk down the narrow dock to get to slot number eighteen, where *Sue's Paradise* floats on the water, filled with enough memories to sink the freaking *Titanic*. My heart races as we make the trek; we're not doing anything wrong just by being here, but I'm still afraid of getting caught.

Sue's Paradise isn't the biggest boat here, but it's close. Like a mini yacht, it's white with a long purple stripe down the middle, two bedrooms, a kitchen, a bathroom down below and a viewing/party area up top. Then, of course, there's the wide deck at the front of the boat, which makes for the best sunbathing a girl could ask for.

"I forgot we can only see the ass end," I say with a little laugh when we reach the boat. There's a small walkway, a ladder up to the top and a narrow door back here, positioned between the two motors.

"They really do have money," Elijah says, using his hand to shield the sun from his eyes. "I mean, Sasha alluded to it but ..."

"Yeah." I kick at a sharp piece of wood that's splintered off one of the boards of the dock. "Mr. Cade is a lawyer. He's uh ... Walter Cade."

Elijah lowers his hand, his brows disappearing into his scraggly hair. "Walter Cade, *the tough Texas lawyer*?" he says, doing a near-perfect impression of the deep voice-over on Mr. Cade's TV commercials.

"The very same," I say, letting out a sigh. The Cades could have afforded to raise two kids, and if Sasha's birth parents had only given them up at the same time, maybe they could have been together.

Maybe Elijah is thinking the same thing, because his expression is tight, almost like he's annoyed. He points toward the boat's shiny backside. "That's probably for us."

I follow his finger to an envelope taped to the boat's back door. I can't read the writing from here, but the pink Sharpie gives it away.

We share an excited grin as I rush over to the edge of the

dock. I pause, looking down at the dark distance of water that stretches about a foot from the dock to the boat's narrow walkway. This is the part I've always hated. That little hop from the shore to the boat, those few inches between safety and safety, where one misstep sends you falling into the abyss below.

"Here," Elijah says. He leaps over the abyss in a quick step, then turns around and offers me his hand.

Eager to read Sasha's note, I slip my cupcake bag onto my elbow, take his hand and jump across. Once I'm safely (and probably illegally) on someone else's private property, I make the mistake of glancing up at Elijah, and our eyes meet. My anxiety only eases up a bit when he blinks. "You okay?" he asks, his hands on my elbows to steady me. He doesn't smell like motor oil today, just the faint scent of soap.

I nod stupidly and turn around, ripping the envelope off the door. I fold the piece of masking tape around the top of the envelope, noticing a black grease thumbprint on it. I wonder who Sasha asked to put this here? Are they watching us now?

"Let's go," I say, leaping back onto the dock without waiting for Elijah's help. He follows me back down the dock and out the metal gate, and then we head to the boat rental booth a few docks down.

"What do you think it says?" He's grinning as he nudges me with his elbow.

I turn the envelope over in my hands: another greeting card by the looks of it. I blow out the breath I've been holding and gaze up at him, glad he can't see my eyes through these massive sunglasses. "Something that will make me cry, I'm sure." I can't deal with this right now.

Mother Nature has blessed us with a beautiful day for

boating out on the lake. The sun glitters on the water, a dark blue oasis in the middle of Texas. There are other boats out, some Jet Skis and an *actual* yacht, but Elijah steers us away from everyone else, cutting the throttle once we're in the middle of an empty bay.

"How'd you learn how to drive a boat so well?" I ask, rising from the squishy seat and attempting to smooth down my crazy hair. This tiny boat is nothing like the luxury of *Sue's Paradise*. It's a ski boat, so it's impossibly small, made only for pulling someone on skis or an inner tube while two or three people sit on board. The pleather seats are cracked and faded, and the inside is covered in laminated safety warnings taped there by the rental company.

Elijah shoots me a grin and then walks the short distance to the back of the boat, where a blue canopy is folded down, locked into place. "You don't want to know," he says while he unbuckles the straps. I help him undo the other side and we both raise the canopy, locking it into position. Now we can hang out for hours without getting baked into human cookies.

"Well, now I have to know." I sit on one of the two long bench seats that face each other. It's not like I'd say it out loud, but I'm not sure how a guy who grew up in a group home would have ever learned how to drive a boat.

He hefts his backpack up on the opposite bench seat and pulls out a small cooler filled with sodas. After offering me one, he takes out a to-go bag from Paco's Tacos.

"I'm waiting," I say, crossing my arms.

"We're supposed to be talking about Sasha, not my boat-driving knowledge."

I reach over and take the envelope, which is still unopened, and hold it threateningly over the side of the boat. It's an empty threat, of course. I'd never toss anything from my best friend.

Elijah shakes his head and says, "Fine. But no laughing."

"I won't laugh."

He grabs three foil-wrapped tacos from the bag, then hands one to me. "I spent like two hours online, watching videos about it. I mean, I figured it can't be much harder than driving a motorcycle."

I'm pretty sure I can drive this boat myself if I need to, otherwise his confession might scare me. Instead, I just think it's really, really cute. I force my lips to remain still. Elijah points at me. "You promised, Raquel!"

His breezy tone makes me think of Sasha. I bring the envelope back into my lap and rip it open.

"Read it out loud?" Elijah says.

"'Hey favorites, it's your favorite dead person again. I'm sorry, is that too soon? When can you start making jokes about being dead? Surely I can do it first, since I'm the dead one. Anyhow, you're getting this note at the marina. I hope you have a kick-ass time at the lake, I hope the weather is beautiful, and if the rules of the afterlife somehow let me hang out on the boat with you, I will.

"'The second part of your adventure today is a quick one. It's not really a big deal, but I'm adding it to the list because it's not every day you get a photo of yourself memorialized forever. Rocki, take him to Karen's Dance Studio and show him that photo, okay? That's all for now. I love you and miss you both. Sasha.'"

"A photo at a dance studio?" Elijah asks, his head seeming to rise and fall as the boat rocks from a passing boat's wake.

"Sasha was a ballerina for several years," I explain between bites of my taco. Even after sitting in a backpack on a motorcycle ride, these things are really good. "Sasha won at the state level, and it was the first and only time someone from that little studio won anything fancy. Ten-year-old Sasha is on a massive plaque hanging on the wall. It's like five feet tall, no joke."

"I definitely have to see that," Elijah says, balling up the foil from his first taco and tossing it back in the bag. He reaches for another one and then slides down in the seat, stretching out his legs and tipping his head toward the sun. "This is going to be a great day."

I watch him, head tipped back, a serene look on his face. I wonder if he ever had days like this as a kid, if he even knows how much he missed out on compared to Sasha's extraordinary life.

I want to ask him. I want to talk about his life, his childhood, his hopes and dreams and biggest fears. But this adventure isn't about Elijah, or me. It's about Sasha. This is her last wish, not mine.

"So," I say, draining the last sip from my Frappuccino. "Which lake story should I tell you first ..."

Chapter Ten

Thirteen days have passed without another word from Sasha. And yes, I'm counting. When your dead best friend sends you messages from beyond the grave, promising adventures, I think it's okay to get a little obsessive when waiting for the next one. My cell phone constantly needs to be charged because I check my emails so often. I've been bitched at by all of my teachers for looking at my phone in class, but I don't really care.

My whole existence has been whittled down to one thing: waiting.

School goes by in a blur. I'm no longer floating in Sasha's popularity cloud, and because of it, I'm getting straight A's in all of my classes again. It's a little awkward to adjust to being just another face in the crowd, but I like it this way. I don't want to talk to people who will just remember how nice and sweet she was all the time. I knew the real Sasha, and she means more to me than any of her superficial school friends will ever understand. I don't exactly *like* school, but I'm grateful for the distraction. Focusing on assignments and homework keeps my mind temporarily off Sasha's last wish.

And Elijah.

He also hasn't emailed me these last two weeks, not that I should expect him to, I guess. I mean, I want to email him, to continue the conversations we had that day at the lake. Talking with Elijah comes easily, even when the subject is something that breaks my heart. Is it weird to wish I could keep doing it even without Sasha's directions?

What had started out as a sobering reminder of how much I missed Sasha had turned into a wonderful day. Lounging on our rented ski boat, I told Elijah every single lake story I could remember, including the details that may not even matter, like how Sasha always smelled like coconut sunblock at the lake. The only details I didn't go into were the ones pertaining to me. Like how Zack spent quite a few lake trips with us out on Sasha's boat.

Then we'd visited Karen's Dance Studio and I'd shown him the epic photo of his little sister in her ballet heyday. We didn't stay there very long, since the whole studio was filled with tiny ballerinas and their parents, and we totally didn't fit in.

Those two days I've spent with Elijah were the only times I've felt okay since Sasha's death … maybe even before. Suddenly I realize I've been on edge pretty much since the day she was diagnosed.

Even though Elijah is just a sack of genetic material that matches Sasha's, and even though I've only just met him and he could be a serial murderer for all I know, it feels like I can breathe when I'm with him. Like I can stop wishing it had been me instead of Sasha, stop mourning every second of the day, if only to have enough energy to share my life — and Sasha's — with him.

* * *

My phone rings bright and early on Sunday morning. As soon as I see Mrs. Cade's name on the screen, I sit up and stretch and try not to let my voice sound like I've been sleeping. She has enough to worry about and I don't need her fretting over waking me up.

Mrs. Cade's voice is cheery, almost like it used to be, before everything. "Good morning, sweetheart. I didn't wake you, did I?"

"Nope," I say brightly. "It's nice hearing from you. What's up?"

"If you're not busy, I was hoping to have you over for lunch today. I have a big pitcher of strawberry sangria — nonalcoholic, of course — and I'm making chicken Cobb salad with extra avocados," she says, practically singing the last part because she knows avocados are my favorite. (The rest of the meal was Sasha's.)

"I'd love to come over for lunch," I say, and I don't even have to fake my enthusiasm. Mrs. Cade's Cobb salads make salad actually good.

"Oh, I'm so excited to hear that," she says. "Want to come around noon?"

"I'll be there," I say. When the call is over, I fall back on my bed, my head crushing into the pillow.

I've had Sunday lunch at the Cades' house a million times, but this is the first time the invitation came directly from Mrs. Cade. I'd promised Sasha that I would always make time to visit her parents after she was gone, but this is the first time I'm actually doing it. I cover my eyes with my arm and make a vow to call Mrs. Cade at least once a week. I swing by Izzy's just before noon and grab a bouquet of daises, but when Izzy hears who they're for, she steers me toward a purple orchid instead. She makes a good point that Sasha's parents have probably thrown out dozens of dead arrangements after the funeral. They need one that will live.

The orchid in my hand, I knock on the Cades' massive front door. It swings open almost immediately, and Mrs. Cade's eyes sparkle when she sees me. Unlike Sasha, my friend's adoptive mother has brown eyes and long, white-blond hair that's always a little frizzy. But her welcoming smile looks just like my best friend's.

It is deeply weird to be here without Sasha.

"This is for you," I say, holding out the orchid to her mom. Sunny appears next to her, his tail thumping against the doorframe.

"How beautiful! Thank you." Mrs. Cade tucks the orchid into the crook of her elbow and then pulls me into a hug, the scent of her perfume overpowering the real flowers. "How have you been, sweetheart?"

"I'm okay." It's the truest thing I've said all week. Okay. Not good, not bad, just in neutral. On impulse, I want to ask her how she is, but I hold back. No reason to make her lie to me.

She gives my arm a squeeze and then closes the door behind us. "Lunch is ready. Since it's such a beautiful day, I thought we'd eat outside. What do you think?"

"Sounds good to me. Is Mr. Cade here?"

She shakes her head as we walk into the large kitchen, where the white granite counters reflect the sunlight from the glass wall behind us. The entire north side of the Cades' house overlooks the lake, and the architect made this wall mostly windows because of it.

"He's at work, on a *Sunday,* if you can believe it," she says with a laugh. "They're looking into acquiring some smaller firms in the greater Austin area, so they do all that work on the weekends so as not to interfere with their daily work."

"Cool," I say, remembering the look on Elijah's face when he discovered that Sasha's adoptive dad is the famous Walter Cade. I bet they would be just as shocked if they knew about Elijah. An uncomfortable feeling settles into my stomach, but I try to ignore it. For now, I have to pretend he doesn't exist.

Two perfectly arranged chicken Cobb salads wait on the counter, their toppings in neat little rows. Mine has two rows of diced avocado and a cup of ranch dressing next to it.

"Looks great," I say. Maybe I'm not doing so well if even a salad can bring me to the brink of tears. Cobb salad was Sasha's favorite — she was of the mindset that a salad isn't worth eating if it's not full of bacon bits, ranch dressing and cheddar cheese. Can't say I disagree with that.

The back of the house has beautiful views of the lake. There's a long porch that wraps around it and a matching balcony upstairs as well. I can't believe Sasha will never see this view again.

We sit at the patio table and Mrs. Cade pulls the plastic wrap from her glass pitcher of sangria. Little orange slices and strawberries float in the ice as she pours our glasses.

Sunny sits between our chairs, his eyes on the table. If any scrap of food drops, he'll be right there to get it. I can almost see Sasha, sitting here with us, tossing him a piece of bacon every few seconds. Mrs. Cade would gripe at her for feeding the dog table scraps and Sasha would apologize. Then she'd do it again.

Having lunch with Sasha's mom isn't that uncomfortable after all. I feared I'd be swallowed up with guilt, but soon, we've fallen into conversation and it's almost like the old days. We chat about school, how my parents are doing and about working at Izzy's. Mrs. Cade is concerned that I might give up my dream of going to vet school just because I picked up a part-time job in a totally different field, but I assure her I'm still excited to work at the animal clinic next summer. I get the feeling that she cares more about my future now that her child isn't getting one.

We live just outside of the Texas hill country, so the land slopes but isn't as jagged and hilly as it is near Austin. The Cades' neighborhood is on a big hill that slopes downward toward the lake, and then the grass turns to rocks and slips into the water a few acres away. Although it's considered a lake house, their backyard is mostly trees and rocks, with some grassy patches between.

Two deer amble through the yard, their ears twitching.

"Go get the bucket," Mrs. Cade whispers, pointing toward a plastic container near the porch railing. I grin and rush over there, unscrewing the cap. Inside is a bunch of dried corn, and the deer freaking love it. I grab a handful and toss it out.

The deer rush to eat it all and then look back up at me, begging for more. I toss another handful, my elbows warm on the wooden deck railing as I lean over and coo at the adorable wild whitetails. Soon, more appear out of the trees and I'm feeding about twenty of them while Mrs. Cade comments on how cute they are. It's not nearly as much fun without Sasha here to give them all funny names.

"I come out here every morning and give them a little snack,"

Mrs. Cade says, handing me a glass that she's refilled. "They're getting an extra treat now."

"They're little gluttons," I say, tossing out another handful of corn.

"I remember how much corn we went through when you girls were little," she says, reaching into the bucket to toss some toward a fawn that's ventured near us. "I'd be inside cooking and all I could hear were giggles and I knew y'all must be feeding the deer."

I smile at the warm memory of our childhood. I loved coming here when I was younger. "I miss her," I say, breaking my own rule of not saying anything that will make me sad.

"I think we always will," Mrs. Cade says softly. When she turns to me, her eyes are brimming with tears. "Every day I just tell myself how lucky I am to have had her in my life, even if only for a little while."

I nod, my throat too tight to say anything. Which is lucky, because I'm afraid I'll blurt out what I'm really thinking. It is killing me to keep Elijah a secret, especially now when Mrs. Cade and I are sharing this moment of raw pain.

I think meeting Elijah would be good for her. But I can't break my promise to Sasha, no matter how much I wish I could, so I bite the inside of my lip and put on a smile.

"Thanks for having me over," I say.

"Anytime, Raquel." Mrs. Cade's hand wraps around my shoulder. "You're a part of the family, I hope you know that. I'm here for you anytime."

Before I leave, I lie and say I need to use the restroom. Since Mrs. Cade is busy loading dishes into the dishwasher, I bypass the half bath in the hallway and rush upstairs, Sunny on my heels. I don't even realize what I'm doing until I'm standing in Sasha's doorway.

Her room is just the way she left it, bed made, a stack of romance novels on her nightstand.

Tiny pictures of us from photo booths are taped to the side of her vanity mirror. Her curtains are pulled open, revealing her familiar bay window.

My hand rests on the doorframe. I don't go inside because I know I can't bear it. After a moment, I breathe in deeply, the scent of Sasha's room igniting every memory I have of my best friend. Sunny appears beside me. I lean down and wrap him in a warm doggie hug. He licks my forehead and I smile, despite the pain. "I miss her, too," I whisper.

I close my eyes and set every part of her room to memory. This room is still Sasha, even though Sasha is gone.

Chapter Eleven

There's a package waiting for me when I get home from school on Monday. It's about the size of a shoebox, with unfamiliar handwriting addressing the package to me. The return address simply says "A friend" and I know it's from Sasha.

In my excitement, I almost call Izzy and say I won't be coming into work today. Then I think better of it and take the package inside, sneaking past Dad, who is passed out in the recliner. He just got home from an eighteen-hour truck route so he's going to be exhausted for a while. He'll probably sleep until he goes back to work on Wednesday.

In my room, I close the door and rip open the box, Hulk-style. Adrenaline and excitement have me tossing handfuls of packing peanuts onto my bed as I dig out the contents. Five brand-new DVDs, all of them movies I've seen a million times with Sasha.

The Breakfast Club, Ever After, The Princess Bride, Mean Girls and *Harry Potter and the Prisoner of Azkaban.*

As I flip through the stack of movies, each one sends a tidal wave of emotions rolling over me. At the very bottom of the box is another greeting card, Sasha's handwritten *To Raquel* on the front. I rip open the envelope. This greeting card has three fat little puppies on it, all wearing sunglasses. I smile and open the card. The pink Sharpie note is simply a web address.

Heart pounding, I rush to my laptop and yank it open to type in the URL, which is just a random assortment of letters and numbers.

A video pops up on an otherwise empty web page. Below the video are four other links of random letters and numbers. I click play.

It's kind of a routine now. Sasha's face appears on the screen, and I start crying. I wipe away the tears and watch her leaning in close to the webcam on her computer. She's wearing a lime green tank top and her hair is piled up in a bun, a headband covering her thinning hairline.

"'Sup? It's me, your favorite friend and sister. So, Rocki, you're probably wondering why I sent you a stack of movies that you already own. Easy. They're for Elijah. He told me he owns exactly two DVDs, and they're both stupid boy movies with guns and action" — she gags at this — "and I decided he needs to own my five favorite movies of all time. Also, he only gave me his work address and I didn't want to send a box of DVDs to a body shop."

Now I know why Elijah smelled faintly of motor oil that day. Sasha's still talking. "But that's not all, of course. My next adventure is a movie night. If you click on the links below, you'll see my project took some major commitment. I want you guys to get together and watch each movie. The links below are videos of me watching each movie as well. I'll tell you when to click play, and then we'll get to watch it together. Cool, huh?"

She pauses, her eyes watching the camera, and I almost reply out loud. The rest of the video goes by in a blur, and I have to watch it twice to get all of her instructions.

She's giving us one week to do this, and then we'll get our next adventure.

Sasha looks into the camera and says one more thing before the video ends. "Have fun with these movies, okay? The next adventure on my list is a hard one. But I guess that's life, huh? Sometimes it's beautiful like the lake and hilarious like these movies. Other times ..." She pauses and looks down at her hands, then her wide blue eyes seem to bore into mine. "Other times it hurts like a motherfucker."

* * *

I read over my email again. Those gut-wrenching feelings of low self-esteem kick in, and I analyze every single word, wondering if I said or did something wrong. It's been twenty-four hours since I emailed Elijah with a link to Sasha's videos and a picture of the DVDs she sent me to give him. I asked when we could meet up and gave him my cell number. No reply.

No text.

What is going on?

Meanwhile, Zack won't stop blowing up my phone. His newest tactic is to ask for a date, just a "simple date," and then berate me for saying I'm not sure if I feel like going on a simple date.

And of course I can't tell him why I seem so distracted because not only is Elijah a secret, the fact that he hasn't replied to me is also a secret. How can I tell someone what's wrong when *I can't tell them what's wrong*?

Today I really do call in to work. Izzy doesn't mind and doesn't seem to care because she says Tuesdays are the slowest days of the week. Since Homecoming was last Friday, flower buying has slowed down for a while.

I eat dinner with my parents, and Dad says I look like I've grown up in the short time he was away for work. I roll my eyes and stab a bite of Mom's shepherd's pie, and everyone laughs like everything is totally normal.

At eight thirty, my phone gets a new email. I rush over to my computer, wanting to see Elijah's reply as big and bright as possible because reading it on a phone screen right now might drive me insane.

> Raquel,
> Hey there. I'm off work Wednesday and Thursday …
> we could probably watch them all over two days
> after you get off school? Let me know?
> Elijah

I type back quickly, hoping he's still at the computer. I can't stand the idea of waiting another twenty-four hours to hear from him.

> I'm free Wednesday and Thursday. We could meet at
> your place? I don't mind the long drive.

His reply pops up in the corner of my screen. He's activated the email chat feature.

> Elijah0Delgado: Can't do it at my place, sorry.

RockiBoBocki: Ugh. Well we can't really do it at mine,
either.

Although Dad will be back at work, Mom will most certainly
be home. I can't even fathom bringing over a new guy my
parents have never heard of or met before. And then asking if
we can chill in my room for nine hours, watching movies?

Yeah, not happening.

The screen tells me that he's typing a reply for what feels like
an eternity. Thanks to my sophomore keyboarding class, I type
ninety words a minute, and Zack types like twice that fast since
he's a massive computer nerd. I've never had to wait more than
a few seconds for Zack's email chat replies.

Finally, his message pops up.

ElijahODelgado: Why not? Boyfriend won't like it?

He doesn't know I have a boyfriend, does he?

Wait, I *don't* have a boyfriend. Not really.

RockiBoBocki: Not sure how I can explain some
strange guy who happens to look exactly like Sasha
to my mother ... If I were lucky like you and didn't
have school, then we could watch them in the
daytime when she's at work.

ElijahODelgado: ....

RockiBoBocki: What does that mean?

Elijah0Delgado: Means you could skip.

RockiBoBocki: ….

I'm guessing Elijah has probably skipped school a day or two in his life. But the closest I've come to ditching school is mildly exaggerating a sickness so that Mom will encourage me to stay in bed all day and get better.

But I did miss four days to mourn Sasha and nothing bad happened. I lean on my elbow, biting my nails as I stare at the chat window. He's willing to drive all this way and spend a whole day watching movies with me and a digital version of Sasha. I pull up another internet window and add up the length of all five movies. With Mom's workday, plus her long commute to the city, we'd technically have enough time to watch them all. While I'm weighing the pros and cons of ditching school and the possibility of getting caught, he sends another message.

Elijah0Delgado: I wonder how strict she is with the one-week rule?

RockiBoBocki: I can't break her rules, even knowing that she's not here. I just can't. We need to do this.

Elijah0Delgado: So you'll skip?

RockiBoBocki: What if we just watch the movies separately on our own? I can send you the movies. I have my own copies.

Elijah0Delgado: I don't have my own computer. :(
I'm on my boss's.

RockiBoBocki: You have a TV, right?

Elijah0Delgado: Yup

RockiBoBocki: So we could talk on the phone and I'll
play her video commentary for you?

Elijah0Delgado: No phone. Maybe we could meet
somewhere? Rent a hotel room … Hahahaha.

I don't realize I am biting my tongue until I taste blood. I let
out a long sigh. He doesn't have a phone? Or a computer? He
lives somewhere so secret he wouldn't even tell Sasha? What is
up with this guy?

Now that I think about it, I don't really know him at all. I
take a deep breath and trust in Sasha. I send him my address.

RockiBoBocki: Can you get here at 7 am tomorrow?

Elijah0Delgado: I don't want to contribute to the
delinquency of a minor. Truancy is a big deal, you
know.

RockiBoBocki: I can break the rules just this once.
You coming or not?

Elijah0Delgado: I'll be there.

RockiBoBocki: Cool. :)

That smiley face is an understatement. The chat window says he's typing for the longest time, and then it stops. I start to type something but then it says he's typing again so I wait to see what he'll say. A few moments pass with him typing and then not typing. Maybe he doesn't know what to say. I put my hands on the keyboard, figuring I'll say something, and then his reply comes through.

Elijah0Delgado: Looking forward to it. See you at 7.

Elijah0Delgado has signed offline.

Chapter Twelve

In my dream, I'm in the guest bedroom of my grandparents' house. It's supposed to be my own house, I guess, but dreams are weird and the dream version of myself doesn't care what room I'm in.

Because Sasha is here.

We're wearing matching pajamas from Victoria's Secret, the pink ones with sunglasses all over them, the word PINK big and sequined across the front of the matching tank top. (Mom had freaked when I came home with that pink striped bag, saying that anything from that store was entirely too expensive and I shouldn't let the Cades spend excessive amounts of money on me.)

Vaguely, I wonder why my dream has drudged up those pajamas from the deep recesses of my memory, but mostly I'm just excited. Sasha is here, sitting on the bed with me, her bright eyes shimmering from the glow of the TV.

And it's not the twenty-two-inch flat screen like what I have at home or a wall-mounted monster like what Sasha has in her room — it's an old box TV with wood-grain paneling, the kind I've only seen in movies.

"Ready to watch the greatest movies ever made?" Sasha says, her voice giving me chills.

Although the edges of my dream are blurry and white, I look right in her baby blues. "I miss you."

Her eyes roll straight up. "You can't miss me, we're in a dream."

I shake my head and wonder if this is what lucid dreaming feels like. "Don't be funny right now. Be Sasha. I need Sasha. I know this is a dream, but I miss you."

I wonder if I can cry in dreams. "I miss you so much."

"You don't have to miss me," Sasha says. She reaches out, wraps a hand around my arm and I swear — I swear to God — I can feel her skin on mine. "I'm with you always, Rocki."

Everything is blurrier now, the edges of my consciousness poking through this dream. I squint and focus on my best friend, wanting to memorize every feature on her beautiful face. As I stare, her soft smile morphs into a smirk, her eyes getting a little shadow from scraggly black bangs. Suddenly Sasha is Elijah. Now his hand is on my arm. I reach out to touch him.

And then I wake up.

* * *

A real movie marathon with Sasha would mean pajamas, messy hair and possibly a dozen bottles of nail polish to keep us busy during the scenes we know by heart. But I'm up thirty minutes early for a movie marathon with Elijah. I hide anything remotely embarrassing from my bathroom (zit cream, box of tampons, printed photo of Andre from the band Zombie Radio) and then put on a pair of jean shorts and a T-shirt that looks nice but not like I'm trying too hard.

And then I ruin the entire look by wearing enough makeup to perform on Broadway. With a sigh into my vanity mirror, I wash it all off and reapply some powder and mascara. Good. I don't need to impress Elijah.

Say it again, Raquel: You don't need to impress Elijah.

Mom always leaves for work about fifteen minutes before I go to school, so at six forty-five, I emerge from my bedroom, backpack slung over my shoulder.

"Morning!" Mom says while she empties two creamer packets into her travel cup of coffee.

"Blah," I say, as I heft my backpack to the kitchen table and then dig in the pantry for a Pop-Tart. I need to keep up the facade that I'm going to school.

She doesn't suspect a thing. My doorbell rings at exactly seven, and I nearly pee myself as I'm walking to the front door. Why is this so nerve-racking? I'm excited to watch movies with Sasha, and Elijah is a cool guy. No need to fret.

With a deep breath, I open the door. He's wearing those same jeans and another black T-shirt, only this one has shorter sleeves and it's a little smaller, hugging tightly to his arms. His biceps are taut as he holds a drink tray with two coffees in one hand and a white bakery bag in the other.

Stop checking him out, you idiot, I tell myself.

"Hey," I say lamely, stepping aside so he can enter. "How'd you drive a motorcycle with coffee?"

"I'm not that talented," he says with a little laugh. I close the door behind him and he turns around to face me in the foyer. He seems two feet taller than usual and I wonder if that's because we never really stand this close together.

"I borrowed my roommate's car. Traded him the motorcycle for a day, actually. He was pretty psyched."

"You have roommates?" I say.

"Three," Elijah says, avoiding my gaze. He turns around to where the foyer opens to the living room on the left and a small dining room to the right. "Where we going?"

"Straight ahead," I say, pretending like this isn't awkward as hell. "What's in the bag?" I ask as I lead him to my room.

"Bagels." When we enter, Elijah makes no effort to hide the fact that he's checking out my room.

"Awesome." I take the bag from him and peek inside.

Elijah sinks onto my bed, nodding approvingly when the foam mattress conforms around his hands. It was a gift from my grandparents, and it's nicer than my own parents' bed.

"Damn, nice bed. And I am particularly liking those Barbie dolls," he says, inclining his head toward where the Barbie versions of Sasha and me sit in the same place on my bookshelf that they've been since I was ten.

"Shut up," I say, grabbing my laptop. "We'll watch the movies in the living room. Can you get that box of DVDs?"

His smirk makes my chest ache, but I ignore it. "The bathroom is down there if you need it."

"You have a nice house," Elijah says. He sits on one end of our couch while I sit on the other, propping my laptop on the coffee table in front of us.

"It's nothing compared to Sasha's." Our furniture is dated and our kitchen needs remodeling. Everything we own is at least a decade old.

He sinks down, stretching out his legs and resting one hand

on the armrest, the other across the back of the couch. "It's a *home,* and that makes it nice."

"You don't live in a home?" Immediately, I wish I hadn't said that.

"I live on a couch in an apartment." Elijah takes the remote and studies it. "How do I turn this thing on?"

"You've never had a real home," I say, turning to face him. "You went from a group home to a couch?" God, I can't shut up. "No foster homes or anything?"

Elijah's lip quirks like he's either pissed or trying not to laugh, and I have a horrifying feeling that maybe it's the first one.

"A few foster homes," he says after a painfully slow moment. "Sharing a room with eight other orphans and elderly fill-in parents who spout Bible verses at you doesn't *really* count as a home, I don't think."

I bite my lip and reach for a coffee, just to have something to do. "I'm sorry I asked."

"It's just a thing that happened to me, Raquel. My past doesn't dictate my future. My *present* does, I guess. I mean, what I do next, now that I'm already two years older than most college freshmen."

"You want to go to college?" I ask. Suddenly I remember Sasha mentioning this in her video at the cemetery. It sounded like she was trying to help him get into school or something.

He lifts one shoulder. "I mean, yeah. I do. I wasn't sure at first but Sasha kind of talked me into it. I've spent all of my life just … surviving." The back of his head is suddenly very itchy. "I want more than survival."

"You deserve more than survival," I say, wishing I had the courage to grab his hand. Sasha would have done it, and her touch would have soothed the pain behind his eyes. But that was her skill, not mine.

He shrugs again like it's no big deal. I get the feeling he wants to change the subject, but I'm compelled to drive Sasha's point home. "You do," I say. "College is for everyone, not just rich, smart kids."

He flattens his palms on his jeans. "You know, they act like scholarships are just handed out left and right, especially if you're underprivileged, but I haven't seen that. You walk onto the community college campus and they stare at you like you don't belong. Tell you to look shit up online as if *that's* easy for everyone."

"Maybe you should try somewhere better than the community college. Go to the University of Texas or Sam Houston State or A&M. A real university."

He chuckles. "You sound like my sister now. Always encouraging me to do something better for myself."

"Good," I say, feeling a swelling of pride in my chest. Something tells me she'd want me to have this talk with him. "She was always taking care of the people she loved. And she was very good at it."

"She was helping me pick colleges," he admits. "You know, before … just, *before*."

That Sasha would spend her remaining weeks on earth helping someone else is just so like her. I smile without meaning to, and a silence stretches out between us. Now I want to help him, too. I'm just not sure how to do it.

"Ah, here it is," Elijah says, pressing the power button. The TV turns on, and then he reaches for the first DVD in the box. "Ready to watch *Mean Girls*?"

Sasha's face appears in a little rectangle in the middle of my laptop screen. Elijah leans forward, resting his elbows on his knees. Whatever weirdness we had is gone because Sasha is here now, and she's all that matters.

I reach for a bagel and a container of cream cheese while she talks. "*Mean Girls* came out when I was four, but it wasn't until fifth grade that Rocki and I found it in the DVD bin at the grocery store. Mom bought it for me because she always bought anything I wanted, and Rocki and I watched it three times the first night we had it. Remember?"

She looks straight ahead, not trying to guess where I'm sitting. It was obviously filmed on a different day than the other videos, because she's wearing a gray PCHS hoodie and the circles under her eyes are prominent, meaning she's a little deeper into her sickness. She's sitting in one of the black leather movie chairs in their small movie room.

"Is she in a theater?" Elijah asks, leaning over and tapping the space bar to pause the video.

"Yeah, they have a room on top of their garage that they converted into a theater. It has a ninety-inch flat-screen TV in there. Sasha and I made a fort out of the box it came in."

"Whoa," he mutters, reaching for his second bagel. He taps the space bar and Sasha's frozen face becomes animated again.

"We fell in love with the movie, and that day can be marked as the day I also fell in love with Tina Fey and Amy Poehler. I mean, is there anything they can't do?" Sasha lifts her hands, her eyes wide. "You should listen to their audiobooks when you get a chance, Elijah. These women are amazing and creative souls. They're also best friends — they remind me of me and Rocki. Anyhow, I love this movie. Mom saw us watching it a few weeks later and she freaked because she walked in on the part where Coach Carr is talking about STDs and having sex and stuff. But when she saw that we'd seen it so many times already we could quote the damn thing, she just rolled her eyes and was like 'whatever' and let us watch it."

Sasha grins and sits back a little, leaning over to grab the remote. "Get your DVD on the menu screen," she says. "I'll wait."

I pause the video and queue up the DVD on my TV. The tension in Elijah's jaw is gone. I turn to him. "You ready?"

"I'm not overly psyched to watch a girl movie, but I'm excited to hear what Sasha has to say."

I scoff. "You're gonna love this movie. It's hilarious and there's a ton of hot girls in it to keep your attention."

The skin between his brows creases. "Why would I care about hot girls in a movie?"

"Oh," I say. "I mean, if you're not into girls, the guy who plays Aaron Samuels is also hot."

He takes a slow sip of his coffee, his eyes peering at me from over the plastic lid. I shouldn't care if he's not into girls, but why is my stomach clenching in agony while I wait for him to confirm it?

He sets his coffee cup on the coaster on the end table next to him. "I'm into girls," he says, settling back into the couch, his arm reaching dangerously close to mine while he taps out a rhythm on the seat between us. "I'm just not into girls in movies. It's not like I'll ever date them, so why should I care?"

"You're weird," I tell him, looking at my half-eaten bagel. Zack wouldn't pass up an opportunity to comment on a hot actress in a movie.

Sasha tells us when to press play and her plan works perfectly. The movie starts and Sasha snacks on a package of candy, the camera watching her every move while she sits sideways in her chair with her knees tucked up to her chest. She laughs at the funny parts with us, and every so often, she'll quote the words along with the actors. I find myself watching her more than the movie. I'll never get tired of watching her.

After three movies, we take a quick break so I can order a pizza for lunch. I refuse to let Elijah pay for it, even though he offers. He bought the breakfast and wasted all the gas money driving over here. I've got lunch.

We queue up the next DVD and hang out while we wait on the pizza delivery guy. I make it a point not to ask anything that will send us back down the black hole of awkwardness, and it turns out that leaves me with pretty much nothing to say.

My phone beeps from its place on the coffee table and I lean forward to check it, seeing Zack's name on the screen.

You're not at school. You sick?

Ignoring it, I put the phone on silent and then check my email out of habit.

"You might want to hang out around the phone tonight," Elijah says. He scratches the back of his head, his shirtsleeve rising up and revealing a ring of lighter skin around his biceps.

"What do you mean?" For some reason, I think he's talking about Zack and my heart seizes up in my chest.

"You know, those automated phone calls letting parents know their kid missed school?" He makes a blank expression and then talks in a robot voice. "To the parents of Raquel whatever-your-last-name-is," he says, and I laugh. "Your child was absent from school today, Wednesday the twenty-first —"

"It's the twenty-first?" I say, jumping to my feet. "Oh my God. No. It can't be."

Eyes wide, I pace the length of the living room.

Elijah appears in front of me, two strong arms holding me in place. "What's wrong?"

I shake my head, but he takes my chin in his fingers and tilts my head up to look at him. I squeeze my eyes shut, not wanting to see the concern that I know is splashed across his features.

"The twenty-first," I say, my throat dry. "It's been one month."

"Since …" he says, realization dawning.

I nod and a tear rolls down my cheek, which he brushes away with his thumb. I reach up and grab his hand, holding it close to me. "A whole month since she died and I almost forgot."

"But you didn't," he says, pulling me against his chest as I hold back tears.

Elijah's hugs are something special. Warm and welcoming, the smell of laundry detergent comforting me as I press my face against his chest. I feel his arm around my waist, the other one holding the back of my head, his chin resting on top of my hair.

Within moments, I feel better, but I don't let go. I want to stay here forever, tucked into his embrace, my arms wrapped tightly around the only living piece of Sasha's DNA.

And then the doorbell rings, and the pizza delivery guy breaks us apart.

After lunch, we play the next movie on Sasha's list. *The Princess Bride* normally makes me cry because I'm a huge softy for the poor farm boy, but now that Sasha's watching it with us, I'm not sure I can survive without flooding the living room with tears.

"As you wish," Sasha says longingly, putting a hand to her chest. She frowns into the camera and bats her eyelashes. "God, this is such a great movie. I always wanted to marry Westley, but not until after he became the Dread Pira — oh shit, never mind! Forget I said that. Spoiler alert, right?"

"Was she always this chatty?" Elijah says, stealing a quick look my way before turning back to the TV. "Or is she talking a lot for the sake of the video?"

"She was always this chatty. I was the quiet one in school, always in her shadow."

"Did that bother you?"

I shake my head. "No way. I liked being the shadow. Sasha always knew what to say and do. People liked her. I was just … there."

"She really loves romance. She gets real quiet during the mushy parts of these movies. She didn't seem that mushy in our emails."

"She was the biggest romantic I know," I say wistfully. "She liked the way the love unfolds in a good story. I always preferred the moment the hot guy takes his shirt off, but she lived for the slow parts that led up to it."

"I agree with my sister. The slow parts are the best parts." Elijah looks like he might want to say something but he turns back to the TV. "Hey, is that Andre the Giant?" he asks, his face lighting up like a kid's.

"Yep," I say, making my voice low. "Anybody want a peanut?"

"Huh?"

I wave a hand, dismissing my stupid joke. "You'll see what I mean in a minute."

When the fifth movie is over, I stand to take it out of the

DVD player, stopping to stretch my limbs. "I don't think I've ever been on the couch this long in my life," I say, twisting to the side and stretching my arms up until my back cracks.

Elijah leans forward and looks at my computer screen. "I don't think we have enough time for the last movie," he says, looking at the back of the Harry Potter DVD. "It's over two hours long."

"Let's just start it and watch as much as we can," I say. For the fifth time today, I click on another movie link and another video of Sasha appears on the screen.

She's redone her hair since the last one, and now it's down, hanging loosely around her shoulders, the black headband still pressing against her forehead. She takes a sip from a soft drink can with a hot pink straw. "Okay guys, this is the last video of the day."

She tells us about how much she loves Harry Potter and how Elijah *should* read all of the books and see all of the movies, but she won't make it a requirement for now. I close my eyes, letting my head fall back against the couch as I listen. If I keep them closed, I can almost imagine that Sasha is right here with us, sitting on the recliner.

The trill of a phone ringing interrupts Sasha's monologue and I open my eyes. "Hmm," she says, holding up her phone to the camera. "Looks like Rocki is calling me. This will be fun," she says, winking at the camera. She answers the call and puts it on speakerphone.

"Hey, Boo," Sasha says, her standard greeting for whenever I called.

"What are you up to?" I ask, my voice sounding weirdly echoey and not at all like how I think I sound. "Can I come over?"

Sasha's eyes dart to the screen, her lips widening in this apologetic way. "Sorry, I'm kinda busy for the next" — she turns the DVD over in her hand and studies the back of it — "hundred and forty-two minutes. Can I call you as soon as I'm free?"

"Yeah," I say with a heavy sigh. "It's just Zack. You know the drill."

"Girl, break up with him!" She puts a hand over the phone and leans in close to the video, whispering, "If you're still dating him when you watch this, I'm gonna be pissed."

Then she goes back to the phone call, the one I'm starting to remember making since her 142 minutes comment struck me as weird back then, and she says, "I didn't mean to yell. I love you, Rocki, but you need a better man than Zack. You'll find him one day, I promise."

"I don't know about that," I say through her phone. "I mean I'm too fat and too pathetic for anyone to care about."

At that, my cheeks go red and I want to throw my laptop across the room so Elijah can't hear any of this. But it's too late — he's heard every word. And he can still hear our conversation, because it's still playing. I cover my face with my hands and bend forward, burying my face in my knees.

"Oh my God, this is so embarrassing," I say, while the recorded version of me goes on and on, bitching about how gamer girls send Zack sexy photos and he keeps them and it pisses me off.

I groan in real life. A warm hand touches my back. "It's okay," Elijah says, his voice low and soft. "You want to fast-forward?"

I look up just as Sasha ends the call. With his hand still on my back, Elijah and I watch Sasha make this "mom look" at the screen.

"Listen to me, Raquel. I know you won't listen when you come over in a couple of hours, but maybe you'll listen now that I'm dead. You are a beautiful, wonderful person. You're the greatest friend I've ever had, and if we were gay, I'd have asked you out years ago," she says with a grin.

I try not to feel so freaking embarrassed in front of Elijah. Sasha continues, "Zack treats you like shit. He walks all over you, flirts with other girls both in real life and online, and he does it because you let him. Stop being a doormat, Rocki. You are better than that. And stop calling yourself fat. I think you're hot, okay? And the opinion of a dead girl is a hell of a lot more reliable than that of your own low self-esteem. Got me?"

She points to the screen, her eyes narrowed. I choke out a laugh and Elijah's hand slides up and down my back in a comforting way.

While Sasha gets up to put her copy of the DVD in her own player, Elijah turns to me, brushing my hair behind my ear. "You okay?"

I nod.

He shifts over until he's sitting in the middle seat right next to me. "Sasha was a really good friend."

"The best," I croak.

"Are you still dating that guy?"

I look up and he's even closer now, his hand wrapped around my shoulder. I shake my head. "No. Not really."

"Well then, you've made her proud," he says.

"I hope so."

Elijah's hand squeezes my shoulder and it all happens so fast. I slide over just a little, letting my head fall into the crook of his collarbone. His arm stays wrapped around me, his fingertips gripping my upper arm. His heartbeat is strong and steady, a constant reminder that a piece of Sasha is still here on earth with me.

Sasha tells us when to press play, and that iconic Harry Potter theme music fills my living room with its magic.

"She's right, you know," Elijah whispers as the movie starts.

"About what?" I ask, letting my hand rest on his stomach.

"You are beautiful," he says, staring straight ahead. A muscle in his jaw twitches. "It's a shame you don't feel that way."

Chapter Thirteen

The next email comes a day later, while I'm at Rancho Grande eating dinner with my parents. My dad is of the old-fashioned variety, and he can't stand phones at the table, especially since he works so much and our family time is limited. I've hidden my phone in my lap, under my cloth napkin. When it vibrates and I secretly check it, there's an email from TheFutureSasha. I know I have to stay cool.

I manage to force down two more bites of my tacos al carbon, although now the normally delicious food is just another obstacle between me and that message.

"I need to use the restroom," I say, folding my napkin and setting it on the table. My parents barely acknowledge me and continue their conversation, and I walk as quickly as a normal person might walk on their way to the bathroom.

Once inside, I slip into a stall, lock the door behind me and lean against the cool, colorful Spanish-tiled wall.

Hey favorites,

I hope y'all had fun watching the movies. Like I said before, this one's a hard one. Rocki, take Elijah to my grandma's place. There will be a letter for you under the gnome on the porch. Try to go in the morning and do not get caught. Dad should be at work and Mom won't notice because she never goes over there.

Sorry for the pain this will cause. Two more adventures and then I'll send you on a fun one.

Love you both, always,
Sasha

I let out a breath and look up at the stucco ceiling, clenching my phone to my chest. She was right. This will be a hard one. Sasha's gran was a troubled soul. She lived in a small apartment on the Cades' property, and Sasha and I would sometimes go over there for tea and cookies when we were kids. Sasha thought the world of the woman, but to be honest, I was a little scared of her.

Gran killed herself in that home when we were thirteen.

I don't want to go there, not even to show Elijah this pivotal piece of Sasha's history. But if that's what she wants, then that's what I'll do.

"As you wish," I whisper, then I join my parents back at our table.

* * *

Elijah meets me at Izzy's right after school on Friday. We'd agreed to meet here so my parents wouldn't get suspicious, and

Izzy didn't need me to work today, so it all works perfectly.

I roll down my window when he backs his motorcycle into the spot next to me. "Get in," I call out. "Let's get this over with."

He peers at me through his helmet. "What does that mean?"

I shrug, my hands on the steering wheel. "Just not looking forward to this one. It's ... sad."

"Oh," he says, nodding. He jerks his head. "Get on."

"Or you could get in *my* car," I say, tapping the outside of my door. "I know how to get there and you don't."

"Yeah, but Sasha's parents know your car, right? What if they see it parked on their road?"

I heave a sigh and roll up my window. He has a good point. Elijah straddles his bike, the motor rumbling. He hands me his helmet and I grimace at the idea of sharing his head sweat, but I put it on. Safety first and all that.

My breath catches in my throat as I realize what comes next. Elijah revs the bike and I climb on, settling my feet on the back pegs. "How will you know where to go?" I yell over the roar of the motor.

"I know the subdivision," he says, his black hair blowing all over his face in the breeze. "Just squeeze my arm when we're close. I'll park a few houses down."

"Okay," I call out.

He drops it into first gear and slowly pulls out of the parking space. I grab on to his sides, trying to be all casual about it, but as we pull onto the highway, I lean forward and hold on tighter. His abs are flexed beneath my grip, and I have to focus on breathing normally, on thinking about *Sasha,* not her dreamy-as-hell brother.

Luckily, Gran's house isn't very far away. I signal for him to slow down at the little rec center building at the front of their neighborhood. It'll be a bit of a walk, but better safe than sorry. Plus, we can cut through the wooded area that leads to the Cades' backyard, and it'll keep us off the roads in case Mrs. Cade happens to be driving by.

The thought of her seeing me with Sasha's male look-a-like sends a chill down my spine. For the first time since meeting Elijah, I wonder what will happen to us when this is over. If we stay friends, there's no way to keep this secret forever.

"You okay?" Elijah asks.

"Perfect," I say, handing him back his helmet as I shake away the slimy feeling of lying to people I care about.

"The bike didn't scare you?" He eyes me with this cocky look. Is he trying to impress me?

"Daddy has a Harley," I say. "I'm no stranger to motorcycle rides."

"Ah, I see how it is." He taps the cracked leather seat on his bike. "My old Honda isn't as cool as the Harley."

"Nope," I say, playfully shoving him in the arm. "Let's get going. And wipe that smile off your face. This one is gonna suck."

"Why's that?" he asks as he falls into step next to me, hands shoved in his pockets. I swear he wears the same jeans every time I see him. Meanwhile, I'm putting more thought and effort into everything I wear each new time we meet up.

"Not sure I should tell you now," I say, my feet crunching over pine needles. This strip of land is mostly trees and rocks, and up ahead I can already see the Cades' house and the abandoned log cabin home that used to be Gran's.

"Here we are," I say as we approach the small one-bedroom

house. It has a big back porch with a slightly obscured view of the lake. I gesture toward the mansion a couple acres over. "That's Sasha's house."

There are no cars in the driveway, but Mrs. Cade parks in the garage, so there's no telling if she's home or not. Still, enough trees separate Mrs. Cade's yard from Gran's house to make me confident that she won't see us. I'm pretty sure she likes to pretend this little house no longer exists.

"The gnome is around here," I say, leading Elijah around an overgrown rosebush at the back of the house. I'd forgotten about the porch swing until I see it looking lonely and faded in the afternoon sun.

Next to the back door, a ceramic gnome sits like a goofy little security guard, its paint flaking off. Elijah puts a hand on the gnome's head and tilts him backward, revealing a plastic bag with an envelope inside. It contains a handwritten letter on Hello Kitty stationery.

"Who's reading it?" I ask.

Elijah walks to the end of the wooden porch and sits, putting his feet on the bottom stair. "You read. I'll listen."

I sit next to him and unfold the letter.

"'Hey favorites,'" I begin. "'This is my gran's house. My parents had it built for her before I was born, so for as long as I've been alive, this little place has been in my life. I only had one grandparent when I was growing up. My dad's parents both died before I was adopted. Cancer, ironically.

"'My mom's dad died in a train wreck when I was a baby. So I only ever had my gran.

"'Gran was the coolest adult I ever knew. She was into tarot cards in this ironic way that made you sometimes think maybe she was serious, and she was the best cook ever. Her chicken and dumplings were the greatest food on earth, and no matter how many times Mom and I tried, we could never replicate her recipe.'"

I stop to clear my throat, which is really just an excuse to look over at Elijah. I know what's coming next.

"'Gran also loved genealogy. She had binders of research on her family tree, and we'd spend summers at libraries and public county buildings going through old birth records and marriage documents while she pieced together the lives of her ancestors.

"'Gran encouraged me to think about my birth parents. My own parents never talked about them and they didn't like me bringing it up. Not Gran. Gran said it mattered where you came from, and she encouraged me to find my own roots. Always. Even if we had to keep it from my parents.

"'Unfortunately, I never found anything about my birth parents back then. There wasn't much to go on since my parents kept the details of my adoption to themselves.'"

Elijah lets out a sarcastic snort, lacing his fingers together while he stares at the ground between his shoes.

I turn back to the letter. "'Gran killed herself when I was thirteen.'"

Elijah looks surprised. I give him a sympathetic frown and keep reading. "'The doctors said she'd been depressed all her life. It was a disease, an error in her brain that she couldn't overcome. But since I was thirteen and adored my gran, I felt betrayed. See, the week she killed herself was the week we'd been researching my birth parents. At first it was like she had betrayed me, dying before we figured it out. Then I realized I had failed her. An entire section in her genealogy binders would forever remain empty because I couldn't figure out the names of the people who created me.

"'I held this secret shame for a long time, even though now I know the binders had nothing to do with Gran's inability to stay alive. Rocki probably knows even though I never told her. That summer after Gran's funeral, I didn't do anything and we barely saw each other.

"'I'm sorry, Rocki. Thank you for still being there when I came out of mourning. If Gran were still alive, I know she'd be so psyched to meet you, Elijah. She'd bake you a batch of snickerdoodles and make you a cup of tea and tell you you're welcome at her home anytime you want.

"'I know Gran would be so proud of me for finding you. And I guess now she does know, if only in the afterlife, huh?

"'I wanted you to come here because Gran is the reason I found you, Elijah. Without her love of family trees and history, I probably wouldn't have thought too much about my birth parents. God knows my own parents didn't want me to find out where I'm from ... but Gran did, and she ignited a fire inside of me that burned brightly until I finally found you. Gran taught me that family matters. You matter, Elijah. I may be gone now, but I know you'll make something wonderful of yourself.'"

I reach the end of the page and flip it over to the back. Elijah drags in a deep breath, tilting his head toward the sky. His eyes are closed but they're leaking tears.

I lean over and rest my chin on his shoulder as I read the rest of her note.

"'Your fifth adventure is related to this one. You'll get an email soon. I love you and miss you both. Love, Sasha.'"

We sit on the porch for another half hour, both lost in our own thoughts. I think about telling him what I remember of Gran, but the words die on my tongue. Silence feels like the right thing at the moment.

It's a beautiful September day, the lake sparkling a dark blue in front of us.

"My sister was a really cool person," Elijah says, breaking the silence. "I can't believe she put all of this together, while she was fighting cancer, no less."

"It's the greatest gift she could have given us," I agree. I bend down and pluck a long blade of grass, then begin breaking it into bits. "I'm sorry you never got to meet her."

"It's okay," he says, leaning back on his hands. "She's making sure I know her, and that's all that matters. She's right, you know. Even if I had met her in the few months before she died, she'd still be dead now. It would have been a fleeting relationship and it would have hurt like hell. Instead, she's left us this enormous keepsake to cherish forever."

"I'm glad you're not mad," I say, reaching for another blade of grass.

"Nah. I don't get mad easily. Especially not at someone I care about."

Our eyes meet, and for the first time since that day in the cemetery, I see Elijah staring back at me, not Sasha. I see the lost boy he used to be, the wholeness he found in Sasha. I see hope and resolve. I see a future.

"She was right about what she said." I hold up the letter. "You missed out on a lot in your life, but that doesn't mean the rest of it has to be that way."

"You sound just like her," he says.

"I'll take that as a compliment."

"Toward the end of our talks, before I got the letter asking me to go to the cemetery, she'd almost convinced me that my life could turn around." His elbows rest on his knees and he stares down at his shoes. "I told her something embarrassing and she took the idea and ran with it." He chuckles, shaking his head slightly. "She almost had me fooled into thinking it'd work."

"Embarrassing?" I nudge him with my elbow. "I want to know."

He looks over at me, a sly grin dancing on his lips. "Not telling."

"Elijah! Please tell me." I glare at him. "For all we know, one of her next letters will tell the secret anyhow. So ... you might as well warn me."

"It's not *embarrassing,* really. Just ... foolish. Lame."

I bite on my bottom lip. "You don't have to tell me, but I do want to know."

He shakes his head. I know I've won him over. He gives me a look. "Okay. No laughing."

I hold up my hands, portraying innocence.

"Remember what I said during movie day about not wanting to just survive anymore?" He turns back to the lake, a bashful grin on his face. "I guess I've always had these pipe dreams of growing up and finding a way into the system. Like ... running my own group home, or at least working at one. Every home I went to was such a shit hole. They treat the kids like criminals when they're just orphans. I mean, don't get me wrong — some of them are criminals, but could that have been prevented? If they'd just had someone who actually gave a shit about them, would they have stayed away from crime?

Would they care more about school and being a good person? It's hard to care about anything when no one cares for you."

He looks at me for a long moment, and I wonder if he wants an answer from me, but then I realize he's thinking. "I always got good grades in school and I barely screwed up along the way. I'm one of the lucky ones. I've seen my friends end up in jail, or drugged out, or working minimum wage to support three kids before they're even old enough to drink. The system could be better. I wanted to make it better."

"And Sasha wanted to help you," I say.

He nods and blinks. "She was convinced I could get a college degree and make that happen. She said I could name my group home The Delgado Group. *Where everyone is family.*"

I smile. Elijah shrugs. "We were still working on the motto."

I grab his arm. "You should still do that, Elijah! I know all about the college admissions process and I've gotten my own scholarships from writing essays and stuff, so I could help you. I even have a computer. We can do it together."

His smile seems a little forced now. He rises to his feet. "I wish it were that easy. I'm already working my ass off to keep my bills paid. There's no time for college."

"It's not easy, but it's doable." I stand, too, folding the letter and putting it back in the plastic bag. The air around him is filled with negativity, so I probably shouldn't push this idea on him right now, but I save it in my mind for later. "You should keep this."

"Thanks," he says, taking it. "I gotta go. Work stuff."

I nod, trying to hide my disappointment. "Same. I have a five-page paper to write this weekend so I guess I should go, too."

"Fun," he says, popping me on top of the head with the letter. He smiles, and it almost hides the sorrow behind his eyes. "Sometimes I forget you're still in school."

"Shut up," I say, sticking out my tongue.

He pops me again. "How could I possibly forget you're only seventeen when you display such maturity?"

I gnaw on the inside of my lip to stop myself from grinning like a fool.

Chapter Fourteen

I spend the whole weekend watching Netflix with Mom and helping her reorganize the office. Sorting through old tax papers and throwing out user manuals for appliances we no longer have isn't normally my idea of fun. But with Sasha gone and my resolve set firmly on the Ignore Zack button, I don't have much to do. I know I should work on making new friends, but I'm still not ready to move on. A best friend like Sasha only comes around once in a lifetime.

"So how are things?" Mom asks while she flips through the bottom drawer of the filing cabinet.

"Fine." My voice is jagged and on edge. Talking about Sasha is like walking on a tightrope — sometimes I can get across it just fine, but other times I feel like I'm falling to my doom.

"That's good. And your job?"

"Perfect." At least that's not a lie.

Mom pulls out a thick folder, plops it on the carpet and goes through it. "I knew we'd have a life after Sasha, but it's still hard without her."

"Hmm."

"Yeah, I just miss her bright personality," Mom says, giving me a sad smile. "Since you two were little kids, I can't remember a single week I went without seeing her. Now it's been over a month."

"Yeah." The imaginary tightrope wobbles beneath my feet. I really, really don't want to talk about this.

"I'm proud of you, honey."

I look up from a box of Dad's fuel receipts. "For what?"

Mom studies me. "For being so strong. You know you can always talk to me, Raquel. Anytime you want, and about anything."

"I know," I say quickly. But it's a lie.

I can't talk to her about *anything*. Not about Elijah. Not about Sasha's last wish.

And lately, that's the only thing worth talking about.

* * *

The next email comes on Monday night at exactly seven p.m., as if someone had timed it. I've checked my other emails from TheFutureSasha, and they're all sent right on the hour. I'm pretty sure she set up an account online that sends her prewritten emails at the date and time she specified. What I'm having trouble understanding is how she knew when to send them. What if she had lived another month?

Her clandestine accomplices must have a way of knowing what to do, and when. I'd love to meet them, to find her secret message-board friends, find out about their friendship with Sasha and how they orchestrated her ultimate last wish. Of course, that would go against the very spirit of her wish, so I guess I'll never know.

This email tells us to meet at the Mount Horeb Baptist

Church as early in the morning as possible. I have to Google the place because I've never heard of it. It's a little church from the 1800s and it's a historical landmark that hasn't been used as a real church in a century. Weird.

Sasha believed in God and had full faith that she'd be going to heaven when she died, but it's not like she ever went to church except on Christmas and Easter — and she'd been slacking for the last few years.

Still, I get that bubbly feeling of excitement in my chest at the thought of going on another adventure for Sasha. With her brother.

I send an email asking Elijah when he's free to visit the church at sunrise. I feel awful that he'll have to drive all this way so early in the morning, so I tell him it's okay if we're not there right at dawn.

He doesn't reply immediately, his username a grayed-out line on my email chat screen. I guess I can't expect him to always be online waiting for me, but after twenty-four hours of no reply, the knot in my stomach has doubled in size, all filled up with worry and angst.

The knot only grows when Mrs. Cade calls me on Tuesday and invites me over to dinner. I love her and Mr. Cade, but a tragic dinner is about the last thing I'd seek out right now, when I am finding flashes of happiness. But I tell her yes, obviously, because I'd never say no to my best friend's mom.

Mrs. Cade opens the door, wearing a smile as bright as her yellow dress. "Hi, sweetheart," she says, pulling me into a hug. At my feet, Sunny's tail is wagging and he's looking out past me, like maybe he thinks I brought Sasha back from an extended vacation he didn't know about.

"Save some hugs for me," Mr. Cade says, entering the foyer.

Their foyer is about the size of my bedroom, and it's lined with priceless artwork, a Tiffany lamp and an umbrella stand.

Mr. Cade squeezes me so tightly all the air in my lungs whooshes out.

"Thanks for having me," I say, lacing my fingers together in front of me. "Dinner smells good."

"We're having chicken Alfredo," Mrs. Cade says, as they lead me into the dining room. "With homemade cheesy garlic bread."

"My favorite," I say, though they already know. "Sasha's favorite, too."

"It was always a struggle to get any of that bread," Mr. Cade remembers. "Sasha would eat the whole damn loaf if you didn't pay attention."

We share a laugh and settle into the plush high-backed chairs around their formal dining table. Mrs. Cade has gone all out tonight, using the same fine china she uses for Christmas dinners.

"You didn't have to go to all this trouble," I say as Mr. Cade hands me the tray of garlic bread. "I'd be happy eating out of a pizza box in the kitchen."

Mrs. Cade's diamond earrings sparkle under the chandelier and she waves a hand dismissively. "Nonsense. I love cooking a good meal every now and then, and since Walter actually got home at a reasonable hour tonight, I thought it'd be a perfect opportunity to have you over as well."

"I appreciate it," I say.

Mr. Cade talks about his work and how they're going through the boring process of auditing the firm they recently acquired. I nod politely as we eat, trying to ask an interested question every so often, but eventually Mrs. Cade tells him to stop talking about work at the dinner table.

"We don't want to bore our guest," she says.

"I'm not bored," I say, reaching for another piece of garlic bread. "People think it's so cool that I know Walter Cade, the tough Texas lawyer." At that, Mr. Cade's face lights up, and I continue, "I think it's really cool how you put so much effort into helping people."

"Thank you, Raquel. I'm one of the good guys in a field of sharks," he says with a hearty chuckle. "Of course, that doesn't mean I don't play the role of shark occasionally. It's all for the greater good in the end, though. That's why I call myself *tough* in the commercials. I didn't think that phrase would stick as much as it did."

"That reminds me," Mrs. Cade says, taking a sip of her wine. "Remember that commercial we did when Sasha was about four? That was the cutest thing."

"What?" I say, eyes wide. "I didn't know about this!"

"Oh, we have to watch it," Mrs. Cade says, hand over her heart. "It was so adorable. Sasha said something like, 'My daddy will fix your problem because he's the tough Texas lawyer.'" She makes her voice high and childlike as she imitates Sasha.

I thought I knew Sasha nearly as well as I know myself. I wonder what other secrets I'll discover now that she's gone. "I can't believe I never knew about that," I say, recalling all of the Walter Cade commercials I'd seen over the years. They'd always just featured Mr. Cade and sometimes his happy clients.

"She might not have remembered it herself," Mrs. Cade says. "It was a long time ago."

Talking about the past makes me think of Elijah, and I realize I've never learned the answer to the biggest question of all.

"What made you adopt Sasha?" I ask in the contented silence

that lingers. Now that I know Elijah was out there, orphaned and alone, I need to know the answer.

Mr. and Mrs. Cade exchange a look, and then Mrs. Cade answers. "I couldn't have children of my own. Once the doctors confirmed that, they offered all those medical options, but I just had this feeling — this hunch, I guess you could say — that we should adopt."

"We went to an adoption agency in Austin the very next day," Mr. Cade says, sitting up taller. "We were just going to talk to them, look around and see how the process worked and all that."

"Oh, honey, you make it sound like we were picking out a puppy or something," Mrs. Cade says, rolling her eyes. She turns to me, one hand still on her wineglass. "We had arranged a consultation with the agency, but on the walk down to the woman's office, one of the caretakers walked by carrying baby Sasha. Sasha was crying, so I tried to cheer her up by making these goofy faces and stuff, and it worked. She looked up with those beautiful blue eyes and stopped crying. She even gave me a little laugh, and that was it," she says, lifting a shoulder. "I knew she would be my baby girl. It wasn't as easy as that, of course, but we got through the long adoption process and soon she was ours."

The warm memory makes me feel all good inside, but only until I remember that Sasha's brother never had the same thing happen to him.

I twirl a strand of pasta around my fork. "Did you ever think of adopting another child?"

Something dark flickers across Mrs. Cade's eyes as Mr. Cade clears his throat. "We thought about it, but in the end, we just wanted to give all our love to our little girl. We're too old to adopt now, but …"

Mr. Cade wipes his mouth with his napkin and looks over at his wife. "We're thinking about maybe fostering some kids. Just one or two at first, see how it goes."

"Really?" I say, looking to both of them. "That's amazing. I think Sasha would like that."

Mrs. Cade's eyes seem far away and she nods. "After that speech Sasha had you give at her funeral, we started talking about it. We certainly have the means to take care of other kids, and I think Sasha would approve. It could be something we do in her memory."

For the millionth time, I wonder why Sasha won't let me tell them about Elijah. Sure, he's an adult now and doesn't need a foster family, but they'd definitely want to meet him. Now they want to foster more kids, but they should have sought out more when Sasha was a baby. Elijah needed that same love that Sasha bragged about in her letter. He needed the Cades. I bite down on the inside of my lip to keep from saying anything.

After dinner, Mrs. Cade walks me out to my car and gives me another one of her motherly hugs. "We'll do this again soon," she says, pulling away and holding me by the arms. The dark circles under her eyes have eased up a bit, and that makes my heart feel lighter. "Next time, bring your parents, okay?"

"I will," I say.

"Are you still dating that same guy?" Mrs. Cade asks, almost as an afterthought. "Zack?"

I shake my head. "Not really. We broke up yet again and now he's been calling a lot but I'm just ignoring him."

She squeezes my arm. "Good girl," she says with a wink. "Sasha never liked him, so I didn't either."

I snort. "Yeah, she told me." A few thousand times.

"You'll find someone better," Mrs. Cade assures me.

A sudden image of Elijah appears in my mind and I nearly choke on my own spit as I try to shove the thought away.

"I hope so," I say, opening my car door. My heart is now going all jackhammer inside my chest. "Thanks for dinner. I'll see you soon."

Before I go to bed, Elijah replies to my email. I sit up in bed, my hands shaking as I read the message on my phone.

> Hey,
> I could do Friday morning at 6? The rest of the week is kinda tight for me, and I might not get back online before Friday, so if you can meet me, I'll see you there. If not, no worries.
> Goodnight,
> Elijah

He's already offline, so I can't talk to him. I reply anyway to let him know I'll be there.

Friday is three mornings away. Three whole nights of lying in this bed, staring at the ceiling and wishing time could go by faster. Two more days of suffering through school, pretending to give a single shit about what my teachers are talking about in class.

In three more mornings, I'll finally get to hang out with Elijah again, and I might be more excited about that than learning what makes this historical church so important to Sasha.

And that scares me.

Chapter Fifteen

Thinking ahead, I tell my parents I have a chemistry study session before school. I know it's a pretty risky lie and one that I can't believe they buy, since school has been the last thing on my radar lately.

Still, they bought it. I'm out the door at five forty-five on Friday morning, following the GPS on my phone to get to Mount Horeb Baptist Church.

This is the first one of Sasha's adventures that doesn't have a backstory that I already know, and curiosity has been clawing at me since I first got her email. Peyton Colony is a small town in the Texas hill country, forty miles southwest of Austin. We have a population of five thousand people and a ton of historical sites along our main highway. None of them have been of any significance in my life, since they're all just landmark signs with some kind of story on them about how so-and-so from the Confederate army did such-and-such a couple hundred years ago.

But Mount Horeb is more than just a big metal sign on the side of the road. The church is located on the outskirts of our tiny town, nothing but cow pastures and empty land sloping all around it. I steer onto a gravel road that's not on the GPS and drive slowly, my car jolting over the bumpy and unused gravel road toward the small white chapel that's tucked away at the bottom of a hill. I guess you can spend every day of your life in the same little town and still not know everything about it.

I don't see Elijah's motorcycle anywhere, so I park and climb out of my car, surveying the area myself.

The church is ancient and abandoned, a white building with a shabby wooden roof and two steeples on either side of an ornate wooden door. The windows are pointed at the top, with dark-blue-tinted glass. Overgrown weeds crawl up the steps that lead to the door.

The rumble of a motorcycle makes my heart leap. I'm about to see him again, and a giddy grin jumps to my face. I hold my hand up to block the harsh white beam of Elijah's headlight.

He rolls up next to my car, cuts the motor and pulls off his helmet. We're here before the sunrise, but only barely. His skin is darker in the predawn morning, the blues of his eyes seeming to glow in the residual moonlight.

"Morning," Elijah says, knocking the kickstand with his foot. He eases off the bike and leans it until the stand catches the gravel road.

"Good morning." My words come out in a breath, and I almost shake myself like a freaking cartoon character. *Get it together, Raquel.* Yeah, he's hot. And yeah, a muscular guy climbing off a motorcycle in the shadowy clutches of dawn is sexy as hell. *But get over it.*

"I think there's a note on the door," I say, turning to face the church instead of the guy.

It dawns on me now, in front of a church of all places, where the term *heartthrob* comes from.

"Looks like it," Elijah says, falling into step with me. His hand brushes my arm in a hello and our eyes meet for just a second — then he dashes up the two stairs to the church's front door and pulls off the envelope that's taped there.

He peers at the note scribbled on the outside of the envelope in pink Sharpie. "'If possible, read me before the sun rises.'"

We both gaze upward, judging how long it'll be before a ball of orange ascends into the cloudless sky above.

Elijah flicks his wrist toward me. "You want to do the honors again? I like the sound of your voice."

"Um, sure." I take the envelope and slide my finger underneath the seal, taking out another handwritten letter. "It's kind of long," I say, pulling the two pages apart. "Maybe we should sit down?"

Elijah gestures to the steps in front of us, then sits on the top one. I join him, and try not to think about how he doesn't pull away when my knee touches his.

"Okay," I say, exhaling. "Ready for this?"

"I'm ready if you are," Elijah says, his voice like honey.

I glance at the emerging orange glow above the tree line, and then focus on Sasha's words.

"'In the 1800s, Peyton Roberts was born a slave in Virginia. At the end of the civil war, he became a free man and moved west, settling right here in our hometown. That's how Peyton Colony got its name. From a man born a slave. I find that really inspiring, that how you're born doesn't reflect how you'll die. Peyton's community founded this church in 1874, and like all good and noble things, it's fallen into disarray.

"'But at least it got historical landmark status, amirite? You can read the history in more detail on that metal landmark sign by the road.

"'You're probably wondering why I brought you here, especially since my parents are nondenominational Christian and not Baptist. Well … that day Gran died … Rocki, you might remember, well, I ran away. My mom called an ambulance for Gran, and in the crazed nightmare that followed, I hopped on my bike and got the hell out of there. I pedaled for what felt like freaking years and years, but it was really only 11.4 miles, and I found the landmark and decided to read it, if only for something to take my mind off Gran.

"'I was really inspired by the story of Peyton Roberts, since earlier that week, Gran and I were talking about how I probably have some African-American relatives in my biological family tree. After reading the sign, I biked up the gravel road and saw the church. I had a good ol'-fashioned yelling match with God, right then and there. I balled my fists and I screamed at the little cross on the door, and I told God that I hated him for doing this to me. To Gran.'"

I stop reading because my mind is blown. So that's where she went. She was here that night, and she never told anyone. Not even me.

"You look like you've seen a ghost," Elijah says, his knee pushing into mine a little.

I lick my lips and stare at the paper. "She never told me this."

"So keep reading. She's telling us now."

I nod, let up on my bottom lip and keep reading.

"'Soon it got dark, and I got scared. I wasn't sure how to get home and I knew that crazy murderers drove around at night, so I broke into the back door and went inside the church. It was terrifying, being in there all alone in the dark. I was heartbroken over Gran, feeling guilty that maybe it was my fault and pissed at God. I didn't know what else to do, so I lay on a pew and fell asleep. When I woke up, it was dawn. The blue windows beckoned to me, and I followed them until I saw the sun rising up over the farm to the right. I went back outside and I sat on the front steps —'"

The energy between Elijah and me ramps up at this. We look at each other, almost as if we both expect to see Sasha right here, right now. I take a shaky breath and return to the letter.

"'It may sound silly now, after the fact, when we're all grown up and all, but back then, this moment was magical. I sat on the steps and watched the sun rise, and I swear to you both, I met God that day.

"'I felt him. I felt his warmth and love, and I felt him grieving for my loss. He didn't actually say anything — this wasn't like Moses and the burning bush — but I *felt* it. I just knew. I just knew that God existed. That Gran died and that it sucked, but I wasn't abandoned. I've never felt anything so crystal clear in my life, never had anything more reassuring since then. I just knew he was there, and that it would all be okay.

"'I cried, I thanked God and I went home. The cops were looking for me, and my parents were freaked the hell out, but once they saw me, it was all okay. As I knew it would be.

"'For the most part, things have been okay since then. And now, as I'm sitting here on these stairs again, writing this letter to you guys, I think I finally understand. Maybe Gran died just so I'd have that moment, that clarity and assurance. I am not afraid to die. I know I'll be okay. I don't think the same would have been true if Gran had never taken her life and I never came here as an angry kid who needed answers. Maybe everything does happen for a reason.'"

The sun is rising, spilling out golden rays all over the dew-coated grass. To the right, we watch the farm from Sasha's letter, a small shadow in the enormity of the sunrise. And then it happens. Subtle, like the rising rays of sun, I feel her.

"Whoa," I whisper. I feel her everywhere. My eyes tear up but I don't bother blinking them away as I picture a frightened Sasha sitting on these same steps all those years ago, taking hope and grace from the last place she thought she'd find it.

Elijah takes my hand, his rough fingers lacing between mine. No words are needed to know he feels it, too. It only takes a few seconds for the sun to do its thing, but those few seconds are every bit as powerful as they were when Sasha felt them, judging by the way he clutches my hand in his. I lean against his shoulder, my cheek pressing into his T-shirt. His head lowers on top of mine.

"It really is magical," Elijah says. Hand in hand, we watch the earth wake up before our eyes. Sasha was right; in this moment, everything does feel okay.

Everything *will* be okay.

"Is that all she said?" Elijah asks a few minutes later, his voice softer than the singing birds nearby.

I shake my head, then pull my hand reluctantly from his so I can pick up the note and read the final line. "'I love you and miss you both, Sasha.'"

Elijah turns around, the tendons in his neck flexing as he gazes up at the church. "A town founded by a freed slave," he says, looking back at me with a sparkle in his eyes. "I bet he started out with nothing, just like me. I think my ancestors would want me to attend college."

"They totally would," I say. It looks like he might say more, but he doesn't.

"I remember that night," I say, both because I want him to know and because I don't want him to leave just yet. There's still an hour until school starts and I want to spend it with him. "Mrs. Cade called my parents asking if Sasha was at our house, but she wasn't. Everyone was freaking out and I spent a lot of time praying for her to be okay. I didn't know Gran had died yet. In the heat of the moment, Mrs. Cade hadn't even told my parents."

"Do you think she's right?" Elijah says, staring at the calluses on his palms. "That everything happens for a reason?"

"I don't know. I think Sasha *believed* that, and maybe that's all that matters."

"I think we met for a reason." He says it so quietly, I almost think I imagined it. Then he reaches over and takes my hand in his, my cold, trembling hand in his rough, warm and weathered one.

I go absolutely still, not wanting to ruin a single second of this moment. Elijah's thumb slides across my palm. He stares at our hands as if they contain all of the answers to life and all of the secrets to mending a broken heart.

"I've never had a friend like you," he says. He shakes his head, looking out at the sunrise. "I'm not sure I ever had a real friend — not until Sasha. And now you."

"I'm honored to take her place," I say, squeezing his hand. "I wish it wasn't under these circumstances, but yeah." *I also wish you didn't see me as just a friend.*

After a tense moment where I'm embarrassingly hoping something might happen, he moves my hand back into my lap and then lets it go, leaving behind a cold ache.

"Well, I guess I should get to work," he says. He stands and then reaches out a hand to help me up.

I check the time on my phone, then slide it back in my pocket. "I guess I should get to school."

Our shoes crunching over the gravel is the only sound for a full minute. When I get to my car, I turn to him, my heart beating so hard it might fly out of my chest and knock him out cold. But it needs to be said, so I pull on some courage hidden deep in my subconscious and say, "You're my best friend, too."

He grins, his head tilting a little as he looks at me. "Have a good day at school."

"Have a good day at work." I look at my car keys, flipping through the keychain until I get to the right key. I'm not sure how I can go to school after a morning like this. When I look up, Elijah is right in front of me, his head blocking the bright sun. He pulls me into a hug, and I wrap my arms around him, letting my cheek press against his shirt. "You're really good at this hugging thing," I mumble as he slowly pulls away.

He laughs, a genuine chuckle that resonates from his stomach. I roll my eyes, trying to play off my serious comment like I didn't really mean it that much. "I wish you could talk more," I say. "You're always so hard to get in touch with."

"Sorry, Raquel." He grips my elbows for a second and then lowers his hands. "My roommate had a laptop but he pawned it a few months back. I can get online at the library, but they close before I get off work most nights, and only in the rare occasion that my boss is gone can I sneak on his work computer. Believe me, though, I am constantly wishing I could email you."

"So," I say as lighthearted as possible because that last thing he said felt heavier than he meant it to be. "I wonder when I'll see you again?"

His shoulders lift as he takes a step backward, toward his bike. He turns up his palms and gazes at the sky. "Whenever Sasha wants you to."

Chapter Sixteen

You know that saying, the one about how we only use ten percent of our brains? Not true.

There is simply no way my entire brain isn't working at full capacity in the days that follow. I'd thought there was no room left to feel anything besides pain, and then the first letter arrived and somehow my brain found more room to feel, love, miss and rejoice.

And then I fell for Elijah.

Suddenly I'm running at one hundred percent brain function.

I'm not sure when it happened, not really. Maybe that first moment I hugged him standing near the fresh grass covering Sasha's grave, maybe when he took my hand on the steps of Mount Horeb Baptist Church. Maybe it doesn't even matter *when* it happened, just that it did.

And now I'm not sure what to do.

Before, my mind was a hurricane of grief, leaving a path of destruction.

This thing with Elijah, it's a tornado. It fills my every waking thought, always spinning. Scientists don't know a damn thing about brains when it comes to love.

I am guilty, I am mourning, I am falling for my dead best friend's brother.

Sasha believed that everything happens for a reason. But this? It can't possibly be a good thing.

With a deep breath, I focus on the tulips in my hand, arranging them just the way Izzy taught me. I work quickly, my fingers relying on muscle memory because my mind is elsewhere. Thinking about how I don't even know Elijah, not really. I don't know his favorite color or food or song. I don't know what keeps him up at night, if he's ever broken any bones, if he's allergic to anything. His first kiss, his first heartbreak. These are the things you should know about a person before you go and fall in love with them.

Just thinking about the L-word makes me cringe. He's Sasha's brother. This can't happen.

The herbal stink of expensive marijuana announces the arrival of my boss from the back of the shop. She floats into the room, humming a song to herself.

"This order is ready," I say, doing one final fluff of the sprigs of baby's breath before moving the vase over to the shelf of today's orders.

"Girl, who took the sunshine out of you?" Izzy asks.

"Huh?" She looks like she could punch someone, and that's saying something because this woman wouldn't hurt a fly.

"Something's bothering you," she says. She reaches into her skirt pocket and pulls out half a dozen glass vials, searching until she finds the one she wants.

"Hold out your wrists." I do as she asks and she rubs a clear oil on both of my wrists. It smells fresh and fragrant, like a garden after a rainstorm.

"Bergamot," she says, watching me intently as she caps the vial and puts it back in her pocket. "It'll help with your ... depression, my dear."

"Um, thanks. I'm not really depressed." My stomach aches as I reach for the next order slip, a bouquet of pink assorted flowers. "I don't know what I am, but I don't think it's depressed."

"It happens to all of us," Izzy says, taking the next order slip after mine and setting up her vase next to me on the table. "If I didn't know any better, I'd think you were ... happy. And maybe worried about that."

I laugh before I get the good sense to hold it back. Running a hand through my hair, I shake my head. "You might be right about that. I don't deserve to be excited about anything right now."

Except Sasha's next adventure.

"Never be ashamed of your emotions," Izzy says, tapping my shoulder with a long-stemmed rose. "The world is a rough place. We need to find happiness where we can and hold on to it with fury."

* * *

Hey favorites,

"I never knew love until I met you / I never knew pain until I lost you."

Ah, Zombie Radio. Is there any better band in the world? Don't bother replying, the answer is no. Four guys from Corpus Christi, Texas ... four super-cute guys ... formed this band when they were in high school. They worked their asses off, indie-produced their first albums and then got a small record deal just two years ago. Now look at them, on posters at Walmart and shit. Elijah, this band is my jam. My favorite musical group on earth. I know you've never listened to them from our talks together, so I, being the greatest sister and best friend on earth, have arranged something special for you guys. Friday, October 7th, Zombie Radio is playing a show in Houston at a place called The Engine Room. See the attached PDF of your tickets, complete with parking pass because I am awesome. God, I wish I could be there, but if they let my spiritual body hang out on earth, I promise I'll be there. Not with you guys in the crowd, of course, but with JJ and his drum set. *drool*

Those boys know how to write a love song better than they know how to rock a pair of skinny jeans, and trust me, that's saying a lot. I love love and I love this band.

You guys have fun, okay? Jam out, rock out, dance, sing, have a blast. Do it for me.
You're going to love this.
Almost as much as I love you guys.

Love you and miss you both,
Sasha

P.S. Rocki, sneak into my bedroom and steal that size

large ZR shirt from my closet. It's the one with the skeleton on the front and we got it at their Austin show that time they were sold out of every other size, remember? Elijah should wear it to the show, because I am NOT going to let my fam show up wearing a regular shirt. No way.

Houston is two hours southeast of Peyton Colony, and although I've never gone to a concert that far away without Sasha, I try not to let the logistics worry me. The first thing I do is rush into the kitchen and check Dad's work schedule. He'll be gone on the seventh. Perfect. Dad is about a thousand times more overprotective than my mom, and that means I have six days to come up with a plan. Easy. It won't be the first time I've bent the truth a little to stay out all night at a Zombie Radio show. Those guys are the best band in the world, after all, and three of the four members were my epic crushes from fifth to tenth grade. JJ has always been Sasha's crush, so I let her have him like a real best friend should.

Now that I have an excuse to contact Elijah without it seeming weird, I email him asking if he wants to meet up halfway between Austin and Peyton Colony and ride the rest of the way to Houston together. My heart does this little pitter-patter of excitement. After two heart-wrenching adventures, we're getting a fun one. Zombie Radio puts on an amazing show. I haven't seen them live since before Sasha's diagnosis. It feels like ages ago.

I try not to let it bother me when Elijah hasn't replied to my email the next day. Or the day after that. He hasn't let me down before, so he won't let me down now, right?

Wait. Sasha. Not me. He won't let *Sasha* down.

Three days before the gig in Houston, I stop by the Cades' house after school. I'd called Mrs. Cade from the school parking lot, so she's expecting me. She greets me with a warm smile and a hug at the front door. Sunny greets me with cheek licks. Mrs. Cade's white-blond hair has been pulled into a sleek ponytail, and instead of a nice dress like usual, she's wearing a velour tracksuit, deep maroon, with a pink tank top under the jacket. It's a little odd, if I'm being honest.

"How are you?" she asks, closing the door behind me.

"I'm good," I say, still kneeling so I can ruffle the fur on Sunny's head. There's a life-sized witch standing near the door, her crazy eyes and green hair reminding me that Halloween is just a few weeks away. "I like your decorations."

Mrs. Cade delights in decorating her house for each holiday, and since Halloween in their neighborhood includes a hayride for all the kids to go house to house, Mrs. Cade really goes all out for this one. There are spiderwebs covering the bricks around the front door, foam spiders as big as my head lining the steps.

The Cades have three custom-made tombstones with their names on them and silly little sayings about how they died. They've always been prominently displayed on the front lawn with a spotlight focused on them. It doesn't escape my notice that she's omitted them from this year's decor.

"It gives me something to do," Mrs. Cade says as she leads me into the kitchen to where she's already made two cups of tea for us. "I almost didn't decorate this year, but Walter talked me into it. He said Sasha would want me to, you know?"

"She totally would," I say, nodding. "I remember we even had this conversation with her. She said to keep doing things that make us happy."

Mrs. Cade nods, that sad smile permanently etched on her face. "I remember. So that's what I'm trying to do."

She spoons sugar into her tea and then gestures toward her clothing.

"So what's up with that outfit?" I ask, allowing myself to grin because Sasha would want me to.

Her cheeks turn rosy and she looks into her teacup. "I joined a club for women my age. It's silly really, but we meet once a week at the community center and play games or talk about books, drink wine … that kind of thing."

"Sounds fun," I say, squeezing the bottle of honey onto my spoon. "Do y'all wear matching tracksuits?"

She laughs, a deep sound coming straight from a place she hasn't used in a while. She looks down at her outfit and shrugs. "Kind of. I mean, I showed up in a dress the first time and all the other ladies were dressed very casual, so I felt out of place. I thought I'd try this one out today. The lady at Nordstrom said it would be perfect."

I put my spoon in my mouth, licking off the remaining bit of honey. "Okay, here's a tip, Mrs. Cade. If you want to fit in with a group of regular women, you probably shouldn't shop at Nordstrom."

She laughs again. "You're probably right. Maybe you can take me shopping sometime. Show me how to dress like a normal mom."

"I'd love to." Wherever Sasha is now, I hope she can see this. I hope it makes her proud that her mom is trying to move on, because I know that's what Sasha wanted. I clear my throat and decide to go with an honest approach to getting what I need from Sasha's bedroom. Well, as honest as I can be without breaking my promise.

"Mrs. Cade? I was wondering if I could borrow a shirt from Sasha's closet. Just for a couple days and then I'll return it."

She sets her teacup back on the saucer and waves me away with her hand. "Of course, of course. Go get it."

That was easy. Much easier than trying to sneak it out like Sasha asked. I thank her and then dash off to Sasha's room, Sunny bounding after me. I stop dead in my tracks when I get to her door. Last time I was here, I didn't go inside. Now, I have to.

Her room still smells exactly the same. That scent of Sasha, not quite like anything specific, but I'd know it anywhere. There's a lump in my throat as I cross the threshold, my feet sinking into her plush carpet. I helped her pick out this carpet after the nail polish–shattering incident that left her former carpet ruined. It's still fluffy and even nicer than the carpet in the rest of the house.

Drawing in a deep breath, I make my way toward her closet, pull open the door and flip on the light. The huge walk-in is filled with clothes, shoes, old toys from her childhood that she could never get rid of and one giant cardboard cutout of Captain America. I glance back and find Sunny hopping up on Sasha's bed, walking in a circle before settling down on the crumpled sheets. My heart aches as I wonder how long he waits there each day, waiting for his human to come back.

I move toward the back corner row of hangers, the solid swath of black T-shirts, all Zombie Radio official merch. This girl has every shirt they ever made, around thirty of them. The only large-sized one is on the far right, and it's a crisper black color than the rest since it wasn't worn as much.

I take it off the hanger, fold it gingerly and take it home, hoping that when I get there, I'll have an email from Elijah. I have to have faith that he won't let us down for this adventure.

He can't. He needs this just as much as I do. Right?

Chapter Seventeen

Dad eyes me over the green glass of his beer bottle. "You doing okay, kid?"

"Yeah, Dad." I smile as I sling my backpack against the wall near the back door and head into the kitchen for a snack. "Why?"

Dad takes another sip of his beer. It's only three o'clock, but he's just returned from a trip on the road and he drinks a cold one when he gets off work, no matter the time. My dad is tanned, rugged and manly. He's always sporting a beard and wearing something mentioning his favorite football team, the Texans. Despite the masculine exterior, my dad has always been a big softy when it comes to Mom and me. So far, he hasn't needed to kick anyone's ass for me. But he's kind of looking like he wants to.

"Honey, come here," he says, pointing his beer at the chair next to him.

I rip open a packet of Pop-Tarts and sit, taking a bite. "What's up?" I ask.

"Something's wrong with you." It's not a question, but a statement. "Want to talk?"

I take another bite, needing to eat quickly so I can get to work. "Nothing's wrong, Daddy. I promise."

He shakes his head and reaches over, breaking off a piece of my second Pop-Tart. "I haven't seen Zack around here lately."

"Oh," I say, staring at the red sprinkles on top of my overprocessed pastry. "We broke up."

"Really?" He sounds more impressed than surprised, though his eyebrows shoot up anyway. "I'm sorry to hear that."

I roll my eyes. "No you aren't, Daddy. You're probably just as happy as Sasha is."

Right after it's out of my mouth, I wish I could take it back. Instead, I do this weird backpedaling thing, and the half-eaten Pop-Tart crumbles in my fingertips. "I mean, you know, she never liked him. So she's probably psyched that we're over, I mean, if she was here, you know? Like, maybe in heaven, she's happy about it."

"I get it," Dad says, taking another sip of his beer. "Honestly, I don't think any of us liked that boy very much. You're better off without him, but I don't think you should be sad about it."

"I'm not," I say quickly. "I'm fine with it. Seriously."

Dad's tanned skin crinkles between his eyes. "Then what is it? I go back to work in the morning and I hate leaving knowing you're upset."

Once again I've been asked a question I can't answer. The concert is tomorrow night and I still haven't heard a word from Elijah. *That's* what's bothering me.

Lies fall out of my mouth so easily these days. "I want to go to this movie marathon tomorrow night," I say, making my face all insecure and angelic, like the lying daughter that I am. "It'll be like five hours and I'm afraid to ask Mom if I can go … because, well, Sasha …"

"What about Sasha?" Dad asks.

"I guess I just feel bad about going out with new friends when Sasha hasn't been gone very long. I'm afraid it might disappoint Mom."

I feel so dirty saying all of these lies. But I know exactly what Dad's going to say in reply, and if it works, then I'll have permission to go to the concert.

"Oh, honey." He reaches over and puts a hand on my arm. "Sasha was your best friend and that means she wanted what was best for you. You should definitely go to the movies. I'll talk to your mom for you."

All of this shame will mean nothing if Elijah doesn't show up. I plaster on a sad smile and run a hand through my hair. "Thanks, Dad."

* * *

Izzy takes my wrists and rubs some essential oils on them before I've even had time to put my purse and car keys under the front counter. "Your aura is troubled, kiddo." She caps the oil bottle, sets it on the counter and then presses my wrists together, rubbing them until the oils are absorbed in my skin. "I know I'm just an old lady, but you can always talk to me."

"I'm fine," I say, even as I heave a massive sigh. Wordlessly, I move to the back table and survey the order slips for the day. Since it's October, we have a few fall harvest baskets of flowers and two Halloween-themed spooky vases that come with black roses and plastic vampire teeth, along with one birthday bouquet for a woman turning ninety-nine.

I get to work, well aware of the fact that Izzy is watching me, probably wanting me to spill my guts to her. But I won't. I can't. This secret is mine, Sasha's and Elijah's. And neither of them are talking to me right now.

It's less than twenty-four hours until the show, and Elijah hasn't confirmed if he can go or not. Deep down, there's a tiny little voice that tells me maybe he doesn't have internet access right now. Maybe I should chill out. It's possible, right?

But the larger voice, the one that consumes me wholly, knows that's not the case. He works at a place where he can use the computer and he's currently in the middle of the adventure of a lifetime from his dead sister. There's no way he hasn't checked his email.

He's avoiding me.

He knows. He totally knows that I am falling for him. That my heart is so freaking stupid it can't simply be friends with a guy like Elijah; it wants more.

And clearly Elijah doesn't want that, or he'd be replying. He'd be seeking me out.

Tears cloud my vision as I work, taking another rose as black as my heart. Sasha gave us the best gift ever and I went and ruined it by falling for her brother like some kind of lovesick idiot. Of course he wouldn't feel the same way. Why would he? Sasha trusted me, and I let her down.

A sob rises in my chest and I force it down. Unfortunately, the only thing that *does* go down is the black glass vase in my hand. It hits the concrete floor and shatters, large pieces of black skittering all over the place.

I curse and start crying all at the same time. Izzy calls my name but I turn my back to her, blinking away tears as I reach for the broom and dustpan that's propped against the wall.

"I'll do that for you," Izzy says, reaching for the broom.

I shake my head. "I've got it."

She watches me sweep up the mess, her hands on her hips. "I'm really sorry," I say, dumping the glass in the trash can. "I'll pay for it."

She waves a hand. "No need. Why don't you tell me what's wrong? I could help."

With a heavy breath, I reach for another vase and look over at her, wishing she wouldn't waste all of her kindness on me. "It's nothing. I'm just … I miss Sasha." *And I made the mistake of liking someone who doesn't like me back. And now I might have ruined my best friend's dying wish.*

"Would you like to go home early?" Izzy pulls a hair tie off her wrist and wrangles her long curly hair into a low ponytail. "You could take home some flowers to cheer you up."

"I'd rather stay, if that's okay." I'm just grateful that no customers are in here. "I don't want to be home right now."

"Fine with me," Izzy says. "You're always nice to have around. And I'm always here if you need to talk."

I almost tell her everything right there. It would be so easy to bleed my heart out in front of all of these beautiful flowers. I wonder if she has an essential oil for someone as screwed up as I am.

But I can't break my promise to Sasha, no matter how much I might want to, so I just get back to work.

At midnight, I stare at my computer screen, the glow the only light in my bedroom. My inbox has zero new messages.

I start a new email to Elijah, leave the subject blank and stare at the blinking cursor for half an hour. I should tell him I'm sorry if I made him feel weird, tell him I'm totally not into him, so he shouldn't let worries of my stupid and nonexistent crush stop him from seeing Zombie Radio in Sasha's honor.

In the end, I send him one final email that doesn't say any of that. I'm not sure if it matters. All I do know is that I won't break my promise to Sasha, even if Elijah does.

> Elijah,
>
> I have Sasha's shirt for you if you do end up going to the show. I'll print out both tickets in case you don't have access to a printer. If you want the shirt or the ticket, you can come find me. There's usually a long line before a show at The Engine Room. Hope you're okay.
>
> Raquel

Chapter Eighteen

A burst of chilly air hits me in the face, sending a tingle down the back of my shirt. It probably wasn't a good idea to wear the Zombie Radio shirt that has a holey skeleton back, courtesy of Sasha's scissors. I have other, non-sliced-up shirts, but this one makes me look older, sexier and unafraid.

Which is another reason I shouldn't have worn it. What am I trying to do? Will Elijah appear because of some magical cleavage and off-the-shoulder skin action? *He doesn't even like me.*

All of my efforts will no doubt be for nothing, since I don't see his black motorcycle anywhere. Zombie Radio fans walk through the streets of downtown, toward The Engine Room, grouped in twos or threes or more. Everyone has someone, except for me. I keep my head down, my bag weighing heavily on my shoulder as I make my way toward the growing line outside the entrance. Sasha's T-shirt doesn't weigh that much, but to me, it's like a ton of bricks.

I search the crowd, hoping for a familiar face. But the Mohawks, tattoos and brightly dyed hair all belong to people who aren't my friends. I wish Sasha was here.

I move forward in line, checking the time on my phone. Doors opened three minutes ago, so we're all steadily trickling into the darkened club. Once we're inside, it will be nearly impossible to find anyone. I stare at a black splotch of old gum on the dirty concrete as I slowly move forward in line. *I'm sorry, Sasha. I should have stuck to your plan.*

"ID?" I look up to find a portly hipster guy staring at me, eyebrow raised. He's holding a permanent marker with the cap off.

"Oh," I say, realizing I'm now just a few feet away from the doors. "No, sorry." I hold up my hands and he crosses a big black X over the tops of them. As much as I love Zombie Radio, I don't know how I'm supposed to get through this show. I should turn around, go home and forget this day ever happened.

"Hey." The sound is coming from behind me. Footsteps thump to a stop right next to me, and Elijah drops his hands to his knees, panting for a few seconds. "Damn, I haven't run that far in a long time."

"Where'd you come from?" Elation pours into every cell of my body, and I step out of line, walking with Elijah over to the club's brick wall. I try to act cool.

"That Exxon three blocks north," he says, his chest rising and falling with heavy breathing. "I saw people walking inside so I ran to find you before I missed you." Those crystal-blue eyes slice into me, reaching into my soul and touching all the parts of me I try to keep hidden from the world.

"I'm glad you're here." I blink a few times and focus on a red Volkswagen Bug in the distance. "Sasha ... she'd be glad."

"I'm sorry I missed your emails," he says, rocking back on his heels. "I only just got a chance to check them, since I can't really be on the computer at work and I have to wait until my boss leaves. I saw what time it was and hauled ass. I swear, Sasha was watching over me to make sure I didn't get pulled over or die." He says it with a laugh, but I narrow my eyes.

"You shouldn't drive recklessly. It's not worth it."

"I couldn't miss this show," he says, shaking his head. "Indie punk rock is totally not my thing, but I couldn't leave you hanging."

I shiver. He must realize it, too, because he quickly adds, "And I couldn't screw up Sasha's last wish. So I'm here." His lips stretch into a smile that feels a little bit forced. "Do you have that shirt?"

Only now do I take the time to realize what he's wearing. Oil-stained jeans even more worn out than his usual pair and a light blue button-up shirt with dark blue pinstripes and a bright red name patch sewn on. *Elijah Delgado* is embroidered under a Monterrey's Auto Body Shop logo.

"Yeah," I say, digging into my bag and retrieving the shirt. "I have your ticket, too."

"Awesome," he says, our eyes meeting as he begins to unbutton his work shirt. Heat rises in my stomach and my toes get all fluttery. I should probably look away. But he slips his shirt off and then playfully tosses it right over my face. I catch it, the scent of boyish body wash and motor oil filling the air before I pull the shirt down and fold it into my arms. Elijah's bare chest awakens parts of me that should be embarrassed, but I can't stop staring as he slides his arms into Sasha's shirt and pulls it over his head, finally tugging down the bottom until his perfect abs are covered. *Damn.*

"Ready?" he asks.

I nod dumbly, shove his work shirt into my bag and then hand him his ticket. As we make our way to the back of the line, there are so many things I want to say, from personal feelings that should definitely be kept to myself to fun stories about Sasha that I'd normally tell him on one of these adventures. But I can't bring myself to talk, to break this easy silence between us as we have our tickets scanned and venture inside.

They don't even ask to see Elijah's ID. His stubble and the crease between his eyes must make him look old enough to drink. We step through a metal detector and into the club.

House music pumps through the speakers and a cool rush of air blasts us as we enter the darkness. Elijah reaches back for my hand and I let him take it, even knowing how much it'll screw up my heart.

"Where's the best place to watch?" Elijah asks once we're inside. We're standing near the back of the crowd. In front of us is the stage, over to the right is the bar and to the left is a little raised area with tables where the drunks usually congregate.

"Sasha and I usually push our way to the front," I say, yelling over the music. "But we're also always the first in line so it's a little easier. We should probably just hang back there. There's no way we'll get through a crowd that big."

"Challenge accepted," Elijah says. He grabs my hand again and begins walking toward the mass of Zombie Radio fans right up front.

"Oh my God, you can't do this," I shout, grabbing his elbow to lean in closer to his ear. "We'll piss everyone off!"

"Nah, we'll be fine." His breath is minty in my ear, but I don't have time to let his nearness affect me because he tugs me along, into the crowd, saying things like "Excuse me, sir" along the way. We inch and slide and move past people until at last I can see the metal railing that separates the audience from the stage.

Elijah's hand slides up my arm. He moves me in front of him, stepping back behind me. "Here you go," he whispers into my ear, his breath hot on my skin.

I grip the railing with both hands like I've done so many times with Sasha, and although she isn't here, I can practically feel her right next to me. The opening band is a small-town indie rock group from Corpus. I don't know any of their songs, but I enjoy their performance. It might be because every time the crowd bobs and sways to the music, Elijah gets pressed against me, his hand on my shoulder, his chest against my back.

At the close of the fifth song, the singer wraps his hand around the mic and thanks Houston for coming out to the show. Then he launches into a passionate rant about the country's political climate but I don't really hear any of it. I'm keenly aware of Elijah's hand on my lower back, keeping contact with me as many people around us shift and move. The band begins to take apart its set.

A short woman with bright blue hair and two beers in her hands moves past me, stopping when she sees Elijah. "You're hot," she says in a low voice, winking.

I take out my phone, pretending to check for messages. Elijah's lips press against my ear as the house music pumps back up to fill the space between acts. "Please tell me Zombie Radio isn't as bad as this first band."

I turn around to face him, ignoring the goose bumps on my neck. "Sasha didn't make you listen to them?"

Though the crowd has lessened, we're still jam-packed near the railing. Die-hard ZR fans want the best view and won't budge for a fifteen-minute set change. This forces Elijah to stand insanely close to me, and I hate myself for how much I like it. This entire adventure is supposed to be about Sasha and Elijah, not my fucking hormones.

He has to tilt his head down to look at me, his eyes like sparkling snow globes under the bright disco ball above us. "She sent me some YouTube videos, but I could never listen to them. No speakers on the work computer, and at the library you have to bring your own headphones, which I don't have."

"You might be the only person in the country without constant internet access," I say, trying to sound like I'm teasing him, but it comes out accusatory. Guess I'm still bitter that he didn't reply to me. "Or a cell phone for that matter."

Something odd flashes in his eyes, then he blinks and it's gone. "There were two computers at the group home, but I didn't see the appeal unless I was researching Sasha. Putting pictures of yourself online is kinda creepy, don't you think? I *hated* when Sasha made me send her one of myself. I made her swear not to post it on social media."

Someone bumps into us on their mad dash to the front, knocking Elijah into me. I wince as my back presses against the cold metal railing. Elijah stumbles, his hands grabbing the railing on either side of me.

"Sorry!" a guy calls out, his hands wrapped around his very drunk girlfriend's shoulders.

"It's cool," Elijah says back. Then he turns to face me, and he doesn't straighten up, doesn't take his hands off the railing. He's so close it would only take a tilt of my chin to kiss him. People crowd around us, returning from the bar or the bathroom or whatever they did after the opening band finished. We're pressed in, covered on all sides except for the railing behind me.

Elijah's eyes meet mine and I swear the whole world stops. Then he says, "What were we talking about?"

"The internet," I choke out. A wave of light-headedness makes me lean on the railing harder.

"Ah, yeah." His tongue flits across his bottom lip. "I'm not really a fan."

"We wouldn't be here if it didn't exist," I say. He laughs, his skin vibrating next to mine.

"True. Very true. I guess I have to like it a little bit."

"Only a little?" I say, pouting. "The internet brought you Sasha."

"And you."

The way he gazes at me makes my heart stop. The air goes cold, the only warmth coming from his hand as he slides it around my waist, tugging me off the railing and against his body. On stage, the curtains whoosh open behind me, the sound of JJ's drums and the roar of the crowd drowning out the silence between Elijah and me.

"The band is starting," I whisper. Somehow he hears me, because he nods.

"I see that."

"We should probably watch it."

He nods, his other hand sliding around my waist until he's holding me so tightly not even the crowd could knock me over.

I swear I'm not breathing.

"Just one more thing," he says, his eyes dropping to my lips. I breathe in, my entire body ablaze, and then he does it. With just a tilt of his head, he closes that tiny space between our lips.

My hands slide up his chest, up Sasha's shirt, and they grab his face and hold it tightly as he kisses me, his lips moving like he's always done this, like kissing me is as natural as breathing.

A guitar rhythm plays and the crowd jumps, and Elijah kisses me like we're all alone in this packed room.

The lead singer, Andre, introduces the band, and I know we should stop. We should turn around and watch the show, but I've never wanted something so badly in my life. We don't stop kissing until Andre says, "I dedicate the first song to this couple in the front. If that's not love, I don't know what is."

I break away from Elijah and look back, my head spinning and my body reeling, and find Andre looking straight at me.

He winks.

Chapter Nineteen

Nothing can kill my high for the next week — not even the ever-pressing and gnawing fact that Elijah hasn't contacted me since the concert. He'd promised that he would try and told me not to give up on him.

Something in his eyes made me believe in him. Sasha's eyes wouldn't betray me, not ever. Her brother's won't either.

I'm going on with my days, school and work and school and work, and I'm pretending like everything is peachy. Sasha has more adventures for us, and Elijah promised to be at every one, no matter how crazy his life at home became or how many extra shifts he picked up at the body shop. He finally admitted that he's been working more to save up money for college tuition, or at least the computer he'll no doubt need once classes start.

I swallow a lump in my throat and drag the broom across the floor at Izzy's, sweeping up glitter, ribbon cuttings and little pieces of floral tape. After the concert, Elijah and I had a wonderful time together. We held hands and walked to a coffee shop that had a poetry reading on the balcony. We didn't kiss any more after that earth-shattering embrace in front of the lead singer of Zombie Radio, but something in us changed. Now I know he wasn't avoiding me.

Still, no matter how passionate he seemed when he promised that he was fine, that he'd be there for Sasha's next adventure, I can't shake the feeling that something is wrong. It's hard knowing someone isn't accessible every second of the day, thanks to cell phones and social media. This distance truly keeps us from getting to know each other.

The bells on the door jingle, so I abandon my broom in the back of the shop and head up front. Izzy is at a chiropractor's appointment this afternoon, and she's left me in charge for the first time ever.

I open my mouth to greet the customer. Then I see a sweep of white-blond hair and yet another velour tracksuit, so I rush up and hug her instead.

"Mrs. Cade!" The real flowers all around us are no match for her floral perfume. It has a nostalgic appeal that will always make me feel at home. "How are you?" I ask, instead of *What are you doing here?*, which is on the tip of my tongue. I know why she's here: because the flowers on Sasha's grave need to be updated. It just sucks to be reminded.

"Sweetheart, I'm doing just fine," she says, releasing me with a good squeeze on my arms first. "How's business?"

"Everyone wants black roses for Halloween," I say, glancing toward the wall of the shop that we've decorated for the holiday. "It's kind of morbid."

"I'll say!" Mrs. Cade looks over the Halloween display and purses her lips. "Do you think Sasha would like those?"

"We have black roses coated with glitter. I think she'd like those the best." The stabbing pain in my chest from talking about Sasha is still there, but it's getting more manageable every day. The only problem is that now there are so many other things I can't talk about.

"I'll take a dozen black glittery roses," Mrs. Cade says, reaching into her purse for her wallet. "I agree that Sasha will totally get a kick out of them."

"Are you taking them to her grave?" I ask as I pick out the prettiest roses we have and wrap them up with purple and orange ribbon.

She doesn't say where she's going, but she knows I know. "You could come with me, if you'd like …"

"I get off at six," I say, glancing at the clock. Still twenty minutes to go.

"Perfect. I'll just have a coffee across the street and then come back and get you, okay?"

"Sounds good." I smile, but I am feeling some pain. I'm not only keeping this epic secret about Sasha's life, I'm also lying to Mrs. Cade about my own life. Elijah is my friend now, maybe something more. But it won't ever happen if he has to stay hidden in the dark.

* * *

Seven days. No emails, no carrier pigeons, no message written in the clouds. Nothing from Elijah. I sit cross-legged on my bed, my laptop in front of me, checking again. It blows my mind that he doesn't have a phone. They sell cheap prepaid phones at gas stations. If I didn't think he'd stubbornly refuse it, I'd buy him one myself.

I take a deep breath. It's Saturday, and I have a lunch date at the Cades' house in an hour. Mrs. Cade invited me over when we were at the cemetery yesterday. I don't know how I'll get through yet another meal with my best friend's parents and pretend that nothing has changed. Still, I have to do it for Sasha.

Before I take a shower, I walk into my closet and stare at the bag on the floor. It's hidden, a shoulder bag slumped next to a bunch of my other crap, and only I know what's inside. Elijah's work shirt.

Bending down, I reach inside and pull out the shirt, like I've done almost every day since the concert. It's embarrassing, but this is my only link to the guy who disappears until Sasha calls us back together.

I run my fingers over the stitching of his name. It's the only thing that confirms he's a real person, not just some email address of ones and zeros online, pretending to be real. He is real, and I've seen him and touched him and talked to him. I just have to have faith that I'll hear from him again. Then I get an idea.

Monterrey's Auto Body Shop stares at me from the patch on Elijah's shirt. I pull out my phone and search the business name, finding an address in just a few seconds. It's a fifty-minute drive from my house. A surge of excitement rises in me as I stare at the shirt in my hand.

After lunch with the Cades, I'm going to give Elijah's shirt back.

* * *

The smell of takeout Chinese food fills the air on the Cades' patio. I fill my plate with some of everything. Mr. Cade is in a cheery mood today, and he's even wearing cargo shorts and a polo shirt, which is about as casual as the man gets. Mrs. Cade wears a lavender pantsuit and a string of pearls around her neck. They're a picture-perfect wealthy married couple, from the outside. Inside, they're still broken with grief.

Sunny, who usually begs for food at any opportunity, lies on the patio with his head against the leg of Sasha's chair. When I call his name, his eyes flit to me but he doesn't move. I slide my chair back, take a piece of chicken off my plate and kneel down next to him.

"Sweet and sour chicken," I say, holding it out to him. "Sasha's favorite."

He eats the chicken, then leans into my hand when I scratch behind his ears. He's seventy in dog years, so in a way, he's spent more time with Sasha than even I did. "I love you, doggie," I whisper to him, repeating what Sasha always said. He just stares at me, his unmoving tail a sign that the happiness has been taken away from him.

I have an okay time at lunch. We talk about Mr. Cade's job and how he's had several successful wins for his clients lately. Mrs. Cade tells us about her new ladies' group and how she's made a few friends. She hasn't told them about Sasha, and we agree that she shouldn't feel pressured to talk about it if she doesn't want to. For now, the Cades are just trying to find a new life, one that goes on day after day without a daughter.

They ask me about school and work, and if I'm still planning on becoming a veterinarian after I graduate. I have to stop myself several times from mentioning anything too ... revealing. Basically, I spend an hour talking in circles around the safe topics of school and work.

I stay for a cup of coffee, not exactly because I want it but because Mr. Cade gets a work call and heads to his office, and Mrs. Cade acts like she doesn't want me to leave just yet. I plan on heading straight to Austin when this is over, but I'm not going to rush this time with Sasha's parents. They need me more than I need them.

Mrs. Cade messes with her coffee maker. There's a weird vibe in the air, and I get the feeling she wants to tell me something but hasn't quite worked up the guts to say it yet. A sliver of fear slips up my spine. Can she tell I'm hiding something from her?

But when she finally turns around, stirring her sugar cube into her coffee and taking a seat next to me at the kitchen island, I'm pretty sure it's not that.

"Are you okay?" I ask just to break the silence.

"Oh sweetheart," she says slowly, staring into her coffee. "I don't think I'll ever be okay again. But yes, I am fine right now." She takes a sip and then cradles the coffee mug in her hands, her soft brown eyes searching mine. "There is something I wanted to talk to you about."

The way she says it eases my nerves. I know it's not about Elijah. "I'm here," I say. "For anything you need."

"Well," she says, "I've been meaning to talk to you about Sasha's room. You were her best friend, so if there's anything of hers you'd like to keep, I want you to take it."

Whatever I'd been expecting, it wasn't that. "That's ... really nice of you," I say as I think it over. But I don't have to think it over. I look over at the sweet furry Labrador cuddled at my feet. Sunny. *I want Sasha's dog.* A little flutter starts in my stomach. Sunny is the only living part of Sasha that Mrs. Cade has left.

Mrs. Cade's hand is extra warm when it covers mine and

squeezes. "Anything you'd like, okay? Clothes, trinkets. You can take her TV if you want. I know she'd want you to have it all. It'd make her happy."

"I don't think her TV would fit in my room," I say with a laugh. "But maybe I'll just go and look around?"

"Of course. Take what you want. You can always come back for more." The woman is selfless, healing in the only way she knows how. She would want to help Elijah. I just know she would.

In Sasha's room, I struggle with the feeling that I might look over and find Sasha sitting at her vanity, doing her eye makeup. Or emerging from the closet in a dress entirely too short. I go to the closet first, opening the door and stepping inside, letting the scent of Sasha fill my lungs. I take two Zombie Radio shirts, then a PCHS shirt from last year when we drew all over it in permanent marker. Sasha used it as a sleep shirt, and it'll be my sleep shirt now. Tucking the clothes under my arm, I venture back out into her room and sit at her vanity. Sunny sidles up next to me, resting his chin on my leg.

My eyes have dark circles that makeup can't hide. My hair is a darker brown than it was this summer, and it's almost long enough to make a tiny ponytail at the base of my neck. Not that I would do that, because it'd look hella tacky. Tacky enough to make Sasha roll over laughing.

Pictures of us are everywhere, ascending in age from eight to seventeen. I have copies of them all at home, so I leave them where they are.

On Sasha's computer desk, I take a tiny glass elephant that we got at the county fair a few years ago. Mine is in my room, sitting on the windowsill. Sasha's will go next to it.

I turn around, holding tightly to Sasha's shirts as I survey the room. I don't really want her *things*. I want her *here*. I walk to the door and then turn around, taking one last look at her room.

Then I rush back inside and take her pillow. It's memory foam, encased in her favorite Egyptian cotton pillowcase, and it smells just like her strawberry shampoo. I grin as I clutch it to my chest. Mrs. Cade said anything I want, after all. I choose this.

A soft thump hits my foot as I step into the hallway. I look down and find a silver flash drive that has fallen out of the pillowcase. My blood runs cold as I bend to pick it up.

A hidden flash drive can only mean one thing. But how could she have known I'd find it here?

My heart thudding, I return to her room and turn on her laptop. It powers up quickly, showing Sasha's wallpaper photo of a famous library with three floors of books connected by a tall, rolling ladder. Sunny is watching me curiously.

I try to swallow but my throat is too dry. The flash drive slips into the USB port and my hands shake as I wait for it to load. Only one file appears. A video named MAYBE_DELETE.

My pulse thunders in my ears. My finger hovers over the mouse pad. Should I click or not? My eyes blur and then I see the tiny little camera lens on the laptop. This is the same camera she used to record so many of the videos she's sent us. She sat here, at this laptop, and planned her entire last wish without me even knowing.

Whatever this file is, she thought about deleting it.

But she didn't.

I bite my lip and double-click.

Sasha's face appears on her own computer. She looks more vibrant than in the last few videos. This one must have been recorded a long time ago. "Hey guys," she says, a flirty grin on her face.

Chills prickle down my arms as I sit in the same spot she was when she recorded this. Sunny hops up next to me on the bed, ears perked at the sound of his human's voice. He looks around the room and then flops down. "So ... you've probably figured this out by now. I mean, right? Look at you two." She leans forward and wiggles her eyebrows.

No, I haven't figured it out, I think.

"Maybe I've read too many love stories and it's turned me into a hopeless romantic, but I just have a feeling about you two. Rocki, you're adorbs and loyal and a little bit stuck in your shell, but I think Elijah can break you out of it. Elijah — not to be gross because you're my brother — but you are totally gorgeous, judging by the pictures I forced you to send me."

Sasha rolls her eyes and looks directly at me. "Can you believe his Instagram account isn't filled with selfies? He's hella retro, but I like it. I think there's nothing more worthy of a fairy-tale ending than the dying girl's brother and best friend falling for each other."

I can't believe what I'm hearing. I guess I should have known she'd be onto us. The girl picks up on everything, even in the afterlife. Why didn't she send us this video, then?

Sasha tilts her head. "So if you're hearing this and you're like, ew, gross, then okay." She holds up her hands. "Maybe I'm wrong. Totally NBD. But I just have a feeling, and I wanted to let you know it's okay. Don't feel bad for finding happiness outside of my death, okay?"

She waits a beat. "As for my parents ... don't tell them. Not yet, okay? They'll be upset that I planned this huge adventure for you and left them out of it, and I still feel a little bad about that, but they never wanted me to find my brother in the first place. They need to be eased into this."

A shadow moves into the room and I nearly launch out of my seat. My hand slaps the space bar on Sasha's laptop and her video pauses. Sunny saunters by, not realizing he nearly caused me to jump out of my own skin. What if he had been Mrs. Cade? "Shit." I breathe, willing my heart to slow down. I need to pay better attention.

I play the rest of the video. Sasha gnaws on her bottom lip. "I just — I don't know. I've been thinking about this video for a few days. I think you two will make a great couple, and I just have this gut feeling that maybe it'll work out for you. I'm still working out how you should tell my parents. I feel like asking you to lie to them about who Elijah is forever is kind of epically wrong, but" — she shrugs — "I'll make a new video as soon as I figure out what you should do. That is, you know, if you two start liking each other. Totally not a big deal if you don't."

She winks and the video ends.

I rip out the flash drive, shove it in my pocket and close Sasha's laptop. My thoughts are everywhere at once. It's not like the heavens part and white doves fly out of the sky to the chorus of a thousand angels singing hallelujah, but it's close.

Sasha just gave me permission to have this huge crush on her brother. I never realized how heavy the guilt of liking Elijah was weighing on me until it finally lifts away ...

... and I am free.

Chapter Twenty

My parents are planning a date night tonight. It's an event that was nearly nonexistent when I was a kid, but now it happens maybe once every other month when Dad's schedule aligns with having a day off on a weekend. The glorious news is that I can practically run off and join a cult and tell them about it, and they won't care because it's date night. The bad part is that now I'm more than a little nervous to show up at Elijah's work.

With the next few hours free and Elijah's shirt in my passenger seat, I begin the drive while replaying Sasha's secret video in my mind. The landscape grows hilly as I near Austin. Interstate 10 is pretty barren until I'm on the outskirts of the city, which is exactly where my GPS is leading me. I turn onto a side road and meander through an older neighborhood, passing a couple of gas stations and laundromats. This is unquestionably the bad part of town. I try not to imagine a world where one sibling is adopted into a life of luxury and wealth, while the other sibling ages out of the system and ends up here.

My chest constricts as I near Monterrey's Auto Body Shop. It's a long metal building with a faded plastic sign near the road. The driveway is gravel and full of potholes, broken-down cars and a black motorcycle. I park in the very first spot, on the other side of a tow truck and out of sight from the small window near the only door. A neon *Open* sign lights up the narrow window.

I hold Elijah's work shirt in my hands, my shoes crunching over the white rocky driveway.

I can't wait to tell him about the video. Maybe he'll be so thrilled he'll ask me on a date, and I'll get to feel the wind in my hair on the back of his motorcycle. I bite the inside of my cheek to keep from grinning as I walk up to the weathered door and pull it open. A rush of cold air hits me as I enter into a small tiled room that looks like something straight out of the early nineties. Dark wood-paneled walls are covered with posters and brand names of car parts, plus some old award plaques from the Chamber of Commerce. Two ratty chairs are against the wall to my left, and an old desk is in front of me, the ripped leather chair empty. It smells a little like old coffee and a little like mildew in here, and the place is eerily quiet. I'd expected to hear machines rumbling, cars idling or, I don't know — the hiss of spray paint or something.

"Hello?" I call out. This room is tiny and no one's in here. There's another door to the right, but it has big red letters saying EMPLOYEES ONLY and DO NOT ENTER, so I take a step back and hover near the worn-out chairs in the corner. I won't risk ruining my jeans by sitting down.

After a few awkward minutes, I can hear voices behind the employee door. The longer I sit here, the lamer I feel. But I know Elijah will be excited to see me. With a burst of courage, I walk over to the door and twist the handle slowly.

It opens into a vast metal building that looks like the mechanic shop that services my car in Peyton Colony. Two wrecked cars hover in the air on lifts, panels removed and lying crumpled in a pile off to the side. I see them before they see me: four men standing in a circle, a cloud of tension hanging in the air. Two have their arms crossed, and they look absolutely terrifying. Like they're competing for an award for most pissed-off guy on the planet.

They're arguing over something, and one guy, an older man with thick-framed glasses and a lumberjack beard, shakes his head violently in protest.

I'm about to close the door, but then I see him. Elijah stands off to the side next to another guy who looks about his age. One hand rests in his pocket, the other runs across his face. He seems stressed. Is it because of the argument?

Maybe I should sit in my car and come back in a few minutes. I turn to go, but one of the older guys sees me and stops talking, his eyes widening as he gestures to the man with the beard.

"Who is that?"

"Oh, hi," I say, my voice high-pitched. I put on a big smile and consider lying and saying I'm a customer.

Elijah turns around, almost bored at first. But then he sees me and his eyes go wider than golf balls.

"I got it," he says quickly. "She's no one."

He jogs over to me so fast I don't even have time to feel offended.

"What the *hell* are you doing here?" he growls as he shoves me back through the door, pressing it firmly closed behind us.

Startled and a little freaked out, I can't seem to form words, so I just hold up his shirt.

He snatches it from my hand. "You have to go," he whispers even though we're the only two in this room.

"Wha — I don't —" I shuffle backward.

From the other side of the door, someone yells, "That better be a pizza delivery girl."

Elijah's jaw tightens. He grabs my arms and says, "You need to go. It's not safe here."

"Why?" I say. "This is a business."

"Just leave," he says, his voice low and pained. "You can't be here. Don't ever come back. Please."

I fight tears and grab for the doorknob.

"Sorry." It sounds like I have a mouthful of marbles as I burst back out into the crisp autumn air, hating myself and hating Elijah and hating every single thing about Sasha's death.

"Raquel," Elijah calls out. I turn around and he's standing in the doorway, his hands on either side of the doorframe. "Meet me at the church in an hour."

"I don't want to," I snap, turning toward my car.

"*Please*," he says. Even with my back to him, I can feel the weight of his stare. "Please," he says. "I'll explain, okay?"

I keep focused on my car.

"I *am* glad to see you, you know. Just give me an hour, and please drive safely."

* * *

Mount Horeb Baptist Church is just as isolated and sad looking as the first time we were here. It's such a shame to let a place of history go to waste like this. Remembering what Sasha's letter said, I drive to the front of the site and read the historic marker sign to get the whole story of Peyton Roberts, and now Elijah is fifteen minutes later than he'd promised. *Maybe he got stuck in traffic,* I tell myself. Another voice inside my head says, *Maybe he's just not coming.*

I sit on the grass beside my car, my back leaning against the tire. My phone is nearly dead, so I put it on battery-saving mode and stay off it, just in case there's some emergency later and my parents need to get a hold of me. It's not like I need it to wait on a call from Elijah.

I snort and pull up a blade of grass.

My entire life is now a collection of weirdness. This long-distance thing, all the secrecy, whatever just happened at the body shop? That's not a healthy foundation for a relationship. Hell, it makes my thing with Zack seem ideal.

I gaze up at the sky and listen to the sounds of birds and the wind blowing through the trees. And I wait. Much longer than I should, but I wait.

Two hours after I left Austin, I hear the rumble of Elijah's motorcycle. I'm still excited to see him — though he doesn't deserve that. I keep my head down, my fingers tearing grass into shreds.

He sits next to me, then leans over and kisses the side of my head. "I'm sorry about earlier. I shouldn't have talked to you like that."

I just nod.

He continues, "I was a little freaked out and I wanted to keep you safe." He lets out a breath. "I don't work at the best place, Raquel."

"It's a place that fixes cars," I say, finally looking at him. "I wasn't expecting a five-star hotel."

He shakes his head slowly. "It's not a body shop."

"What does that mean? Of course it's a body shop." I know what I saw.

His shoulders lift and then fall. "It is a shop, and that's the part Anthony and I work in, but that's not all it is. Our bosses are into ... well, we're not sure, but we think they're money laundering or something. The shop is just a way to hide it."

Oh. Suddenly I realize he could be in trouble. "I'm sorry I showed up. I just wanted to see you, I guess, and the shirt was an excuse to find you." I am babbling.

"I've been wanting to talk to you all week, Raquel. I didn't want to wait until our next adventure. I wanted to see you now."

"Tell me about it," I say. I know the feeling.

Elijah reaches into his pocket and pulls out a small cell phone, turning it over in his hands. It's an older model, worn around the edges.

"Did you just get that?" I ask.

"No," he says, heaving a sigh as he slides it back into his pocket. "It's for work. My boss pays for it. I can't use it for anything other than work, though."

"Why would you need a cell phone for the body shop?"

"We *mostly* work on cars. But occasionally we drive bags of cash to other body shops."

What? "This sounds like some action-movie shit."

He laughs and reaches for my hand, pulling it into his lap. He laces his fingers into mine and stares at his thumb while he slides it across my palm. "Sometimes, it is just like a movie. So much drama. I only work there because Anthony found the job for us. We were in the same group home and we aged out together. He was a couple months older than me, so he found

Monty and got a job. Then he got one for me, too, when I turned eighteen. Monty just wants guys who work hard on the cars and don't ask questions. He even lets us stay at one of his apartments with two other guys who work at a different shop, so we get both a job and a house out of it. I know it's shady, but it seems like a miracle when you've got nothing."

Finally, he's opening up. "So you work at a body shop that's not really a body shop?" I confirm.

"I *do* work on the cars, so at least my work is legit. But lately things are getting weird. My boss had two guys quit on him and one went to jail, so now he's all hinting that he's going to have me or Anthony running more side jobs soon. *Side jobs* means huge boxes of cash that we're supposed to pretend are car parts."

He rubs his eyebrow, then takes my hand into both of his. "I may be an orphan and I may be broke, but I'm not a criminal and I never will be."

My mouth tastes like copper and I realize I've been chewing on the inside of my lip this whole time. "You could have told me this from the beginning," I say, trying not to sound judgmental. "It would have saved me a lot of time worrying about why you barely contact me."

"I don't want there to be lies between us, Raquel," he says. "But it's hard to tell you the truth. You mean something to me."

I look at him. Is there more he wants to say?

"Maybe we could be more than friends, I don't know," he adds.

"You don't know?" I say, trying to smile playfully, but it comes out all wrong.

"It's up to you," he whispers. "But you're too good for me."

He's just inches away, his hand in my hair and his gaze on my lips.

I should probably hold back.

But I give in. I lean forward and kiss him, sweet and quick at first. But then he pulls me into his lap, and soon I'm straddling him with his back against my car, my knees on either side of his hips. I run my fingers through his hair while he kisses me somehow sweeter than he did at the concert. My entire body melts into his.

He slows until he's just holding me, his lips pressed to my forehead. "I am not too good for you," I murmur. I can feel his chest vibrate when he mutters something in disagreement. His warm hands slide up my back and then settle on my hips.

I look up and put my hands on his chest. "You should quit that job and move to Peyton Colony."

"I wish it were that easy."

"It is," I say, sliding my finger around the collar of his white T-shirt. "Just quit and move."

"Where would I go? How would I find another job?"

"You could go to school," I say, resisting the urge to kiss him again since we're having a real conversation. Well, as real as it can be with me sitting in his lap. "You can apply to TSU. You could live in a dorm. And next year, I'll be at the same school."

He doesn't have the same self-control, because he leans forward and kisses me. "And where would I get the money for that?" he says against my lips.

I feel his abs tighten under my hands and it sends heat flushing all through my body. "Scholarships ... and stuff," I say, my breath hitching as he buries his face in my neck and places a soft kiss near my collarbone. "How am I supposed to think when you're doing *that*?"

When he pulls away, he's all serious. "All this school talk is sounding a lot like Sasha."

Hearing her name reminds me. "I can't believe I haven't told you yet! I found another video from Sasha." I cover my mouth with my hands, trying to remember exactly every word from the video.

Elijah quirks an eyebrow. "Are you going into detail, or is that all I get?"

I know I'm grinning like a maniac, but I can't stop the rush of giddiness. I sit back on my heels. "I found a flash drive hidden in her pillow. There was only one video on it and she didn't send it to us. I don't know why, but in it she says she thinks we'd make a cute couple."

"Really."

I grab his wrist. "Do you know what this means?"

"That she figured out the obvious?" he says with a snort. "She had to have known I would like you."

I shake my head. "It means I don't have to feel mind-numbingly guilty every time I — well ..." I can't seem to say the words.

"Every time you check me out?" Elijah says with a flirty wiggle of his eyebrow.

"Well, yeah. She gave me the task of being your tour guide through her adventures and I've been feeling horrible for liking you. But this video, I don't know, it's like it's giving us permission."

"Why didn't she send it to us?"

My happiness deflates at the question I've been avoiding. "Maybe she will. We haven't seen all of her adventures yet. Maybe she's saving it until the end or something."

"I know why." Elijah brushes the hair from my eyes. "She

doesn't want her parents to know about me. She was very clear about that from the first video. If we got involved … well, our future would be tricky."

"But it's *our* future," I say, leaning into his chest. "We get to make the decisions."

Elijah's chin rests on top of my head. "I'm going to email you more often, okay? I'll buy a cheap tablet and I can go to the McDonald's near my apartment for the free Wi-Fi. We *will* talk more."

Now I'm grinning like a goofball, all those awkward feelings be damned. "And then you'll quit and move here and go to college with me?"

He chuckles. "We'll see."

I sit up. "No laughing. I'm serious. I care about you, Elijah, and you have to get out of that job."

"I do *hate* that job," he says softly, his gaze focused on the church. "Give me time. I'll figure it out."

Hearing him agree to leave that place makes me want to jump up and dance, but I play it cool. "This is our first real conversation," I say, poking him in the chest. "One that's not about Sasha's adventures or her plans. I like it."

His hand slides into mine. "You know, I never felt guilty about liking you."

"Why's that?" I ask.

He lifts one shoulder. "Sasha wants us to be happy. You are my happiness. She wouldn't want to take that away from me."

Chapter Twenty-One

Raquel,

I think I have an iced coffee addiction. They gave me one free the first time I came here to email you because the lady in front of me ordered one and they accidentally made two. Now I'm ordering one every time I come here. It's a problem, Raquel. Send help. No, send more iced coffee.

I grin as I read Elijah's email. He wasn't kidding about talking to me more. He wrote to me every day last week, and yesterday he sent two emails, one that he had typed up the night before when he couldn't sleep at home and the second from his new favorite McDonald's.

In his first email, he said he'd spent two hours before his shift creating a resume and sending it out to places that were hiring. I replied that he should focus on getting scholarships and applying to Texas State University. A scholarship would mean he'd get to live in the dorms for free, I pointed out, and he could probably start in January. He promised he would look into it, but he hasn't mentioned anything else about it since.

My head drops onto Sasha's pillow. I haven't changed the pillowcase yet, but that's allowed in situations like these. I can still smell her shampoo when I roll over in the middle of the night.

It's nine o'clock and Elijah has just messaged me online, raving about the new caramel iced coffee. We talk for the next hour, and although it's just in emails, I can hear his voice in my head, see his grin when he makes some snarky joke. It's starting to feel like I'm up all night chatting with my best friend again.

My TV plays in the corner of my room, the volume muted while I email with Elijah. I send him a copy of Sasha's secret video and tell him about the little glass elephant. We go back and forth, our talks more casual than they used to be. It almost feels like I've known him forever. It's such a good feeling having someone to talk to again.

My eyes flutter closed, heavy with the weight of the long day behind me. When my phone chimes a new email, I almost don't check it. I'm half asleep, and his message will be there for me tomorrow, a perfect gift when I wake up. He's gotten used to me falling asleep on him over the last few days, so …

My phone beeps again, and then a third time. I draw in a deep breath and blink myself awake. TheFutureSasha just sent us a new email. It's almost like she's a part of our late-night chat, too. I pop up in bed.

The next two messages are from Elijah, probably excited about her new email.

I swipe across the screen, eager to hear from my best friend again.

An audio file is attached instead of a video. I click play and Sasha's voice rings out through my darkened room.

"Hey favorites, it's me, in voice form. I've been doing these videos for a while now, but I'm not feeling it today. In case no one's ever told you: cancer makes you feel like shit. So anyway, I have your next adventure ready. Halloween is coming up, and I am inviting you to Peyton Colony's annual Halloween bash!"

She laughs, though her voice sounds strung out and tired. I should have guessed this one; the Halloween bash is a big deal each year. My phone alerts me that I have yet another message from Elijah, but I ignore it to finish listening to Sasha.

"Halloween is my absolute favorite holiday. You get to dress up, eat candy, bask in all things creepy and scary, and best of all — there's no obligation to buy gifts for everyone you know. I mean, don't get me wrong ... I love giving gifts, but Christmas is kind of a downer. I tend to obsess over getting the right gift for everyone and it ends up being super stressful. Anyhow, Elijah and Rocki, you two will pretend to be a couple on a date. That means a couple's costume, a.k.a. — the best Halloween tradition ever! Rocki will tell you all about our years of couples' costumes. So that's it. Go, dress up, have fun and expect a package from me before the big day. Love you always."

She makes a kissing sound and then the file ends. This is my least favorite message from Sasha so far; she sounded really sick. This had to have been recorded just a week or so before she died. Ignoring the knot in my stomach, I read Elijah's other messages.

The first one was just a reply talking about how if he ever got to run his own group home, he'd allow the boys to do chores to earn money for themselves to buy things instead of relying on state-funded clothing donations. Then, he replied to Sasha's email with: YAY ANOTHER ONE! And then: WHERE ARE YOU, CHICKA?

And finally, fifteen minutes after the first email, he wrote:

> Looks like someone fell asleep at the wrong time! Halloween bash, eh? We had Halloween parties in the group home for a few years, and then it was taken over by a religious organization and that was nixed. Never dressed up, though. Sounds fun. I'll leave the couple's costume ideas to you, the smart one. Let me know if you need money for it, okay?
> Sweet dreams, Raquel.
> — E

As promised, a package arrives a couple days later. The return address says it's from the PCHS Summer Internship Program — a thing that totally doesn't exist. I guess this is Sasha's way of making sure my parents don't intercept a gift from the afterlife.

I have to leave for a shift at Izzy's in a few minutes, so I take the package into my closet and rip it open. Fluffy turquoise, gold and white fabric fills the box, all satin and soft to the touch. On top is an envelope with a long letter inside. I pull out the fabric first.

Soon, there's a full Jasmine and Aladdin costume set spread out on my closet floor.

Puffy pants and a tiny purple vest are all that make up Elijah's costume. I can practically see his drool-worthy abs already.

Mine is really cute, nearly identical to Jasmine from the Disney movie, with a chunky fake-gold necklace and earrings.

It comes with a long beautiful wig to cover my shoddy excuse for hair.

I snap a photo, and then tuck them away in my closet for further perusal later tonight. Leave it to Sasha to pick out the perfect couple's costume for us. She was always the best at costume ideas, and romantic couples from history or storybooks were her favorites. We always took turns playing the boy role each year. This year, I'm the girl, and I'll be going with a real boy. It's like Sasha made sure I'd have a fun time this Halloween instead of being forced to sit through this holiday without her.

A shiver runs up my spine, and I'm grinning so hard it hurts as I email a photo of our costumes to Elijah. I've already made a list of ideas for us, but obviously Sasha's is better. Plus, it's free.

I start a new email.

> Sasha picked our costumes for us! See the attached photo. Here's a link to the park where the Halloween bash is held. Want to meet me there, say around 7?

A few minutes later, the chat feature pops up just as I'm getting in my car to go to work.

> Elijah0Delgado: I will pick you up at your house. 7 still a good time?

> RockiBoBocki: No ... meet me at the park. My parents will be home.

> Elijah0Delgado: Good. I want to meet them. This is a

date, remember? Sasha's rules, not mine. I'll be there at 7.

RockiBoBocki: ... But ... That's scary! And awkward! And ... ahhhhhhh.

Elijah0Delgado: That's dating. :p

RockiBoBocki: *sighhhhhh*

Elijah0Delgado: Sigh all you want. I'm excited. Be there at 7!

Halloween is in two days. This might be the longest forty-eight hours ever.

* * *

Okay. I lie to my parents. Again.

With trembling hands and a speech that comes out entirely too quickly since I have it memorized, I tell Mom and Dad that a guy I met at Izzy's has asked me to the Halloween bash. I say it's just a friendly thing, nothing serious.

Dad asks a few questions about the integrity of *this boy*, but overall, they handle it well and don't ask to perform a background check. I guess they're happy I've moved on from Zack, but the lie burrows into my subconscious and makes me feel sick. I really like Elijah. This isn't the right way to start out ... whatever this is between us. But it's not like there's another way. Sasha pushed us together and then told us to keep it a secret. A tiny, unforgivable part of me is a little mad at her for that.

The doorbell rings and my heart leaps into my throat. "I've got it!" I call out, almost plummeting into Dad as I race to the front door. It's still too early for trick-or-treaters, so that means he's here. All the warm fuzzies I get near Elijah are currently locked in the dungeon of Parental Proximity.

Elijah stands on the other side of the door — at least I think it's him. He's wearing a full-faced werewolf mask, the cheap rubber kind that doesn't exactly look real. It's also not part of our costumes tonight.

"Trick-or-treat," he says, his voice like warm honey on a summer night.

"We don't give candy to weirdos," I say, rolling my eyes as I step back to let him inside.

"You make a *really* cute Jasmine." He says it so softly I almost don't hear it. My throat feels like it's full of cotton, so all I can do is shake my head like he's full of crap, because he is.

As if by some kind of daughter-protection magic, both of my parents appear. Mom's wearing her signature witch costume, complete with green hair and a pointy hat. "Hi," she says a little too cheerfully. She holds out a hand. "You must be Elijah."

"Yes, ma'am," he says, shaking her hand. "That's me."

Dad does not dress up for the holiday, but if you didn't know any better, you might think he's wearing an award-winning Overprotective Father costume.

"It's nice to meet you," Dad says, extending a hand. "I'm Luke Clearwater."

"Elijah Delgado." He shakes Dad's hand and then points to his hidden face. "I found this at the gas station on the way over," he says, the werewolf's mouth bobbing as he talks. "Three bucks. I couldn't help myself."

His little icebreaker seems to set both of my parents at ease. I grab his elbow. "That mask does not match your costume." Still, I give him a look that I hope he interprets as gratitude. This mask, silly as it is, hides that one part of Elijah that I've been scared to reveal to my parents.

"Your costume is in the guest room," Mom says. She scratches the place where her gnarled witch nose is glued over her real skin. "Can't wait to see you two together! I always loved when Raquel and Sasha went as a matching couple. It's nice to see part of the tradition continue."

Dad snorts. "They'll match even better if one of them isn't a shape-shifter."

I get the hidden meaning behind Dad's comment. He wants to see the boy who is taking out his daughter tonight. I figured it would happen, but it still sucks. Elijah chuckles and pulls off the mask, revealing a head of messy hair and those gorgeous, gorgeous lips.

Mom inhales sharply. She punches at Dad's arm. "Those eyes," she murmurs, putting a hand over her mouth.

Elijah glances at me, his expression unreadable. Dad draws his brows together, little lines forming in his forehead as he studies my Halloween date. "What'd you say your last name was?"

Elijah's Adam's apple bobs. "Delgado, sir."

"Hmm." Dad looks like he's about to say something else, but I begin the damage control as soon as possible.

"We have to hurry," I say, taking Elijah's arm and pulling him into the hallway. I shove him into the guest room, where I've already laid out his costume, and then pull the door closed behind him. To my stunned parents, I say, "We'll be back before curfew, don't worry."

Dad nods, getting lost in the television again. Mom just stands there in the foyer, a quizzical look on her face that only goes away when our first trick-or-treater arrives a few moments later.

Elijah emerges dressed as the sexiest Aladdin in all of existence. I was right about the abs. I was *so* right.

"How do I look?" he asks, cocking his head. "Like a real-life cartoon character?" His poufy satin pants hang low on his hips.

"Better than a werewolf," I retort, turning toward the front door. I can't let him know how much seeing him shirtless affects me. I mean, that's Dating 101 right there.

"You think your parents made the connection?" Elijah asks as we step outside into the cool October air. Anthony's car is parked on the curb, and I realize he probably borrowed it to make a better impression on my parents.

"They noticed the resemblance, that's for sure." I resist holding his hand as we set off on the three-block walk to the park. At least until we're far enough away from my house. "They'll think it's impossible that you're related to her, but no one could miss that you have Sasha's eyes."

His jaw flinches. "Maybe I should have left the mask on."

"I'm sorry Sasha is keeping you a secret."

He reaches over and takes my hand. "Let's not talk about sad things tonight. This is a date, after all."

I look over at him and he winks. "Do you go on a lot of dates?" I ask playfully. As much as I want to know the answer, I kind of don't.

"This will be a first."

"Really?" I look over so quickly my fake hair slides an inch to the right. "You're twenty. How did you go so long without dating?"

"This is my first date, not my first *dating*," he says with a wry grin. "You know, all official and stuff. The few times I stayed at a coed group home, the girls were all over me."

An uncomfortable feeling crawls over me, but then he squeezes my hand. "So much drama with those girls. I didn't really dig it. And lately, I work so much I don't think about dating. Except when I think of you."

"I guess that makes me a happy product of coincidence."

We stop at an intersection next to a group of kids in super-hero costumes. Elijah's eyes sparkle under the glow of the streetlights. "The happiest."

Peyton Colony's Halloween bash takes place in the park in the center of town. Surrounded by the historic buildings of old downtown, the park glows in orange and purple strands of lights that line the perimeter. There's a ton of food, games for the kids and a stage with a dance floor and a live band. This older couple in the town always hosts a haunted house they make from a small mobile home that's moved in just for Halloween every year.

Sasha's parents are gold-level contributors to the city's parks department, so this yearly Halloween bash has been a huge part of Sasha's life. I didn't have to ask Mrs. Cade to know they wouldn't be attending this year. It's still too soon for something like this, although being here tonight doesn't feel like a punch to the gut to me. There are too many goblins, ghouls and foam-muscled superheroes running around reminding me that Halloween should always be celebrated Sasha-style.

Elijah holds my hand as we walk into the fray. I choose a park bench that's empty, and we sit to read Sasha's letter. This one is mostly for Elijah's benefit. She tells him all about attending the celebration as a child and then discusses — at length and with no regard to mortifying me — how scared I get in the haunted house. Elijah laughs at this, and I purse my lips and finish reading the letter.

"We are not going in that stupid haunted house," I say, narrowing my eyes at him.

He looks to the right, at the creepy mobile home that's painted black. An older couple dressed like mummies usher a group of kids through the front door while smoke machines pump a creepy fog through the windows and loud music plays the sounds of nightmares.

"We're totally going in," he says, leaning over and bumping me with his shoulder. "You can hold on to me if you get scared."

Heat rushes to my cheeks. I tuck my long artificial hair behind my ears and gnaw on my lip. I have no doubt that Elijah would protect me from the monsters lurking in that smoky haunted house. The very idea almost makes the whole event seem romantic. Still.

"I'd rather cuddle without the haunted house joining us."

Elijah slides his arm around my shoulders, his skin warm even in the chilly night air. His other hand tilts my chin up toward his, and he places the softest kiss on my lips. My insides melt. I inhale a jagged breath and slowly open my eyes.

"I guess we could cuddle *before* the haunted house," he says, pulling his arm tighter around me. I sink into his embrace, my hand on his bare stomach while we gaze out at the carnival. "I never did any of this as a kid. Candy, costumes and running wild for one night? That would have rocked my little-kid world."

He presses his lips to the top of my head, and even though

there's a whole wig between his skin and mine, a shiver of delight runs through me. I reach up, taking his hand that's around my shoulder and lacing my fingers through his.

"Let's get out of here," Elijah says.

"You're bored?" Or maybe he's just tired of talking about everything he missed.

He shakes his head and stands, straightening his poufy pants. "We saw what Sasha wanted us to see, so the rest of the night should be for ourselves." He reaches for my hand.

"I like that," I say, joining him on the sidewalk. And it's not just because he's dropped the idea of going into the stupid haunted house. It feels like we're finding our footing, slipping into a relationship that is all our own, one not orchestrated by Sasha. We feel real now. Not just two people shoved together by circumstance.

Just as easily as he takes my hand, a darkness settles over him as we walk away from the park. I think I'm imagining it, like maybe he's just thinking about Sasha or something, but after we've walked a couple of blocks, the vibe around him is so thick it makes the hairs on the back of my neck stand up.

"Hey," I say, nudging him in the shoulder. "Are you okay?"

He nods slowly, his gaze on the ground. "There are things I want to tell you, but maybe when we're farther away."

I glance around. "No one can hear us. What's up?" I'm glad he feels he can open up.

"It's not the people, it's the location. We're still on Sasha's adventure so I don't want to talk about my personal stuff."

Maybe I have him all wrong. "You're being weird," I say. "The park is way back there. Talk to me."

"I need more time with you. You are the best thing in my life now. The *only* thing." His words are rushed and he gives me a smile that disappears as quickly as it had appeared.

"Is that *all* you wanted to say?" I dare to ask. My nerves are on edge, waiting for the other shoe to drop.

"Not really, but it's still true."

"Elijah …" I stop just a few driveways away from my house. "Please. Just tell me." Maybe I don't know him as well as I thought I did … yet.

His black hair is shaggier than when I first met him, and he doesn't brush it out of his eyes as I stare him down. "Walk me to my car?"

He starts without me, and now I'm totally unsure of what to do. I want to rush up, grab his arm and demand that he talk to me, but that kind of thing never works. I don't know what it takes to piss him off. Or lose his trust.

"If we can't talk tonight, then when can we talk?" I reach up and adjust my Jasmine wig and realize how stupid we look, two troubled teens cosplaying as a couple in love.

Elijah leans against the hood of the car. "Tomorrow? I'm sorry, Raquel. I *do* want to talk. I just —" He runs both hands through his hair. "I need more time."

I am trying very hard not to freak out. This thing between us, it was starting to feel solid. Now it's back to being a cloud of fog.

Anthony's car is filthy. Blankets and clothes in the back seat, a backpack and shopping bags in the front. I heave a sigh and change the subject. "Anthony should really clean out his car."

"It's not his car anymore," Elijah says. "I traded him for the motorcycle."

"So … you're the one who needs to clean out your car?" I

survey the contents through the windows. This is not just some guy's dirty vehicle. It looks like a bedroom in there. "Elijah, what is going on?"

"Tomorrow," he says, taking my face in his hands. His lip trembles just a bit and I realize he's nervous.

"You work tomorrow." I remember his usual schedule. "You work in the day and I work in the evening. We never see each other on Tuesdays."

"I don't work tomorrow, Raquel." He lets go of my face and his whole body seems to slump. "I don't work at all. I quit."

"But ... you don't have a new job yet." How will he support himself? How will he save for his future?

He shakes his head. "I'll get a new job. I've been wanting to quit that place forever and you gave me the push I needed." He meets my gaze. "This is a good thing."

The lump in my throat tells me everything. Elijah kept his job as long as he did because it came with an apartment. Quitting it would mean ...

"Are you living in this car?"

His lack of an answer is all the answer I need. "Elijah! You can't do this. You have to go back."

He shakes his head. "Raquel, that place was toxic. You said it yourself — I need to do something better. That's what I'm doing, starting now. I'll find a job soon and it'll be fine."

"No. Living on the streets is not better." I can't erase the mental image of Elijah sleeping in the back seat of this old car, freezing in some abandoned parking lot just waiting to get mugged. "You can't do this. Sasha wanted you to fix your life." *Or she wanted me to fix your life*, I suddenly think. "This is just ruining it. What about college?"

"I don't *care* about Sasha's plan!" Elijah growls. "I care about you! *You* helped me see that living in Austin was a bad idea. *You* made me realize I could do better. That's exactly what I'm doing. This is my life, and these are my choices."

Tears spring up in my eyes. "No, Elijah. You can't live in your car. It's dangerous. It doesn't help you get ahead, either. You have to go home."

He throws his head back and exhales. "I didn't want you to find out this way. I wanted to tell you at the right time. Dammit, Raquel, I thought you would want this."

I shake my head. "Not this way. Go home, Elijah."

"I don't have a home," he says, his voice like rocks clashing together. Those blue eyes pierce into mine, and there's a fire inside him that's trying to burst out. "I've never had a home."

"Go back to the apartment with Anthony," I say, as much as it hurts me to send him back there. "You can't live on the streets."

"Fine," he says. In one movement, he slips into the driver's seat of his new car. The engine starts and he doesn't look back at me. He just drives away.

Chapter Twenty-Two

I don't sleep at all that night. I split my time between wishing I'd said things differently to Elijah and checking my emails hoping to hear from him. *Yes,* I want him to quit his job, but not like that. He needs stability. And I need Sasha. If she were here, she'd leap into action and help me figure this out.

But Sasha's help won't come to me in the form of a pre-recorded video. It won't show up on my doorstep in an envelope with my name written in pink Sharpie. This is up to me.

It's the end of the school day, and I'm stuck in traffic, ready for another day of work. I definitely miss the animal clinic, but working at Izzy's feels like where I need to be right now. Flowers can die just like the animals at the clinic, but at least I don't mourn a few wilted petals.

While I'm waiting in a long line of cars trying to get out of the school parking lot, my phone alarm goes off, which is a little weird. I glance at the screen and see an alert from my calendar. Tomorrow is Mrs. Cade's birthday, and I almost forgot. When I'd saved the date in my phone a few months ago, I knew I wanted to do something special for her in case Sasha passed away before then. I was going to carry on the tradition of going to Gigi's Cupcakes. A knot settles into my stomach.

When I first got the idea to take her out for a birthday cupcake, I'd felt a rush of excitement. This tradition she'd always shared with her daughter could still be carried on through her daughter's best friend. Maybe we'd even make it our own tradition now, remembering Sasha once a year with stories and cupcakes piled high with icing. I can't stand knowing that our first year of this new tradition will be darkened by my worries over Elijah.

I try to focus on cleaning the flower shop and fulfilling orders, but of course Elijah is always on my mind. His entire life changed when he met Sasha, but he's homeless because of me.

After sweeping, I get the mop out and scrub the floor. Izzy gives me a curious glance as I slide the mop past her feet, but she doesn't say anything. I dust and wipe and organize the flower accessories on the back shelves. I peel off the old *Credit Cards Accepted* sign that was crooked and curling and print out a new one, then tape it neatly to the counter.

When it's closing time, I help Izzy lock up. Then I'm sitting in my car in a dark parking lot, staring at a new message from Elijah on my phone.

Elijah0Delgado: Still mad at me?

RockiBoBocki: Still homeless?

Elijah0Delgado: Yes.

RockiBoBocki: Then yes.

*　*　*

Mrs. S. smells like cigarettes and coffee as she slips through the rows of students, dropping a graded chem test on each desk. I wonder where she gets time to smoke when there's only five minutes between classes. The coffee isn't a mystery; she keeps a coffee machine at the back of her classroom and never lets us have any.

She used a black Sharpie to grade our tests, and my paper still smells faintly like permanent marker. The Sharpie makes me think of Sasha. The grade — a seventy-two — is all thanks to her brother.

How the hell am I supposed to know what happens when a fluorine atom becomes a fluoride ion in a chemical reaction when I can't stop thinking about a boy?

In my next class, I'm attempting to focus on Mr. Green's lecture about the civil war when my phone vibrates in my back pocket. We're not allowed to have phones in school, but people can usually get away with a sly text or two without the teacher caring. The thing is, no one really texts me anymore. Zack has forgotten I exist, and few other people even have my number. When the vibrating doesn't stop, I realize it's a phone call. Maybe it's a wrong number.

I slip the phone out of my back pocket and bring it into my lap, keeping my eyes focused on Mr. Green to make sure he doesn't see. Mrs. Cade's name flashes across the screen. Dread slams into me, making it hard to breathe. The only time she ever called me at school was when Sasha was having a cancer emergency.

Why would she call me now?

I panic until it stops ringing, then a few seconds later, a new voice message notification pops up. I can't stand waiting any longer, so I jump up and ask to use the bathroom.

Mr. Green gives me a sideways look, like he wants to say no, but I still get a little dead-best-friend sympathy, so he lets me go.

"Hurry up," he says before turning back to the whiteboard.

Out in the hallway, I jog toward the nearest bathroom. Getting caught on the security camera with your phone is a fifty-dollar fine that I don't want to pay. Once I'm safely locked inside a stall, I play Mrs. Cade's message.

"Honey, call me back! Hurry!"

A million terrible things flash through my mind, and they only get worse as I realize that she's my parents' emergency contact. Did something happen to them? *Oh God.*

I call her back and lean against the wall on shaky knees while the phone begins to ring.

"Raquel!"

"What's wrong?"

"Oh, Raquel, I can't believe it."

It sounds like she's … laughing? "Mrs. Cade!" I say, my fingers going numb from panic. "Is everything okay?"

"I got a card in the mail."

Goose bumps rise on the back of my arms. I gulp some air, now that I feel safe enough to breathe again. "A card?" I ask, but I'm pretty sure I know what she's going to say next.

"It's a card from Sasha! A birthday card for me that she wrote before she passed." There are sobbing sounds from the phone and I blink quickly, looking toward the ceiling to hold back my own tears. "She wrote me a birthday note and it's the sweetest thing, Raquel."

"That's amazing," I say, choking up.

"I don't know how she pulled it off. She must have had some service mail it at a later date for her, but it arrived today and I can't stop smiling and crying at the same time," she says, laughing. "Isn't that something?"

"That sounds just like something Sasha would do." I leave the bathroom stall and walk up to the sinks, checking my makeup in the mirror.

"It does, doesn't it? My daughter was such a brilliant, caring soul. I was dreading my birthday, but this just made it all better."

"Happy Birthday, Mrs. Cade."

"Oh my goodness, sweetheart," Mrs. Cade says. "I just realized what time it is. You're still in school!"

"For two more hours," I say, fluffing my hair in the mirror. "But I can't wait to get out. I was thinking I could take you out for a cupcake at Gigi's if you'd like."

There's a slight pause on the end, and I think I hear another muffled sob. "I would love that, Raquel. Thank you. I'm sorry to bother you in class. I just couldn't help myself after I got her card. I'll bring it to Gigi's so you can read it."

When the call is over, I stay in the bathroom a little longer, thinking about Sasha and all of her secrets. Though she's set up this elaborate last wish for Elijah and me, she never told me about the plans she had for her mother's birthday. I bet she'll do the same for her dad's birthday, and maybe even mine.

Part of the magic is the waiting, I realize. As long as there's something new to look forward to, it's not like Sasha is really gone. Not yet, anyway.

At Gigi's Cupcakes, Mrs. Cade is an explosion of happiness. I'm not sure she was ever this alive, even before Sasha's cancer diagnosis. We splurge and order two cupcakes each: the traditional Birthday Cake creation, which is vanilla and sprinkles and heaven all baked into perfection, and another one called the Chocolate Surprise.

Gigi keeps our coffee mugs filled, and she bursts into tears when Mrs. Cade shows her the birthday card. I picture Sasha huddled over her desk, writing the note weeks before she died.

> *Happy Birthday, Mom!*
> *I hope this day finds you well and happy and moving on. I know you can probably only think of losing me today, but please know that I'm never truly gone. Please don't ever feel guilty for enjoying a beautiful day, for smiling and laughing, for moving on and enjoying life. I want you to live.*
> *Take risks, go on adventures and smile.*
> *I love you, Mom. Hope this birthday is the best.*
> *Love,*
> *Sasha*

Mr. Cade takes off work early to join us, and he orders another round of cupcakes for everyone. Even though I might get the stomachache of a lifetime, I chow down on my third cupcake and bask in the joy of being with these two people who share so many of my memories. For the first time since I met Elijah in the cemetery, I feel free. I can talk to Sasha's parents about this message after death. We can't talk about *everything*, but this is good enough for now.

Mrs. Cade slides the birthday card back into her purse and

then flashes me a wry smile. "A little bird told me you have a new gentleman in your life."

"Huh?" I swallow. "I mean ... what?"

"Sue," Mr. Cade says. "Don't embarrass her."

"I'm not." She puts a hand to her chest. "I'm just curious. I still want to be in the loop, Raquel. Your mom told me you had a Halloween date. So, who is he?"

"Just a friend."

She leans forward. "Is he cute?"

If my cheeks weren't on fire a minute ago, they are now. Mr. Cade clears his throat. "I think I'll head back to the office and leave the boy talk to you girls." He gives me a quick hug and whispers, "Plead the Fifth if you want to."

Mrs. Cade slaps his arm playfully and I wiggle in my chair as we watch him leave. *Please change the damn subject,* my brain screams at me. But I've got nothing. "He's cute," I say, staring at my empty cupcake wrappers. "But we kind of had an argument. I'm not sure where we stand now."

"I'm happy that you're going out," she says, her hand soft on my arm. "I want you to live your life and be happy."

"Thanks." I try to smile. "I am."

"Good." Mrs. Cade gathers our trash into a neat pile in the center of the table. "This new boy ... would Sasha approve of him?"

I swallow. Maybe this is why Sasha never sent the MAYBE_DELETE video. This thing with Elijah and me — it's too new, too raw. Too steeped in history and blood and loss. I can't keep him in my life and live this lie forever.

I also can't tell Sasha's parents about the brother they never knew she had. "Yeah," I say after a moment. "I think Sasha would love him."

Chapter Twenty-Three

Our sparkly black roses have been exchanged for a cornucopia of Thanksgiving floral arrangements. Literally. I nearly strain my back moving a box of cornucopia horns from the storage room up to the front, where Izzy has me sorting them out by size. There's something hearty and contented about our fall selection. Maroon and orange flowers with yellow sunflowers fill our stockroom, kicking aside the traditional red roses, if only for one month of the year.

If you ask me, red roses are kind of snobby since they're so popular. The more you see them, the more you prefer an exotic arrangement of multicolored petals. Izzy shows me how to make one of the cornucopia arrangements with sunflowers, a sprinkling of orange and auburn roses, and some plastic squash and apples thrown in.

We also have really cute plastic pumpkins filled with flowers. Though my love for our creepy Halloween vases ran deep, Thanksgiving might be my favorite season in the floral world.

It's only the third of November, and already we're filling up order forms with our most popular fall harvest arrangement.

Izzy insists on giving me a bottle of essential oil that smells like orange, ginger and cinnamon, swearing it will give me happiness that will endure the season.

Unless she can bottle up Elijah, she's wasting her time. *He* is what made me happy, back before the fight. I rub the oil on my wrists anyway, because a girl can always use extra happiness (and bonus points with her boss).

"Raquel!" Izzy singsongs from the front of the shop. "You have a visitor, my dear!"

Frowning, I set down the box of plastic pumpkins and check my phone. No new messages. It's probably Mom, coming to buy more flower arrangements we don't need. Now that I work here, she's developed a habit of stopping by.

Izzy makes moony eyes at me when I walk into the front of the shop. Crinkling my brow, I look past her to see what's got her all swoony.

Elijah.

His windblown hair is swept over to the side. He's holding a bag from the burger shop down the strip, his motorcycle helmet tucked under one arm.

That helmet can only mean one thing, right?

"Hey," he says, one dimple forming. "You hungry?"

My mouth opens, but I am too startled to speak. I'm still wearing the leggings and oversized PCHS shirt I wore to school and my makeup is twelve hours old. Not exactly how I want him to see me.

"Of course she's hungry," Izzy says, shooing me with her hand. "Take as long as you need, kiddo."

"Are you sure?" I glance at our table full of order sheets.

She pulls a scrunchie off her wrist and wrangles back her

mess of hair. "I've worked alone way longer than I've worked with you. I'll be fine."

We walk down the historic shopping strip a little way until it ends in a small park that overlooks the lake. "You got your bike back," I say, taking one of the sodas he offers me.

"Yep."

The next part is tricky. "So … why are you here? Are you back to work, too?"

We sit on a bench and he hands me a cheeseburger and fries. He has this playful grin on his face, like he's as weak as I am when I am around him. It's pathetic, but despite everything, I think we could just sit in a room together, staring and smiling, and be happy.

"I got the day off unexpectedly." He shoves two fries into his mouth at once. "The, uh …" he says, scratching his forehead. "The cops were there. I guess they raided the place? I don't know, but when I showed up, Monty's wife told me to leave."

"That seems like a big deal. Why aren't you freaking out?"

He looks up from his burger. "It's probably not a big deal. This kind of thing happens a lot. They never get caught. They're good at what they do."

I nod, staring at my food. Even if it's *not a big deal,* it's still a big deal. The police don't just raid a place for no reason. Sasha would want him out of this job even more than I do.

His fingers slide across my shoulders. "Why the long face, beautiful?"

I love his honeyed voice, the way he talks, the way he'll slip in a compliment like it's nothing.

"I'm worried about you," I say. "I'm glad you're not homeless anymore, but we still need to find you a job and a place to live.

I've been racking my brain trying to think of something."

"That's why I'm here." Elijah gazes out at the lake. "There's this older guy named Mr. Reinhart."

It seems like he's going to continue, but he doesn't. He just grabs another fry and chews it slowly. I poke him in the arm with the pointy end of my fry. "What about him?"

"He lost his son in a drunk-driving accident. I guess it changed his life or something, because he started volunteering at the group home when I was about ten." Elijah's features usually darken when he talks about the group home, that muscle in his jaw always taut during his flashbacks. Now, his forehead relaxes and his lips curve upward slightly. He looks over at me. "I liked him a lot. He took us out to baseball games, me and Anthony and some of the other guys. Even bought us a Christmas present a few years in a row, before I got moved to a different home."

"The world needs more people like that," I say. The tragedy here is that not only did someone as wonderful as Elijah end up completely alone, but there are kids in group homes right this second, probably experiencing the same neglect.

Elijah nods, his eyes crinkling when he looks at me. He reaches out and runs his thumb across my cheek. "One time, he gave me his home phone number and told me to call him if I ever had an emergency and needed help. I lost it a long time ago, but I've been thinking about trying to find him. Maybe ask for a place to crash for a while until I can get my life together."

I shift on the bench until our knees touch. "Elijah! That would be awesome. You need to find him." I set down my food and pull out my phone. "What's his first name?"

"Joseph. Last name Reinhart, and I'm pretty sure the area code of his number was 512."

I'm no private investigator, but I get to work. There are four Reinharts in Austin, Texas, and my heart leaps at the first result. I turn the phone to Elijah. "Is this him?"

He pulls his brows together as he stares at the screen. "How did you do this?"

"Facebook," I say with a shrug. I click on Joseph Reinhart's profile, and it's set to private, but there are a few public photos of an older man and his wife.

Elijah looks up at me. "That's him."

"I'm emailing you the link to his page. Make your own profile and then you can send him a message. Do you want me to do it with you?"

Hesitation colors his gorgeous face and he shakes his head, reaching for another fry. "I'll do it later."

"Okay." I kiss his cheek. "I'm excited for you."

"Thank you."

The days are getting shorter now. Sasha always loved the winter months. In her opinion, nothing was better than curling up next to the fireplace and reading a romance or watching one on TV. It's only five o'clock when we finish eating, but the sun buries itself beneath the tree line, leaving the park covered in shadows.

"I should head back," I say. "We have a ton of orders to fill."

"No worries." Elijah rises from the bench and stretches his arms up over his head. We throw away our trash and then start on the short walk back toward the flower shop. Elijah laces his fingers into mine as we walk, stepping around tourists who are lined up outside of an old-fashioned ice cream parlor for a slice of their famous cherry pie. His hand fits into mine like it was molded specifically for me to hold. I lean against his shoulder as we walk, positively high on the fluttery feeling he gives me, and the hope that this man Elijah knew as a kid will show him kindness now that he's an adult.

"You haven't left yet and I already miss you."

He chuckles. "I *would* say I could stay until you get off work, but I'm not sure your parents would be cool with that."

"On a school night?" I say with a snort. "Definitely not. Although they've been asking about you a lot."

"Oh yeah? Good or bad asking?"

I lift an eyebrow and let him get all nervous about it for a second. "Good asking," I finally say. "I'm sorry for all of that … stuff … the last few days. I just want you to stay safe."

"I know." He stops in the middle of the sidewalk, his hands grabbing my waist and lifting me until my feet are floating and I'm at his eye level. Giggling, I wrap my arms around his neck and pull him closer for a kiss. When I'm in his arms, it's so easy to forget all of the unknowns we still face. "You're making it really hard to go back to work," I whisper, peering down at him.

He sets me back on the sidewalk, his bottom lip rolling under his teeth. "You have no idea." His voice is a low growl that sends a shiver into my toes.

"Maybe you two should get a room."

All of my muscles tighten at the sound of a familiar voice. Zack stands just a few feet away, his fingers woven with the slender fingers of Savannah Weststar, varsity softball player. She smiles uncomfortably at me. We've never really been friends, but she was a part of the Dying Sasha Fan Club for a short while.

My heart crawls up in my chest, but then Zack winks as they walk by us.

"Who was that?" Elijah asks.

"Just someone from my past." I'm actually smiling, believe it or not. "But right now, all I care about is my future."

* * *

When I get home from work, there's a thick manila envelope on my bed. It claims to be from the PCHS Scholarship Fund, not that one exists. Whatever this next adventure is, I'll get to share it with Elijah as we move forward together, finding our place in this world that took away someone special, but also brought us this gift.

I rip open the letter, going through the contents one by one. An envelope of cash, a letter addressed to *The Parents of Raquel Clearwater*, a plastic hotel key, printed-out reservations and a gas station gift card.

Happy tears flood my eyes as I grip Sasha's handwritten letter in my hand. Of course she knew exactly what we'd need.

> *Yep, I'm sending you guys on vacation! Trust me,*
> *you'll have a blast.*
> *Love you and miss you always,*
> *Sasha*

Chapter Twenty-Four

I can't believe Mom fell for it. Following Sasha's instructions, I dropped the fake letter in a mailbox near Izzy's, and the next day, it arrived in our mailbox. Printed on card stock, it congratulated the parents of Raquel Clearwater for their daughter's award, an "Excellence in Education Weekend Getaway" at the Black Bear Lodge in Dallas, Texas, along with ten other high school seniors. My parents then spent an entire dinner telling me how proud they were of me for keeping up my grades, even during the aftermath of losing my best friend.

One week later, I'm tossing my suitcase into the trunk of my car.

"Always keep a full tank of gas," Mom says. She's in her pajamas because it's six in the morning, her feet shifting on the cold concrete. "Fill it up again when you're at half a tank. And keep your phone charged. You never know when there will be an emergency."

It's over two hundred miles to Dallas, and I've never driven even half that far away, so she's sort of freaking out. "You don't have to worry, Mom. I'll be extra safe. I'll walk around with blinking lights and a reflector vest if you want."

She rolls her eyes and then pulls me into a hug. "I'm your mother, Raquel. It's my job to worry."

I start up my car and blast the heater since it takes a while to get warm. Mom puts a hand on top of my open car door and rattles off a few more safety warnings. Don't leave the resort after dark, never drink anything from a stranger, don't carry all your cash on you at once.

"I sure hope you kids have fun. Black Bear Lodge is kind of … juvenile. You and Sasha got bored of it when you were about fourteen."

"Fifteen," I say, recalling two summers ago when we told her parents we'd like to go to the Guadalupe River for spring break instead of the lodge. It was the first year since we were eight that we didn't go to the resort famous for having the country's biggest indoor water park. Mom's right about it being kind of … young. I can't imagine the high school actually choosing Black Bear Lodge for a high school student event. Of course, they didn't.

I wait until I'm out of our neighborhood and on the main road before I set the GPS to the address I'd programmed last night.

Mr. Reinhart took in Elijah the day he messaged him on Facebook. Elijah formally quit working at Monterrey's Auto Body Shop for the second time, and then he moved into the Reinharts' spare bedroom. I had hoped something good would come from Elijah reconnecting with the man who had shown kindness to him all those years ago, but this is better than I imagined. I even sleep easier at night knowing Elijah is no longer sleeping on some shady guy's couch. Things are only going to get better from now on. I can feel it.

The Reinharts live in a little ranch-style house in the suburbs just outside the Austin city limits. As soon as my tires roll to a stop, I notice movement in the open garage. I park and wave at Elijah. He's standing next to his motorcycle, which is parked next to an old Crown Vic. A tall man with a full head of solid white hair is beside him, and they both turn to look at me.

There's an awkward second where I wonder if I should get out and introduce myself, but then Elijah shakes the guy's hand and jogs across the lawn, climbing into my car. The scent of his cinnamon gum is everywhere.

"Hey." He grins, tossing an overstuffed backpack into the back seat of my car. With a jerk of his head, his unruly black locks shake away from his eyes, which lock on mine. "Want to stop for coffee?"

He smells like heaven rolled up in that distinct scent of boy, and that glimmer in his gaze knocks all the breath out of my lungs.

"Yeah," I say, clearing my throat. I put the car into drive and focus on the road in front of me. "Coffee."

I can feel his eyes on me while I drive, but we're silent for a long time. This is the start of something new. Elijah and me, together and figuring out our life. This is big, this is powerful, and I know we both feel it.

"So, that was Mr. Reinhart's house." Elijah drums his fingers on the inside of the passenger door. "Turns out he's even nicer than I remembered. He says I can stay as long as I need to."

"Wow, that's great."

"Sorry my emails have been sporadic. Anthony is pissed at me for ditching him. I had to get as much of my stuff as I could from the apartment with only my motorcycle, so it took me a few trips with a backpack. Then, Mr. Reinhart and his wife are like the sweetest people on earth. They feed me and clothe me and want to talk about things. I didn't want to be rude and ask for the Wi-Fi password in the middle of that."

I reach over the console and grab his hand. "It's fine. You're here now."

After an hour of driving in mostly silence, I pull to a stop at a red light. I can feel him watching me from the passenger seat, so I glance over. He grins, and those eyes make my toes tingle.

"I really want to kiss you," I say.

"Can't." He shakes his head. "That's not what Sasha wants."

Panic colors my vision. "What?" I thought we'd moved past this.

Elijah grins. "We're technically on the next adventure, and she wants us to be kids, right?"

I let out my breath in a relieved laugh. "Right."

That *is* exactly what her email said.

> Black Bear Lodge is a kid's ultimate vacation. There's game rooms, the water park, an arcade, inflatable bounce houses and so much candy you want to eat until you throw up and then eat more. Black Bear Lodge was the essence of my childhood. We went twice a year, every year, and I always got to take my best friend with me. So although it's kind of a haven for children, and you guys are almost adults, just be kids for the weekend, okay? I want Elijah to experience what it would have been like to be a kid in the Cade household. Also, there's something I need you

guys to do when you're there, and being a kid will make all the difference.

The light turns green and I take one last look at him before turning my attention back to the road. "I agree. Let's be kids."

* * *

"Whoa." Elijah is all but pressed against the glass, drooling like a five-year-old.

"Yeah, it's pretty impressive," I say, turning into the parking lot of Black Bear Lodge. Set on top of a hill, the mighty resort has fourteen floors of hotel rooms to one side and a massive water park to the other. In the center, two fifty-feet-tall concrete bears sit guarding the entrance on their steel-reinforced haunches. As a kid, it felt like you were arriving in a magical world when you walked between the bears. Something tells me that as an almost adult, it'll feel just as surreal.

"Cute," Elijah says, eyeing my suitcase as I heft it out of my trunk. It's hot pink with emojis all over it. My only excuse for buying something so delightfully tacky is that it was on sale.

"Shut up," I mutter.

Keeping a nice distance of at least three feet between us, I breathe slowly and concentrate on telling myself not to think about how cute he is, how great he smells, how I sort of love that innocent excitement in his eyes. This trip is not about how badly I want to make out with Elijah. It's about pretending to be a kid for Sasha.

"Have you ever been to a place like this?" I ask, figuring it's a perfectly acceptable platonic thing to say.

He stops right in the middle of the enormous entrance that looks more like it was built for giants and looks at me. "What do you think?"

The lodge feels cozier in November than in the summer. Fewer kids running all over the place, and more older couples who look like they came to get away from the headache of planning Thanksgiving dinner.

Elijah's head wobbles all over the place as he tries to take in the sight. The ceiling is at least five stories high, and a forest canopy of fake trees almost covers the top. Winding stairways go up the tree trunks with little hideout spots to find along the way. Fairies zoom across the room on nearly invisible wires, and life-sized animatronic bears hide in between the fake trees. A waterfall pours straight from the ceiling, emptying into a concrete pond filled with fish you can feed from paper cups of fish food. I have to tug on Elijah's shirt to get him to follow me to the reception desk.

"Your pretend-to-be-a-kid act is convincing," I say, pulling him in between the velvet ropes that form a winding line to the check-in desk.

"Totally not an act," he says, peering down at me. There's a waterfall behind us and a big fake toucan hanging from a branch just above our heads. That single dimple in his cheek appears again. "I'm really psyched for this."

Butterflies hop around in my stomach when I bring my printed reservation up to the front desk. What if we're turned around, identified as frauds? A woman with Susan on her name tag gives me a warm smile and scans the barcode on my paper. The computer chimes, so that must be a good sign.

"You're all set," she says, sliding over two silver wristbands that are made to withstand the water park during your entire vacation. Relief floods through me and I reach for them. "Oh, wait," Susan says, frowning. "There's something else here in the reservation notes. Just a moment."

Elijah slides the wristbands off the counter and slips one onto my wrist, then wraps the other one around his. "Why so freaked out?" he asks quietly, nudging me with his shoulder.

I lift my shoulders, eyes wide. "There's some kind of problem," I say, trying to decipher what Susan is saying to another woman when she points back at us. "What if this doesn't work? Where will we go?"

"Relax, chicka. This is Sasha, remember?" I look up at him and he winks. "She won't let us down."

Susan slips into a back room and then returns a few seconds later, a white envelope in her hand. "This was sent here for you, Miss Clearwater. Now you're all set. Please enjoy your stay at Black Bear Lodge!"

I reach for the envelope, my name in pink Sharpie scrawled across the front. I don't have to look at Elijah to know he's no doubt wearing a smirk the size of the parking lot. In the elevator, I go to rip it open, but stop when I see Sasha's note written across the seal.

Do not open until you check out on Sunday!

Elijah leans over, reading the instructions. "Interesting."

Just as I'd suspected, Sasha reserved the Wolf Pack room for our stay. The coolest and most expensive room option available, it has two queen beds and a "Wolf Den," which is a cave built into the wall, with bunk beds made of treated logs inside. There's a little platform you get to by ladder, and your own private TV mounted on the wall. It is a kids' paradise, and Elijah's jaw falls to the ground when he sees it.

I move into the main part of the room, dropping my suitcase at the foot of the queen bed nearest to the window. We're ten floors high and have a beautiful view of the Dallas skyline. We're also spending this entire weekend together. I swallow.

Elijah's voice echoes from inside the man-made cave. "If you think I'm not sleeping on this kid-sized bunk bed, you're wrong."

Laughing, I go to the window and draw the drapes shut, darkening the room.

"Just wait until you see this," I say, slipping into the cave with him. The light at the top of the cave is shaped like a moon — although why a moon would be inside a cave, I don't know. I wiggle my eyebrows, my grin so big my cheeks hurt. "You ready for this?" I ask, hovering my fingers over the light switch, which is shaped like an inchworm.

Elijah nods, and I flip the lights.

The Wolf Den has a sound system rigged to the light. When it turns off, the sounds of a forest fill the space. The buzzing of bugs, a sweet song of a bird and the occasional wolf howling at the moon. Tiny dots in the walls light up like fireflies, disappearing the second you look at them.

Elijah exhales.

"It lasts for about an hour," I say, turning the lights back on. "The perfect amount of time to fall asleep."

"This was Sasha's childhood," he says, more like he's talking to himself.

I nod. "I was lucky enough to come along. My parents could never afford something like this."

Elijah shrugs off his backpack and tosses it on the top bunk. "So what was on the table?"

"Huh?" Ducking out of the cave, I notice a package on the table, a little white card with our names on it taped to the top.

Ripping it open, I find a letter from Sasha and —

"A wand?" Elijah says, reaching into the box and pulling out a plastic wand painted in so much glitter nail polish you can barely see the brown of the original design.

"Not just any wand," I say, unable to hold back my smile in the wake of all this nostalgia. "That is *the* wand."

"Explain," he says, aiming the wand at me like simply saying the word will compel me to answer. But that's not how the magic works.

"I think Sasha probably will," I say, opening the letter. Pulling in a deep breath, I read.

"'Elijah, this would have been your childhood had we grown up together. This place is literally the place of dreams, screw what Disney says. Rocki's favorite part was the water park and the arcade room, but Wizard's Quest was mine. I want you to have fun this weekend, so I'm only leaving you one rule: play one last game of Wizard's Quest for me, okay? I have bestowed my wand upon the two of you. It has fresh batteries and, of course, it's still registered to my name so that my digital legacy will continue. Make me proud. I love you and miss you both ... Sasha.'"

"Is this some kind of game?" Elijah asks, turning the plastic wand over in his hands.

"You have no idea," I say. Reaching for the wand, I twist the handle to the right, making the tip of it light up purple as it starts a new game. The wand vibrates and a tinny voice sounds from a small speaker in the bottom.

"Do you have what it takes to complete a Wizard's Quest, young warlock?"

There's a spark of adventure in Elijah's eyes, the same exact look I've seen so many times while in the presence of this wand.

"Come on," I say, tapping his chest with the purple light. "Let's go."

Chapter Twenty-Five

Wizard's Quest was ahead of its time back when Sasha and I were kids. State-of-the-art technology plus the genius of a bunch of MIT students who never quite grew out of role-playing games came together to create an interactive masterpiece. The game was installed in Black Bear Lodge nearly ten years ago, and I still remember the first year it appeared. I was wearing my *iCarly* one-piece bathing suit, towel around my shoulders, goggles hanging off my wrist, the scent of chlorine beckoning me from the water park. Sasha had grown too tall for her bathing suit; a problem we didn't realize until it was time to go swimming. So Mrs. Cade took us down to the gift shop on the first floor to buy a new suit while Mr. Cade stayed in our hotel room, ordering room service breakfast and getting some work done remotely.

It was there, just outside the plastic foliage of the Black Bear gift shop, that Sasha saw a standing sign that was as tall as we were. Wizard's Quest, a magical journey throughout the entire lodge. Set up in stairwells, hidden chambers accessible only through fairy doors, with evil witches disguised as waitresses in the lodge's restaurant and the like, Wizard's Quest had lights, sounds and flat-screen scoreboards all over the facility. All you needed were your wand (available for $14.99 in the gift shop), your wits and your imagination. On that particular vacation, we only spent one of our four days in the water park. The rest were dedicated to solving our quest.

"Sasha was the greatest warlock of our time," I tell Elijah as we head to the Bear Cub Clubhouse. It's not really a clubhouse, but more of a long hallway filled with shops and kiosks with fun kiddie stuff to do. There's a build-your-own-bear-cub booth, face painting, jewelry making, hair beads and wraps, an ice cream shop and, of course, the candy booth. At the far end of the hallway of childhood wonder, Sasha's one true talent awaits.

Wizard's Quest.

"It's like we've walked right into a Tim Burton film," Elijah says, eyes wide with awe as we step into the Wizard's chambers. To adults, it's just a highly decorated gift shop with overpriced trinkets and bored teenage employees wearing cheap wizard robes, but we feel like it's real magic.

"Y'all here to start a new quest?" the bored teenage employee says, looking up from her phone only because she wants to avoid being fired. Her Texas twang is as thick as the bouffant of blond hair she wears pinned back with a miniature-witch-hat headband.

"Yes, please," I say, glancing over at Elijah, who is too taken with our surroundings to pay much attention. He's staring at a group of ancient runes carved into the fake cave wall beside us. I know from experience that if you point your wand at them, they'll light up and add bonus points to your warlock's overall score.

"Wands are fifteen dollars," the girl says, gesturing to a caldron of various battery-powered wands to choose from. "Unless you're a Bear Cub member, and then it's five dollars off."

"Actually, I have my own," I say, taking the wand from Elijah's hand and setting it on the counter. "We just need a new quest."

The girl eyes Sasha's glittery wand, quirking an eyebrow. "Purple," she says, leaning forward over the counter. "Nice. We don't see many of those anymore."

A few years after we'd started Wizard's Quest, the wands were upgraded to have green LED lights at the tips. Mrs. Cade bought me three new wands over the years, but Sasha insisted on keeping her original one. Said it brought her good luck.

The girl takes the wand and drops it into a computer-port thingy that has a sticker wrapped around it, making it look like a magical object instead of a piece of modern-day technology.

Behind her, a large flat-screen displays the scoreboard, showing all forty-three players currently logged in. They all have little green dots by their names, and a user named 1D4ever is currently winning with sixty-three thousand points.

As we watch, a new name appears on the scoreboard: PrincessSasha.

"Damn," the girl says, her eyes widening like she's truly impressed. "One of the top five. Never thought I'd meet one of y'all."

She hands me the wand, now that the fake-magic machine has loaded it with a new quest. She seems to regard me with a new respect now that she knows this wand's history. "I know a kid who will totally want to meet you."

"Why's that?" I ask, turning the wand over in my hand.

She presses something on her computer screen and the scoreboard behind her switches to one with only five names.

THE WIZARD'S QUEST HALL OF FAME
1. MaxTheImpaler
2. PrincessSasha
3. JAXLUVSBAY
4. TexasCheerSquad
5. Bobby41

"Whoa," Elijah says. "She's only forty thousand points away from getting first place."

"Yep," the girl says. "You and MaxTheImpaler both stopped playing a few years ago, and those top two scores halted. People fight for the bottom three, but no one is even close to having your top score."

The way she gushes, it's like she's standing in front of two real-life celebrities. Her eyes sparkle as she switches the scoreboard back to display every player that's currently logged in. There, in first place, with a purple dot by her name, is Sasha's account. She has over two million total points.

The girl's rabbit's foot necklace knocks against the counter and I find myself wondering if witches are known for wearing them. I'm also wondering if I should tell her I'm not Sasha, just a proxy.

But she's been transformed from a zombie staring at her phone to a witch who's watching me with an admiration I'm not used to at all.

She reaches for a new quest book and hands it to me, along with a pen that's shaped like a crooked twig, thus adding more to the illusion that this isn't a game, but a real quest. "If you hurry, you can probably get the points to be in first place."

"I wonder if she knew," Elijah says as we venture across the hall to where the quest begins, in a small room with a projection screen that makes it look like you're being taken by dragon to a magical land.

"If she knew what?" I say, gripping tightly to the wand as we climb up the steps and enter the Quest Chamber. A few kids are in line ahead of us, so we have to wait to begin.

"That she was so close to winning."

"She definitely knew." We're in a narrow hallway filled with fake foliage and runes. I point my wand at one and give it a little flick. The rune lights up and a tiny speaker beside it says, "You have found a secret rune. Two hundred points awarded!"

The kid in front of me stares, doe-eyed. "How'd you know how to do that?"

"My best friend taught me," I say, winking at him.

When it's our turn to stand on the mighty rock and begin our quest from the dragon, there's a moment where all of the lights go out, and all that's left is the tinny sound of a waterfall and the soft melody of an ancient Celtic tune piping in through the speakers. Elijah is standing next to me, our arms and hips touching in the cramped space, our fingers electric with the spark between us.

And even though we're in a darkened room on the first floor of a multimillion-dollar resort in Dallas, Texas, right now all I can feel is the magic of this moment, the spirit of my best friend wrapped around my heart and the love Elijah and I both have for her linking us together forever.

* * *

"Whoever … invented … stairs …" I suck in a deep breath and heave my legs up another step, finally landing on the fourteenth floor. I pitch forward, resting my hands on my knees. "Sucks."

Elijah laughs, but then it turns into an out-of-breath wheezing sound. "Come on, zap the rune so we can take a break."

On the bottom of the fourteenth-floor stairwell, hidden in the intricate tile flooring, is a small rune. I zap it with my wand and then slump to the floor near Elijah. I'm panting so hard that I don't even hear what the rune tells me. It was something congratulatory, to be sure.

It's just after ten o'clock at night, and although Wizard's Quest goes on all night long, most of the players are kids with parents who would rather head back to their rooms for a good night's sleep. So it's been just the two of us for the better part of an hour, roaming the hotel, zapping treasure chests and paintings and little fairies hidden in potted plants. My quest book is full of hastily scribbled answers to the riddles each obstacle gave us, and if we understood the tree fairy, Estelle, correctly, we have just one more task to complete until we've won our quest. The last task involved traipsing up the entire staircase, hitting runes in exactly the perfect order.

We screwed up twice.

So if I had to guess, I'd say we've been up and down two hundred flights of stairs today, and the burning in my thighs can confirm that this is more exercise than I've had all year.

I flatten my back against the cool concrete wall and look up at the ceiling, which is painted black like the night sky. Little twinkles of stars are probably LED lights hidden in the ceiling tiles. This place spares no freaking expense when it comes to ambiance.

"There's only one more task left," Elijah says, flipping through our quest book. "You want to go back to our room and finish this tomorrow?"

Completing a whole quest in one day is a difficult challenge, one even Sasha didn't much care for. She liked to spread it out over the whole vacation to enjoy it every day.

I nod and push up from the wall, rising on weary legs. "I could use a hot shower."

It isn't until we're stepping into an elevator that the magic of this day begins to fade away and reality settles in. Amazing how easily I can become a kid again, fighting evil sorcerers and gremlins, pretending Sasha is by my side.

But as soon as the elevator doors slide closed, wrapping Elijah and me in its mechanical embrace, I am once again hit with the reminder that she's gone. This time, I look at Elijah, feeling a sense of gratitude to Sasha for bringing us together. Her last wish had been meant for Elijah, but I know it's for me, too. She's given me a mission, an adventure and a reason to move on.

The way he stands with his hands in his pockets. That little dimple in his cheek when he's thinking about something. How he rocks back on his heels when he's in a good mood, and how that's probably why the bottoms of his jeans are so frayed.

The elevator descends. Elijah quirks an eyebrow, those blue eyes on me, a constant reminder that he's always paying attention, always aware and living right here in the moment with me.

"I don't want to go back to real life after this," I mutter.

His eyes lock on to mine. I'm used to seeing reflections of Sasha when he looks at me, but this time, whatever is going on in his mind isn't something she's thought before. "I don't want to lose you," he says like it's the truest thing he's ever spoken. "It might not be easy being together, but I don't want anything else."

My pulse quickens. I think of the MAYBE_DELETE video, of the warning Sasha gave us in the cemetery. I don't know why she told us to keep Elijah a secret, but I do know she wanted the best for us. But what if what's best is to slip off her path and find our own way?

Overhead, the lights blink and a twinkling fairy sound surrounds us. The elevator lurches to a stop. The screen above the elevator buttons blinks on and an animated Queen Mab herself, the ruler of the fairy world, appears.

"I am impressed with your magical skills, young warlock. Before you go, I would like to grant you the stone of serenity. It is worth ten thousand points and will only be available for thirty seconds after the doors open. Farewell, young warlock. May your magic be as strong as the mighty oak from which your wand was forged."

The screen goes dark and the music stops. The elevator doors slide open on the tenth floor, and Elijah and I share a quizzical look.

Then we run.

Sasha's wand vibrates harder the closer we get to the glass pedestal at the end of the hallway. There's a gemstone the size of a basketball perched on top, Queen Mab's icicle symbol etched into it. I fling my wand at the stone and it lights up pink.

The queen appears on the screen on the wall. With a flourish of her staff, ten thousand points are awarded to PrincessSasha's account. When the animation is over, another one appears in its place. The scoreboard. PrincessSasha has risen to first place.

Elijah lets out a whoop. Before I realize what I'm doing, I'm bouncing on my toes, flinging my arms around his neck in excitement. He lifts me into the air and spins me around, and in this moment, the whole damn world seems to stop. We are the only two people here, and nothing matters but this.

How easy it is to kiss this boy. My eyes close, my hands tangle in his hair. He grips me so tight it's hard to breathe.

I don't even care.

It won't be hard trying to forge my own path with Elijah. I think we're already on it.

* * *

Elijah really does plan on sleeping in the Wolf Den, which is funny and dorky and adorable. I sit on my bed, facing the window that overlooks the Dallas skyline, while he takes a shower. I stare at the iconic green ball of the Reunion Tower lit up in the sky, just below the crescent moon. *Why didn't you send us that video, Sasha?*

Sasha wasn't into dating. She had crushes on the guys in the romance books she read, and she couldn't resist Tom Hardy's charming smile on the big screen. In all of her years on earth, though, she never had a boyfriend.

I was the boy-crazy part of our duo, the one she always ragged on for dropping everything to spend time with some guy. She hated how I changed my personality to make Zack like me better, hated how I was one person with her and another person with him. She always told me to be true to myself.

I *can* be myself with Elijah.

On the table next to our ice bucket, that envelope from Sasha stares at me. The warning not to open till the end of the trip has mocked me from the second we got here.

"Oh *hell*," I say, throwing myself off the bed. I can still hear the water of the shower running, but I can't wait for Elijah now. With a sliver of hesitation, I slip my finger under the seal and rip it open.

It's another one of her fat-cat greeting cards. This one is a tabby wearing black-frame glasses, a cup of coffee next to it.

There's only one sentence scribbled on the inside of the card. *Please tell me you didn't fall in love.*

Chapter Twenty-Six

We spend the better part of our second and last day on vacation at the water park. It's too cold to enjoy the outdoor section, but inside, the water is heated. We float in the lazy river, sipping every nonalcoholic drink they offer, all paid for with Sasha's mad money. With Sasha's name at the top of the Wizard's Quest scoreboard, we did all the other kiddie activities, too, including eating candy until our stomachs hurt, getting matching leather bracelets with our names stamped into them, even building our own stuffed animals (dragon for Elijah, four-foot-long pink snake for me).

I keep my hands, my lips and the contents of Sasha's letter to myself.

Sunday morning comes too soon, and now we're packing up our stuff, getting ready to check out of the lodge. The side of Elijah's face still has a sprinkling of green glitter along the jawline from the glitter lizard "tattoos" we got last night. Holding up his bright red dragon, Elijah says, "I don't know what I'm supposed to do with this thing." It has plastic wings, a foam heart inside and eyes that light up when you press the foot. "Twenty years old, and this is my first stuffed animal."

"You take it home with you and sleep with it on your bed," I say, grinning, as I shove my dirty clothes into my emoji suitcase.

His eyes roll to the ceiling. "I'm a man, Raquel. I don't sleep with stuffed animals."

He chucks it at me and I catch it, hugging it close to my chest and petting its fuzzy head like its feelings are hurt and I'm trying to console it. "It's a dragon, Elijah. They're the manliest animals around."

"I thought that was the lion," he says, zipping his backpack closed. "King of the jungle."

I scoff. "Lions don't have wings and they don't breathe fire."

He shoulders the backpack. "But lions, you know, *exist*, so … I win."

I love that cocky look he gets when we're messing with each other. So much that my stomach gets this floaty feeling and I turn around, pretending to care about packing my makeup. Really I just don't want him to see this shit-eating grin on my face.

"I have an idea," I say, grabbing my perfume. Holding out the dragon, I spritz him all over and then toss him back across the room into Elijah's arms. "Now he'll smell like me. Surely he deserves a place on your bed now, despite how his kind doesn't actually exist?"

The look Elijah makes awakens some kind of mutant butterfly in my stomach. If my life were a soap opera, I'd dive across the bed and pull him down on top of me. Instead, I swallow the lump in my throat and pray that he won't reject the silly dragon this time.

He tucks it under his arm. "Can't argue with that."

After a final inspection of our room, I grab the fancy Black

Bear Lodge pens and stationery as souvenirs and then we head out.

I'm not sure if the Mount Everest–sized awkwardness in the elevator is real or just a figment of my imagination. I think we both want to make out, but we're still honoring the kid rule. But that's the thing. I don't want to live in the past, pretending to be a kid. This is my life, my future, and it's too damn exciting to pretend to be anything else.

Elijah stands still, his gaze focused on the descending numbers at the top of the doors. It isn't until we level out on the first floor that he looks over at me.

The doors slide open and we're thrown into the fake forest of the lobby. "There's something you need to see." Reaching into my purse, I take out Sasha's fat-cat greeting card. "I read it early. You should read it, too, just … not in front of me."

He quirks an eyebrow and I press the card into his hand. "I'm not sure what it means. We can talk in the car." He walks ahead of me.

In the weeks following Sasha's diagnosis, we wasted so much breath talking about what might happen, what *could* happen, what *would* happen. After a while, Sasha shook her head and held out her hands and said, "We can talk all day long. It is what it is, okay? Let's just live in the moment and enjoy what we've got."

Her words play over in my mind as I make my way back through the giant doors and between the towering concrete bears. I've spent my entire life following Sasha's path, taking up residence in her shadow and making myself comfortable there. She was brilliant and confident, everything I wasn't. I'd never questioned the path we walked together.

But now she's gone and I've got some questions.

If she were here, I don't doubt for one second that I'd find the courage to stand up for myself. It's a little trickier now that she's gone, though. Can I honor her while ignoring her instructions?

But she fought her fight, and now I'm going to fight mine.

I tug my jacket around me and walk quickly to my car. Elijah is leaning against the trunk, hands in his pockets, hair all a mess from the chilly breeze. "Does this mean she *doesn't* want us to be together?"

"I don't care what it means," I say, only stopping when my toes are pressed against his. The wind whips my hair back, probably making me look like one of those dogs with their head out a car window, but Elijah looks at me like he doesn't mind what he sees. "I want to live in the moment," I continue. My hands are in my pockets, but I wish they were wrapped in his. "I want to stop hiding and lying just to keep a promise we made to Sasha after she died. I love her more than anything, but she's gone now. We have to live for us."

His head tilts slightly and I let myself get lost in his gaze, in those oceans of deep blue. "Okay, then."

I wait for him to reach out and pull me against his muscled chest, wrapping me in the scent of his cinnamon gum, kissing me in ways that'll make the passing parents toss dirty looks our way. It doesn't happen though, and instead he holds out the card.

"What do you think is on the video?"

"What video?" I ask, just as he flips the card with his fingers, showing me the back. There's a pink URL written on the back, one of those shortened kinds that always take us to a video of Sasha.

I pop my trunk and Elijah picks up my suitcase for me. "Let's watch it when we get home?" I ask.

He closes my trunk and nods. "Then I'll take you on a real date."

* * *

Mr. Reinhart won't let me leave until we've come inside and had some of his wife's triple chocolate cake. I'm reminded of that famous painting of the farmer and his wife when I meet the Reinharts, although they both have silver hair and Mrs. Reinhart is quite a bit bigger in the midsection. She insists that I call her Jarrah, and she serves up a slice of cake that could feed a family of four.

"I can't remember the last time I won something," Mr. Reinhart says. He holds his fork with two fingers and I notice he's missing a pinky on his right hand.

"Oh?" I say.

Elijah clears his throat. "Yeah, it was pretty cool. Raquel is a lucky person."

I lift an eyebrow and he just gives me this look like he wants me to trust him, so I turn back to his temporary family and nod enthusiastically. This must be the lie he told about why we were going on vacation.

"I wish we'd win a vacation," Jarrah says, pointing her glass of milk at her husband. "We could use one."

They chuckle, sharing one of those moments that makes you know they've been a married couple for probably longer than I've been alive. I find myself wishing Sasha could meet them.

Eventually, Elijah walks me back out to my car, tablet in hand.

"Ready?"

I hold my breath while he types in the URL. It could be a video of Sasha making fun of us for liking each other. Or it could be her formal blessing in person — well, in video. I don't even know what to hope for.

Sasha appears on the screen wearing a Hello Kitty beanie with her name airbrushed across it. We'd got it at the Market Square in San Antonio several years ago. Her hollow eyes are darker than ever. This was recorded after the other videos we've seen. The girl on the screen is dying.

Her jaundiced face leans toward the camera. "Hey guys," she says. "I don't know how to tell you this, and honestly, it kind of screws up a couple videos I've already recorded, so now I have to redo them." She holds up a notebook and then drops it into her lap. "I'm trying to figure out how to rearrange some letters now. My whole plan just got a wrench thrown in it."

Elijah and I exchange a glance.

"I'll just spit it out, okay? You can't tell my parents that Elijah exists. Like not just *now*, but ever. I don't think they would be happy about it, and not just because I went against their wishes and looked for my birth parents." Sasha runs a hand over her face, her sullen features seeming to turn darker the longer the video plays. "I just learned something new. So … so here's the thing."

She swallows and looks at her hands, which are somewhere in her lap where we can't see them. "I'd been wondering if I should tell my parents that I found Elijah, but I didn't know how to bring it up, so I tried to be all casual and stuff at dinner last night. I mentioned to my parents that I think blood cancer can be hereditary. Then I wondered out loud if any of my birth family had it as well." On screen, she rolls her eyes. "As you can imagine, my parents just kinda shuffled along and tried to talk about something else, but I didn't let it go. I said I wondered if I had any siblings or cousins or something who should be warned to get themselves tested for cancer. I mean, *right*? It was a legitimate concern. Well, they scoffed and said that it'd be impossible to warn everyone I was related to in the world and that I should just get over it."

Whatever Sasha has to say next, she takes a long time saying it. Her eyes flit downward, her hands twisting together. A cool breeze sends a shiver up my spine and Elijah wraps his arm around my shoulders. Sasha draws in a deep breath. "When I went upstairs after dinner, I overheard them talking. Mom said it might be a good idea to let the adoption people know about my cancer just in case — and I'm quoting verbatim here — 'the boy needs to be warned.' And then Dad said something about how he's probably screwed up enough as it is, and that she should let it go."

She shakes her head slowly. "The boy. So yeah. They know. They know about you, Elijah. And they never told me, and they're not gonna tell you about my cancer. They don't even care what could happen to you."

Her eyes flood with tears and she peers into her webcam, struggling to keep her composure. "I'm sorry, Elijah. I don't know why my parents didn't want you then. I wish they did. I wish we could have been a family. And I don't know why they won't help you now. They're good people, okay? They really are."

She wipes away tears with the back of her hand. "I don't understand why they did what they did, but if they didn't want you back then, they don't get to know you now." She shakes her head. "I'm such an idiot. I actually thought the two of you would make a really cute couple, you know?" She holds up her hands. "You're perfect for each other! But now there's no way you can be together without them finding out and making everything awkward."

Sasha stares at the camera for a long time. "My parents thought you'd be screwed up? Why, just because you were in a group home? I've never been so embarrassed by my family before. I'm sorry, guys. This sucks and it hurts and it's stupid." She looks me right in the eyes. "I have to record another video now. Sorry this one sucked. I love you both. Bye."

Elijah lowers his tablet.

"I'm so sorry." My words are meaningless, of course. Nothing can make up for what we just heard. I grab his arm, try to look at him, but he's focused on the sky beyond the horizon.

"You have nothing to apologize for, Raquel." His lips quiver into a shaky smile. "I guess I just … don't understand. They seem like such great people. That's all I keep hearing — how nice they are."

On instinct, I want to say yes. They are good people. I feel the words rising to my tongue. But then I picture the Cades talking in hushed tones behind their daughter's back, deciding not to contact the orphan boy they know exists, and my reality turns on its side.

"Well, now we know," I say instead. "This is why Sasha doesn't want us to be together."

His hand grabs my waist, his lips pressing a soft kiss to my temple. "I'm not sure that's a good enough reason," he murmurs.

My insides shatter, too many emotions all competing for

space in my withered heart. I lean against his shoulder until he gives me a quick hug and steps back.

"You should get home." His chest fills up slowly and then deflates. "I think I'm going to go for a drive. Clear my mind."

Chapter Twenty-Seven

On Wednesday morning, my phone rings two hours before my alarm is supposed to go off. The number is unknown, but I know who it is — the only person who would call me at this ridiculous hour.

"Elijah?"

"Hey."

The chatter of people talking and phones ringing filters in through the line. It sounds like he's in some kind of office. Or worse — a hospital. I sit up in bed.

"What's going on?"

"I'm in jail."

I sigh, palming my forehead. The hospital might have been a better answer. "What happened? What the hell did you do?"

"Nothing. Well — speeding, but, basically nothing." Exhaling, I cover my eyes with my hand. *Sasha trusted you, Elijah.* "Since when do they take you to jail for speeding?"

"They don't. They take you to jail for a warrant."

I don't know what to say. I *really* don't know what to think. The silence stretches on so long that Elijah starts talking again.

"It's nothing, I am a good person. I swear to you. Last week they raided my old apartment, and Anthony and my other roommates all got busted for cocaine and pot distribution. They had a shit-ton of it in the apartment, and since I was living there, too, up until last week, I got lumped in as an accomplice and charged with Intent to Distribute."

"But you don't live there anymore!" The panic is so consuming I'm only vaguely aware that I shouldn't be yelling this early in the morning. The last thing I need is for my mom to come barging in here, wondering what's wrong. "They can't do that," I grind out in a lower voice.

"They can and they did." He sighs, long and heavy. "My driver's license has that address, not Mr. Reinhart's, and half my stuff is still there since I couldn't fit it on my bike. I'm in Travis County jail. My bail is five grand, and I have no money for that. There's a court date coming up and maybe I can prove my innocence, I don't know." He's normally so laid-back, which is why the tension in his voice sends a chill up my spine.

"Did you call Mr. Reinhart? Maybe he can help."

"Yours is the only number I have memorized."

I take a deep breath. "You need a lawyer. I'm sure you'll get out of this, okay? It'll be okay."

"No money for a lawyer, Raquel. I get a public defender." He snorts. "Wish me luck."

"Elijah —"

In the background, I hear a gruff voice say, "Time is up, Delgado."

"I care about you a lot, for what it's worth."

The call ends.

* * *

Mom doesn't bother going through the motions of putting the back of her hand to my forehead when I tell her I'm too sick to go to school today. She just nods while twisting her graying hair into a bun that she secures with a big hair clip.

"Do you need me to bring you anything?" she asks before she goes to work. "Food? Water?"

"I'm okay, thanks." With my hair a frazzled mess and my blankets pulled up to my chin, I'm sure I look pathetic enough to pass inspection.

Mom nods and then she's gone. I listen to her car drive away, and then I'm up, resetting the GPS on my phone to route to Mr. Reinhart's address right away. I'm not just going to sit back and hope for the best. I'm going to make Sasha proud and help Elijah in any way I can.

An inflatable Thanksgiving turkey greets me in the middle of the Reinharts' lawn. The rose bed in front of their small house has a little holiday scarecrow sticking out of the mulch, and I'm reminded of the Cades and how their lawn is always decorated for the holidays as well.

Mr. Reinhart answers the door wearing reading glasses dipped down on his nose. He's dressed like he's going to work at an office job, though I know from our previous meeting that he's retired.

"Raquel?" He lifts the glasses to the top of his head, and I notice he has dark circles under his eyes. "Elijah's not here. I'm not sure where he is. We've been worried sick."

"He's in jail," I say, twisting my hands in on each other. I'm still confident that this is the best way to help him, but showing up unannounced on a near-stranger's doorstep is a first for me.

Mr. Reinhart lifts a curious brow, and I talk faster, hoping to restore Elijah's reputation before Mr. Reinhart decides to think badly of him. "There was a warrant on him and his old roommates for dealing drugs, but he's *not* a dealer, I swear to you. That's why he left — he wanted to get out of that place and find somewhere safer to live. But they arrested everyone, including Elijah, and now he's stuck with no money for bail."

Hopelessness weighs me down. If only Sasha had planned for something of this magnitude. Left a secret stash of bail money or something.

"Come in," Mr. Reinhart says, stepping back from his doorway to let me inside. "Which jail?" he asks, his voice level. He doesn't seem angry, so maybe he will help Elijah.

"Travis County."

"And how much is the bail?"

I sigh. "Five grand."

Mr. Reinhart pinches the bridge of his nose. "I want to help him, and I'll do what I can, but I can't afford that."

"I can't either," I say, staring at the purple lilacs embroidered on the placemat in front of me. "I just wanted to tell you, so you'd know what happened."

"I appreciate it," he says. "Jarrah is at the grocery store. She's been worried sick, the poor thing. We thought he decided to live somewhere else, but it didn't seem like Elijah. He's not the kind of person who'd leave without saying anything."

"He called me because he didn't have your number," I tell him. "But he wanted you to know he's okay. I think I'm freaking out more than he is," I mutter, letting out a sigh. "He's acting like he expected his life to fall apart one day."

"Elijah grew up with nothing, and he often thinks that's all he is. He cares about you, more than he cares about himself, I'd wager."

I look up at this. Mr. Reinhart nods, giving me a sad smile. "Group home kids don't know love like the rest of us do. I tried my best to be there for him. He wasn't like most of the boys his age when I met him. He's an old soul. Quiet, rational. He's always wanted more for himself, but he thinks he doesn't deserve it."

"We have to help him," I say, my jaw flexing. "He needs us."

Mr. Reinhart meets my gaze. "Then I guess we better get to work."

* * *

The next day, Mrs. Reinhart sets a cup of tea in front of me, right on top of the embroidered flowers. "It might be a little hot," she says, sliding a jar of sugar toward me before she sits next to her husband.

He'd asked me to come over straight after school. Izzy seemed worried about me when I told her I'd be missing work for a while, but I'll explain it to her later. School is already impossible to get through each day; I can't go back to real life until Elijah is free.

"So what's the plan?" I say, spooning some sugar into my tea.

"I'm afraid it's not looking too good." Mr. Reinhart was able to visit Elijah, but only by video call. The jail no longer allows in-person visits through a pane of glass and a telephone, like you see in the movies. It's all done over the internet now, at scheduled sessions. I was stuck at school today and had to miss out on his call.

Mr. Reinhart studies a notepad in front of him, his notes scrawled every which way in handwriting I can't decipher from across the table. "I spoke with his public defender. The evidence against the boys is stacked a mile high, and it turns out his friend Anthony has been dealing drugs for months now. Elijah wasn't aware of it, says he's been spending all his time working and being with you. Anthony is claiming they were all a part of the deal because he thinks he'll be in less trouble that way."

"Elijah wouldn't deal drugs," I say through clenched teeth.

"I believe you, dear." His lips form a thin line. "I believe Elijah, too. But there's nothing we can do. His lawyer is going for a plea deal. He'd only get five years, probably get out early with good behavior."

"*Five years?*" I spit out, raw anger coursing through my veins. "He's innocent! He can't stay in jail, it will ruin his life! He's going to college. He's going to get a degree in social work."

It's not that easy, Raquel. Elijah told me that so many times and I never believed him. But maybe he was right. Nothing in his life has been easy. Things only got a little better for him when he discovered Sasha, and then they came crashing down again when she died. But now Elijah has me. I know I can't make the world easy, but I can damn sure try to make it a little better.

Mrs. Reinhart dips her head down, staring at her intertwined fingers. "That's just how this works, honey. The system has failed him, just like it's failed so many other kids."

"So that's all?" My chair skids across the linoleum as I bolt up. He's just a worthless orphan in the eyes of the legal system. "I'm not believing that excuse. The system sucks, but it's not everything. He's going to get out of this."

"This happens a lot to kids who age out of the system," Mr. Reinhart says, seeming to ignore that last shred of hope I'm still holding on to. "Like we talked about before, even if we could scrape together enough money to get him out on bail, once this goes to court, there won't be much we can do."

Mrs. Reinhart shakes her head while stirring her tea. "If we could afford a good lawyer, he'd be fine. Just like those rich brats who get off scot-free after driving drunk and killing someone. Those are the people the law should throw behind bars."

My jaw hurts. Closing my eyes, I take a deep breath and try to settle down. These people are kind souls and they're trying to help. I can't direct all of my anger at them.

"Thank you for trying," I say, making an effort to smile, but it comes out like a frown. Even with all the despair roiling around my insides, I suddenly feel a spark of something in me. Like the steam from my cup of tea, a warmth rises in my chest.

A sign.

If Elijah had money, he could get out of this. Rich people get out of worse things all the time. My knuckles go white on the table in front of me. My resolve is set, and there's no turning back now.

He just needs a good lawyer.

Chapter Twenty-Eight

At school, I forgo doing my makeup work in an effort to Google everything possible about local lawyers and how to find the best one. I wear an oversized hoodie and hide my phone in my sleeve so I can slouch over my desktop in class and secretly figure out how I'm going to make this plan of mine work. I'm pretty sure the whole process is nothing like what I've seen on TV and in the movies, so I want to go into this prepared and not like an idiot teenager with no clue of how life works. I need to find someone who will believe in me and work with me. Unlike Sasha's adventures, I'm planning this one, which means I have to take the reins.

The Greenwood Group is just down the road from Mr. Cade's office, and they are similarly ranked in online reviews. Even though my best friend's dad is the best lawyer in Texas, I think I've found a good second in Max Greenwood.

There's an online form to request a free consultation, *free* being the key word here, and I fill it out in history class. My research has informed me that I'll need to pay this guy a retainer fee when I hire him, probably to the tune of a few thousand dollars, but I shove that to the back of my long list of worries to deal with later. I'll find a way to make this work. I have to.

By the time the eighth period bell rings, Mr. Greenwood's assistant has replied to my email, saying she can fit me in for a consultation today at four thirty. My heart races with the thrill of possibility and I respond right away.

I rush home after school and change into a pair of dress slacks that I only own from my incredibly short tenure in the debate club freshman year. They're a little tight, but they still fit and I match them with a navy blue button-up blouse that was an ugly gift from my aunt Renee last Christmas. These are the most professional clothes I have, and I'm grateful I let them hang out, ignored and hated in the back of my closet for so long. Today, they're going to help me make a good impression.

The Greenwood Group is a squat building at the end of Main Street, tucked off the road a bit. Unlike the tall, gray building where Mr. Cade works, this place looks like an old house that was turned into a business. There are flowers planted all along the edges of the parking lot and even more flowers at the entrance. I take a breath and open the door.

Soft jazz music plays from somewhere in the distance, and I'm immediately greeted with a smile from the woman at the front desk. She has dark skin and short, curly brown hair and is wearing a gorgeous string of pearls over a shirt that's not all that different from mine. I smile inwardly at my clothing choice, feeling confident that I can pull off the mature vibe for a few more minutes.

"How may I help you?" the woman asks. The name engraved on the brass plate on her desk tells me she's Marietta Brooks, the woman who emailed me earlier today.

"I'm Raquel Clearwater," I say, shoulders back, head held high. This is what Sasha would do, I know, and I am determined to make her proud. "I have a consultation with Mr. Greenwood at four thirty."

"If you'd like to have a seat, he'll be right out," she says, gesturing to a coffee station against the wall. "Would you like some coffee?"

I say yes, because it feels like the mature thing to do, and I pour myself a cup even though my stomach is so nervous I don't think I can swallow a single sip of anything right now. The cup sits warm in my hands as I watch the seconds tick by on the decorative wrought iron clock on the wall. The second hand is only a few seconds past four thirty when Mr. Green- wood walks out.

He looks exactly like his picture on his website. Tall, well- dressed, bright silver hair with a little black left around his sideburns. "Miss Clearwater," he says in a booming voice that I visualize him using in the courtroom as he gets Elijah out of trouble. "I'm Max Greenwood. It's a pleasure to meet you."

I stand up, shifting the coffee to my left hand. I shake his hand, a jagged smile forming on my lips. "Hello," I say feebly. *Ugh.*

I follow him to his office, and I try not to compare its homey vibe to the vast glass and metal intimidation of Mr. Cade's office. A thousand framed pictures of his wife and kids does not mean Mr. Greenwood won't be a tough lawyer in court. Besides, he's all I've got if I'm going to keep my promise to Sasha to leave her parents out of this.

"How has your day been so far?" Mr. Greenwood asks as we take our seats on either side of his desk.

"As good as it can be, considering I had to suffer through school," I say, and he chuckles. This is all part of my plan — to be the kind and upstanding teenager who needs a little help. Maybe in the form of a payment plan, reduced prices and some kind of grant money.

"Try to enjoy it while you can, Miss Clearwater. Sometimes I wish I could go back to my high school years. Back then I could run a five-minute mile and eat whatever I wanted."

Enough of the pleasantries. I sit on the edge of my seat, shoulders straight. I've rehearsed this speech in my head all day. I will explain the situation. I'll lament how the system has failed an upstanding member of society. I'll play on the mission statement on his website: using integrity, excellence, innovation and respect to give legal service to his clients in unique ways that pertain to each client's individual needs. I'll concede that, yes, I am a poor high school student and Elijah is no better off, but I'll urge that I'm capable of paying his fees if we can get creative with payment options.

Before I say a word, Mr. Greenwood pulls his bushy eyebrows together. He presses a finger to his lips and then points it toward me. "How do I know you?" he says, concentrating on me.

"I, uh, you don't?" I say. I know him, though. He graduated from South Texas College of Law and has been licensed to practice in the state since 1989. He's won awards and participates in charity events all over the state, which is one of the reasons I'm hoping he will go easy on me when it comes to his compensation.

"You look so familiar," he says, leaning back in his chair. "Ah, wait a minute." His face lights up in recognition, and then it promptly slides into a frown. "That's where I remember you. The funeral. You were Sasha's best friend who gave a speech, right?"

I'm too dumbstruck to answer. Mr. Greenwood continues, "I'm so sorry for your loss. The Cades are such great people. I'm sure you miss her a lot."

"You know the Cades?" My plan begins to fall apart the moment he nods.

"Oh sure. I'm very close with Walter Cade. We play golf together. Of course, he hasn't been at the golf course since his daughter passed. Understandable."

I don't know what I was thinking by coming here. I thought I could keep Sasha's last wish a secret like she'd asked me to. I thought I could save Elijah and no one would have to know. But lawyers don't exactly grow on trees, and they probably all know each other. Who *doesn't* know the famous Walter Cade?

If I ask for Mr. Greenwood's help, it's sure to get back to Sasha's dad, a slip of the tongue over drinks or a round of golf at the country club. Mr. Cade would find out that his daughter's best friend hired a lawyer to get a strange boy out of jail. He'd inquire about the boy. He'd discover the truth.

He'd find out about Sasha's secret from someone who isn't me.

I stand up, my chair gliding across the thin carpet. "I'm sorry, I can't do this."

"Is everything okay?" Mr. Greenwood asks.

I shake my head. Everything is not okay. But I'm not about to explain it.

"Sorry I wasted your time," I say.

And then I get the hell out of there.

* * *

A chilly breeze dances through my hair and sends fallen leaves skidding all over the cemetery grounds. Some crash into headstones, where they pile up, but others make it all the way down to the water. My butt is freezing, my teeth chattering, as I sit on the mostly dead mound of grass that covers Sasha's grave.

"Listen," I say as I stare at her name etched into the bright white granite headstone. "Elijah needs my help. Actually, he needs your dad's help. I understand why you want me to keep Elijah a secret, but I can't do it anymore."

I stare at the ground and try not to imagine the casket that's buried six feet below. Sasha's bones may lie beneath me, but her spirit is everywhere. I look up toward the sky, closing my eyes as another cold gust of air slams into my face. I've never been one to stand up for myself, especially without Sasha by my side. Maybe I just didn't have the right motivation until now.

"I'm not here to ask permission, Sasha. I have to spend the rest of my life making decisions without you, and this is the first one. Elijah spent twenty years missing out on knowing you. On knowing *anything*. I'm not going to let him spend five more years rotting in jail and missing out on more."

I stand up and brush the dirt off the back of my dress pants. My teeth chatter from the cold, but there's probably some apprehension mixed in as well. "I hope I have your permission," I say as a lump rises in my throat.

"But if not ... I hope you'll forgive me."

Chapter Twenty-Nine

There is no time to come up with the perfect way to betray my best friend and tell her parents about their daughter's last wish. And even if I had come up with a plan, if I'd worked up some epic speech to give them, I'd no doubt botch the entire thing.

With this in mind, I don't even call Mrs. Cade to announce my unexpected visit. I just show up and knock on the door.

Mr. Cade answers. Instead of a hello, I say, "Good. You're home."

"Raquel?" When I give him a tight smile and walk right past him into his own house, he stares at me like I've lost my head. "Is everything okay?"

"No, sir. Everything is not okay. Where's Mrs. Cade?"

"I'm right here, hon." Sasha's mom appears on the other side of the foyer, patting her hands dry on her apron. She gives me a once-over, maybe checking for bullet holes or black eyes, and then her gaze settles on my thumb picking the nail polish from my index finger. "What's going on?"

"I need to tell you something," I say, turning to Mr. Cade. "And I need your legal services. Pro bono, if possible."

If I'd had a plan, maybe that wouldn't have sounded so insane.

"Why don't we sit in the den," Mr. Cade says, ushering us into the adjoining room. As soon as they're seated on a high-backed antique couch, I take a deep breath that does nothing to settle my nerves and sit in the chair across from them.

"Sasha has a biological brother." I study my chipped nail polish, giving them a moment to react to the news they technically already know.

Mr. Cade clears his throat, and I hold up a hand, cringing at how rude I'm being to the wealthiest and most dignified man I know. "Please. Just let me get this out before you say anything."

Nerves twist my stomach into knots, but I stay strong, for her. "Sasha found her brother a few months before she died. They talked online but she never met him in person. She saved that for me. We've been going around doing these little adventures for Sasha so that he can learn about her life and about who she was before she got cancer."

I turn to Sasha's parents, who are watching me with identical expressions.

"What's his name?" Mrs. Cade says, wiping a tear from her eye.

"Elijah Delgado."

They exchange a glance, one that I guess only makes sense when you've been married to the same person for twenty-five years.

Mr. Cade clears his throat. "Why do you need legal help?"

I want to look away, but I need to be confident. "Elijah is in jail, but it's not his fault." I swallow. "He was never adopted, and he aged out of the system. He had absolutely nothing, and because of that, he went to live with some guys he met. They happened to be drug dealers, but he didn't have anything to do with the drugs. Now he's in jail because of it, and his public defender doesn't give a crap about him. He's looking at five years for something he didn't even do."

Again, they exchange a look, only this time I see something like regret in their eyes. Sasha's mom covers her face with her hands, her weeping growing louder until Mr. Cade wraps his arms around her. He strokes his wife's hair, and I look away, allowing them a private moment.

"Walter, we should have done something," she says.

"There was nothing we could do." He shakes his head. "It would have been a legal nightmare. We didn't want that, remember? We wanted a closed, drama-free adoption."

Mrs. Cade dabs at her face with the bottom of her apron, and then she turns to me. "We knew about him. He went into the same agency a few months after Sasha did, but it was by court order, not by choice. His dad kept fighting to keep him, even though his mother wanted to surrender him at the same time she surrendered Sasha. About a year after we adopted Sasha, they called us and said her biological mother had died from an overdose and the biological father had lost temporary custody again and was looking at jail time for drug use. But he wanted an open adoption."

I watch her so intently I forget to breathe. I see the pain in her eyes, the regret notched in her forehead. Her gaze drifts downward, and she presses her hand flat to her chest. "We said no. Walter was a new attorney and we weren't well off back then. Adopting Sasha drained all the money we had at the time. We couldn't afford the paperwork for another child and" — she exhales forcefully — "we knew we didn't want an open adoption. We also didn't want someone who was an addict in our child's life, and the boy — Elijah — he was already a toddler. He wanted his dad more than adopted parents, and we didn't want to risk losing him and then Sasha to the allure of their real father."

"We looked for him a few years later, thinking maybe we could get the kids together for a playdate," Mr. Cade says. "But when I found him, he was in a group home. Not even ten years old, and already suspended from school for smoking pot with a few junior high kids." His lips were pressed together, his jaw tight. "It's a shame, it really is, but we couldn't have someone like that around Sasha. For all we knew, he was on the same path as his dad."

Mrs. Cade can't even look me in the eyes. She runs her fingers across an embroidered rose on her apron. "I felt awful, Raquel. I really did. But I didn't want to share my daughter with someone who didn't even want her. And taking in another child we couldn't afford when we knew his history was just too big a risk."

Here's the thing about hearts: they can hurt even when they're already broken. "Please," I say, fingernails digging into my palms. My chest feels like it's been ripped wide open, and all they're doing is offering me a bunch of excuses. "Please help him. He's not a criminal. He's not using or dealing drugs. He doesn't even remember his dad."

"Raquel," Mr. Cade says, his voice deep and authoritative. I flinch, almost expecting to get chewed out. Mr. Cade stands, so I do, too. He puts a hand on my shoulder, and a few seconds too late, I realize he's in lawyer mode. He peers down at me, the fine lines etched around his lips from years of working around the clock. "You should let this go. A kid like him probably can't be helped, no matter how much you might wish otherwise."

The words sting worse than they should, because I know they're all untrue. Maybe he's still bitter from losing his daughter, and that's why he's refusing to help me. I don't know what's changed, what's happened to the Mr. Cade I've known most of my life. But after seeing Sasha's last video, I guess it's officially true: the man before me isn't who I thought he was.

Chapter Thirty

Jarrah places a slice of coffee cake in front of me. It's still warm from the oven, and the smell should make my mouth water. On any other day, I'd be shoveling the whole thing into my mouth, but today, I can't stop staring at the pathetically small pile of cash on the Thanksgiving tablecloth.

I pick up my fork and poke at the cake. "Do judges negotiate bail, by any chance?"

Mr. Reinhart stares at the money. Thirteen hundred and forty-two dollars. He's also holding his fork midair, also not eating. I notice his missing pinky, wonder what happened to it, but I know it's not the time to ask. This measly stack of green is all the two of us could come up with in the last five days.

"I think," he says, reaching over and taking some bills off the stack of cash, "bail isn't the problem here." He slides my three hundred and forty-two dollars across the table to me. "Even if he gets out, it'd only be for a little while, until the court date. And then what happens? He gets thrown back in jail?"

"But he's innocent." My forehead drops to my palm, and I stare at the perfectly cut piece of coffee cake. "This can't be how this works. Life can't be this bad. First it takes my best friend and now it's wrongly punishing her brother." My other half. My first love.

My voice cracks on the last word. I am so sick of crying. So sick of hurting. "Elijah never had parents, or a home, or a sister he got to meet," I say as the ceramic pumpkin salt and pepper shakers blur beneath my tears. "Now he won't even have his freedom. He won't even have a chance to live his life."

The room goes so silent I'm not even sure the Reinharts are still in here. I close my eyes and wipe away the tears, and then Jarrah's hand is warm on my shoulder. "I have an errand to run," she says simply, her voice a little thick. Or maybe it's just my imagination. She grabs the stack of their money and slips out the door, leaving her coffee cake untouched.

"Well, that was weird," Mr. Reinhart says a moment later. "Guess she wants it back in the bank where it belongs."

"What are we going to do now?" I reach for my money and shove it in my pocket, where it makes a lump in my jeans. A shameful reminder that I'm not the right person to fix this for Elijah. I've let both him and Sasha down.

Mr. Reinhart takes a bite of his coffee cake. "We hope for the best."

* * *

We get the week off school for Thanksgiving break, and the reprieve from homework couldn't have come at a better time. I am worried about Elijah, missing Sasha like crazy and filled to the brim with guilt over the whole situation. But at this point, flunking out of chemistry would only be a blip in the vast galaxy of everything that is wrong.

My parents have to work until Thursday, so I spend my days at Izzy's helping her with the rush of Thanksgiving orders. Unlike at school, where I am a catatonic zombie, I find that I can focus on my tasks here in the flower shop. It's peaceful arranging flowers, and after all the hours I've spent standing at this counter, Izzy's feels more like home than anywhere else.

She takes my wrist on Tuesday morning, turning it upward while she hums along to a David Bowie song on the radio. "You are stressed about something," she says, rubbing an essential oil onto my skin. It's a mixture of peppermint and maybe thyme, and she applies a lot more than usual. "Maybe even ashamed. If I were a betting woman, I'd say you're worried about Thanksgiving dinner with the Cades."

My eyes dart to her. "How do you know this stuff?" I ask. She just shrugs and turns back toward the cash register, her skirt sweeping along the floor, taking fallen petals with it.

Though my head is swimming with worries, I could definitely tack down Thanksgiving dinner as one of my bigger concerns. I haven't talked to the Cades since they all but threw me out of their house last week. Then Saturday morning, Sasha's mom called my mom and invited us all over for the holiday. Mom happily accepted — having no idea what had happened — and I've been weird about it ever since.

I haven't told my parents about Elijah, and I'm guessing the Cades won't bring him up. If I know them as well as I think I do, we will probably all enjoy a large and delicious meal without any mention of things that are awkward. But how can I ever look at them the same way again? These are the people who would have happily given their own lives to save Sasha, yet they couldn't be bothered to consider helping her brother. Not once, but twice, they had the chance to save him. And both times, they walked away.

When I get home from work and find Mr. Cade's SUV in our driveway, I can only guess he's here to talk about Thanksgiving dinner. Too bad that nagging feeling in my gut, the sensation a luckier person might call intuition, is telling me otherwise.

Mom and Dad are sitting with Mr. Cade at our kitchen table. On the counter, the coffee maker is gurgling and spewing out a fresh pot of my mom's go-to drink for company.

All eyes turn to me. Mr. Cade is dressed for work in a suit that probably cost as much as my car. He looks so out of place at our dinky kitchen table, his hands clasped together over our plastic tablecloth. Any other time he's come to my house, it's been for fun things like dinner parties or dropping off Sasha for a sleepover. Now, though, seeing him here is all wrong.

My purse is slung over my shoulder and I hold on to the strap like it's a security blanket. There's a vibe in this room and it's not that of a friendly chat.

"There she is," Mom says, her cheeks rosy from her heavy-handed makeup application. "Walter came to talk to you."

"Okay," I say, my heartbeat ratcheting up to unsafe levels. "Is it about ...?"

"I was hoping to speak in private," Mr. Cade says. "If it's okay with your parents, of course."

"Not a problem at all." Mom doesn't even look at me as she puts her hand on Dad's arm. "We'll go outside and get some fresh air." Funny how they still think Mr. Cade is this wonderful man with upstanding morals. They're not even questioning why he'd be here to see me.

When they're gone, I pull out a chair and sit across from

Sasha's dad, somehow feeling like I'm in trouble for something, even though I'm not the one who abandoned Elijah. Mr. Cade takes off his glasses and sets them on the table. He pinches the bridge of his nose, an action that only takes a couple of seconds but feels like an eternity.

"I owe you an apology," he says. My eyes bug out. Of all the things I imagined him saying, that wasn't one of them. He holds up a hand, then sighs and runs it through his white hair. "Sue doesn't know I'm here. I wanted to talk to you first. I recently had a visit from a woman named Jarrah Reinhart." He lifts his brows when he sees my reaction. "You know her?"

"Yes, sir," I say, tightening my grip on my purse strap. I'm still not sure if this is good news. "I've met her."

He nods, then clears his throat. "She showed me Elijah's eighth grade report card. Apparently, he had given it to her back in the day." He straightens, and a slight smile curves on his lips. "All A's. I was quite impressed. This woman, whom I'd never met before, came to my office at work and spent an hour talking to me about Elijah Delgado. She made a real case for the boy, talking him up as if he were her own flesh and blood."

I press my lips together as I listen to his story. I'm trying to smile, but tears are lingering in the wings. "She's a really nice lady."

"She is," he says. The corner of his eyes crinkle. "She asked for my legal services. Said she didn't have much, but she wanted to give me the entire contents of her savings account, one thousand dollars. She even had it in cash, right there in her hands."

Chills prickle up my spine. While Mr. Reinhart and I were giving up hope, Jarrah was making one last attempt. I gnaw on the inside of my lip until it goes raw.

"Raquel," he says, heaving a long sigh. "I loved my daughter with all of my heart. But the truth is that I kept a secret from her, and although I told myself it was for her own good, I realize now that I made a mistake. I shouldn't have judged Elijah for the sins of his father."

His hands twist together and his forehead is creased with deep lines. "I kept asking myself, what would Sasha think? How would she see me now, refusing to help the boy? How could I do justice to her memory if I didn't do something?"

I can tell this is hard for him to admit, but the anticipation is about to break me in half. "What are you saying, Mr. Cade?"

There are tears in his eyes, vulnerability I've never before seen in the tough Texas lawyer. "When that woman came to visit me, I saw some of Sasha in her. My daughter also sought out the good in people. She loved her brother and she would have wanted me to do anything I could to save him."

He laces his fingers together, elbows on the table, and the wealthiest man I know looks me right in the eyes.

"I guess what I'm saying to you, Raquel, is that I've decided to help."

Chapter Thirty-One

Over the next few days, Mr. Cade works his lawyer magic, and I decide to come clean to my parents about Sasha's last wish. I figure I've already broken Sasha's ultimate rule, so revealing everything to my parents isn't much worse. After Thanksgiving dinner at the Cades' house, I sit Sasha's parents and mine together in the living room and show them Sasha's first video.

Mom didn't cry as much as Mrs. Cade did, but Dad didn't cry at all. He said this was the greatest gift Sasha could have given me. He said a friendship like that only comes along once in a lifetime, if you're lucky. And I have to agree with him. I am the luckiest to have had Sasha, if only for a little while.

While the infamous Walter Cade sets to work on the case, Mrs. Cade wants to meet Elijah through the jail's video chat visitations. It costs twenty freaking dollars just for a ten-minute video call, but Elijah is allowed visitation time every day.

I set up my laptop on the Cades' dining table and log in to the jail's visitation website. Mrs. Cade fusses with her hair as I set up the video chat. "You look fine," I tell her, rolling my eyes.

An empty booth stares back at us as we wait for them to let Elijah into the visitation room. In the corner of the computer screen, our ten minutes have already started. Once it reaches zero, our visitation time will be over and we won't get to see him again until tomorrow. Mrs. Cade exhales. "I'm really nervous," she whispers. That makes two of us.

Even in an orange jumpsuit, Elijah is the cutest guy I've ever laid eyes on. I wave at him, and he grins at me, then turns his attention to Mrs. Cade.

"Hello," he says.

"Elijah," Mrs. Cade says, her voice warm. I don't know how she manages to turn off the anxious vibe she had just a second ago. She leans forward. "I'm Sue Cade. I'm so happy to meet you."

"Same," he says, his smile softening. "I wish it were in person and not like this, but yeah."

Mrs. Cade watches him as the timer on the corner of the screen slowly counts down the minutes. "You look just like her."

He grins. "So I've been told."

"How are you? Are they treating you okay?" Her voice cracks, and she reaches for a tissue. I use the opportunity to give him a look that shows how awkward I feel. He winks at me.

"I'm fine. Really. Mr. Cade is confident about my case. Hopefully I'll be out of here soon."

"Are you sure? No one is messing with you or anything?" Mrs. Cade dabs at her eyes. "Walter could talk with someone. Move you to a safer place."

Elijah shakes his head. "Nah, I'm good. My cellmate is in here for scamming people out of money online, so he's not scary. If anything, I think he's scared of me."

I smile, unsure what to say. I don't want to take up Mrs.

Cade's time with him, so I just sit here and let her do the talking. Just getting to see him fills me with a peace I hope I can hold on to when the screen turns off.

"I'm so sorry I wasn't there for you, Elijah." Mrs. Cade is full-on crying now. "I should have been there. We should have taken you in, honey. I'm so sorry. I'll never forgive myself."

I put my arm around her shoulders. Elijah's lips move like he's trying to figure out what to say.

"You're here now," he says after a moment. "And I really appreciate it."

The ten minutes fly by entirely too quickly, and soon a warning flashes across the computer telling us our time is almost up.

"You're going to be okay," Mrs. Cade says, wiping her eyes with the fifth tissue she's grabbed since this call began. "I can't wait to meet you in person."

"Same," Elijah says. For a quick moment, his grin looks just like Sasha's, and I can practically feel Mrs. Cade thinking the same thing.

"I'll call you again tomorrow," I say.

"You let us know if you need anything," Mrs. Cade says, as if he's at a hotel and not locked up in prison.

He chuckles. "Okay. Thank you."

* * *

The day before Elijah has to be at the courthouse to meet the judge (which has been expedited thanks to Mr. Cade), Mom makes us two gigantic bowls of ice cream and we eat it together while we watch *Mean Girls* with Sasha's commentary playing next to us on the end table. I close my eyes when Sasha talks, grateful that her voice will never fade from my memory. Something tells me I'll still be watching these things when I'm old.

Although I've shared a few of Sasha's adventures with our parents, most of them — the important ones — I've kept to myself.

"Do you have your outfit picked out for tomorrow?" Mom asks, digging her spoon into vanilla ice cream covered in chocolate syrup.

"Yeah, the navy blue dress. Does that look court-ish?" This isn't exactly a court case like in the movies, but Mr. Cade has arranged a hearing with the judge to plead Elijah's case. He explained to us that most good lawyers push this off as long as possible to delay sentencing, but he wants a fresh start for Elijah. So he pushed it forward. He's obtained character references from the Reinharts and people who worked at Elijah's old group homes. It only took a few minutes of the tough Texas lawyer's time to convince Anthony to admit that Elijah never dealt drugs with him or his other roommates. Mr. Cade says we're going to win this one. We're all going to the courthouse to show our support.

"I like the navy blue dress." Mom's lips curve up as she eats another spoonful. "I think you look very beautiful in that dress."

I lift an eyebrow. "That doesn't really answer my question."

Her eyes flit over to me, the look on her face waking up the butterflies in my stomach. "I just thought you'd like to know."

The look she gives me is new for us. She may not have said it directly, but she's talking about boys here. These are the kinds of things I always reserved for talks with Sasha. But now I guess these topics are finding their way into my relationship with my mom.

"Thanks," I say, feeling heat rush to my cheeks. On the computer beside me Sasha says, "None for you, Glen Coco!" before collapsing into giggles.

"So," Mom says a few minutes later. "There's only one adventure left?"

I nod, stirring my chocolate and ice cream until it's a uniform color. "No telling when it will arrive. I'm not ready for them to be over." After that first envelope arrived, I thought I'd go crazy waiting for the rest of the adventures. But now that it's almost over, I find myself hoping the time will pass slower, the mail will take longer and this final adventure from Sasha won't come until I'm fully ready to say goodbye.

Mom watches Sasha's face on the computer screen and then she turns to me. "I'm sure she'll make it a good one."

At night, while I'm lying in bed unable to sleep because the courthouse meeting is tomorrow, my phone chimes from my nightstand. Reaching over, I see that it is 12:01 in the morning, and I have a new email from TheFutureSasha.

Hey there favorites,

The time has come to end this adventure. I think it's only fitting to end by showing you the best day of my life. This one beats out every bad day I've ever had.

Well, what are you waiting for? Watch the attached video!

Love you and miss you both,
Sasha

The video attached to the email is practically glowing with how badly I want to watch it. I should wait for Elijah, probably. But if this is the best day of her life, I don't think Elijah would fault me for my lack of patience.

I play the video.

Sasha grins into her webcam. "I'm just going to get right to it, okay? So this morning, I broke into my parents' filing cabinet. The one they keep in a back closet in my dad's office, under strict lock and key. I've always figured my adoption papers were in there, so today, with both of my parents gone, I just went for it."

She wiggles her eyebrows, and I see a hint of Elijah's eyes sparkling at me through the screen. "There was a DVD included in my folder. It's a file my mom saved from her email because back then she put everything on DVDs instead of flash drives. It was dated a few months after my parents had officially adopted me, so I'm not sure why the lady at the agency emailed this video to my mom, but she did. I guess this is when they found out about Elijah … but I don't want to get into that right now. Right now is about you and me, big brother."

Sasha grins into the camera, her face still vibrant even though her hair had fallen out by then. She reaches up and the video goes blank. Then another one begins to play.

The grainy footage is obviously from an old digital camera, circa 2000 or so. The room looks like a daycare, with colorful walls and toys all over the floor. Kids are playing in the background, but the camera is focused on two kids in particular. A baby sits on a blanket, holding a toy caterpillar on a string. The baby's skin is a creamy tan, her hair black and her eyes the bluest I've ever seen.

Beside her, a boy, about three years old, plays with a toy car. He has the same hair, the same skin tone and those same eyes. Elijah was a chubby toddler.

Watching them play together makes me completely lose track of what the woman is saying, until she moves the camera closer to Elijah.

"This is Elijah. He just arrived and he wanted to find his sister. Elijah, what are you doing?"

"This is my sister," he says, his fat little cheeks grinning as he wraps his arms around Sasha's head. She looks startled, and then bops him in the face with her tiny fist.

"It's okay. I love you," Elijah says, placing a wobbly toddler kiss on top of her head.

The video cuts out and big Sasha appears again. Her eyes seem far away when she talks. "I always thought my biggest regret was that we never knew each other until it was too late. But that's not true, Elijah. We *were* actually together, at least for a short while. We did know each other after all. There was a time in our lives where we were best friends, even if we can't remember it."

She focuses back on the webcam, and I get the chills when her gaze falls on me. "It may feel like that time is gone. But in a universe that is infinite, that moment still exists. It's in the past, but it's there, and it makes me happy. You were the brother I'd always wanted. And you still are."

I think Sasha meant for this to be a beautiful, heartwarming video, but a sadness hits me so hard I turn off my phone and toss it back on the nightstand. I sit up in bed, nausea rolling around my stomach. All those years ago, the future seemed so bright. Two beautiful siblings had the whole world ahead of them.

Now only one of them does.

Chapter Thirty-Two

The blue dress might look good, but a cold front blew in last night and now I'm shivering on the long walk from the parking lot up to the county courthouse. Mrs. Cade throws an arm around my shoulders as we enter inside a set of glass doors.

"Are you cold, or scared?" she asks, her breath smelling like the coffee she holds in her other hand.

"Both." It's the honest-to-God answer. My parents offered to take off work for the day, but I'd insisted that they go about their normal lives. After all, letting my parents meet the guy I'm pretty much in love with during his court appearance? Not ideal. I worried that they would have told me not to miss any more school, but they didn't. After all, my best friend has only been gone a few months.

This is something I have to do.

The courthouse has a life of its own, with people going every which way. Lawyers walking quickly in their tailored suits, faces bored or determined, or too focused on their cell phones. Worried mothers fussing over their sons' ties, silk formalities that are only pulled from the closet for rare occasions like these.

We have to go through a metal detector before we're let in the main part of the building, and then Mrs. Cade and I spend a few minutes staring at the map in the lobby to figure out where to go. There are several courtrooms hearing many cases today. Some of them are simple things like people trying to get out of speeding tickets, and others are more severe, like trying to get a drug charge dropped. Mr. Cade told us this morning that Elijah's meeting with the judge is closed door, and if we want to be here for moral support, we have to wait outside.

I focus on breathing exercises as I sit on a hard bench next to Mrs. Cade, who is reading an ebook on her cell phone. She acts calm, but I notice she hasn't flipped to the next page in a long time. The only reason we came today is because we want to be here the moment the judge releases Elijah, not that it's guaranteed. But he has the truth and the tough Texas lawyer on his side, so I refuse to believe the judge would rule against him.

When the doors swing open, I feel like it hasn't been nearly long enough for the judge to rule in our favor. I bolt off the bench, my heart pounding and my teeth digging into my bottom lip. Does a quick meeting mean Elijah is screwed? Or —

Mr. Cade seems ten feet tall as he strides out of the courtroom, shaking hands with colleagues as he passes. Behind him, Elijah wears a suit that's too baggy and a subtle grin.

"Well?" I practically shout at Mr. Cade and I rush to meet them.

"All charges dropped," Mr. Cade says, clapping a hand on Elijah's back.

All sense of propriety disappears into thin air as I rush forward and throw my arms around Elijah. He hugs me back, lifting me off the floor. I get lost in the scent of his shampoo, the fresh minty smell of his breath as he places a kiss on my cheek.

When he sets me down, the whole world is spinning. I can't take my eyes off him — not that I'd want to.

"Thank you *so* much," Elijah tells Mr. Cade. "I can't ever repay you for helping me."

Mrs. Cade inhales sharply. "Oh Elijah," she says, grabbing him in a tight hug. "It is so great to meet you in person." His eyes go wide as he looks at me over her shoulder, and all I can do is smile.

When she pulls back, she holds his face in her hands, and even though he's taller than she is, she seems to be looking down on him with the utmost approval. Her lips curl at the corners. "You *do* have her eyes," she whispers, tears filling her own.

"So I've been told," Elijah says, his gaze darting to me.

"I think we should celebrate," Mr. Cade's voice booms. "I spoke with the Reinharts, and they're happy to meet us for lunch. What do you say, Elijah?"

He blinks. "Sounds … great, thanks."

We walk out of the courthouse together, this weird group of people who are all somehow related in ways that aren't blood.

As we step out into the chilly December air, I gaze up at the sky, a cloudless blue, and then close my eyes. *I miss you, Sasha. And I did the best that I could.*

We pile into Mr. Cade's SUV, Elijah and I in the back seat. He marvels at how creamy soft the leather interior feels, and then he takes my hand. My pulse quickens.

In the rearview mirror, I catch Mrs. Cade's eyes as they trail to our clasped hands. She looks away. And grins.

Leave it to Mr. Cade to take us to the fanciest restaurant in the county. The Blue Crab is an upscale seafood restaurant only accessible to members of the country club next door. Elijah's eyes widen as we enter and are taken to our reserved table. The Reinharts are already here, and although they introduce themselves, it feels like we're all family, right from the start.

Mrs. Cade directs Elijah to the seat next to hers. "I want to hear all about you," she says, fawning over him the same way she used to fawn over Sasha. "Tell me everything."

"Everything would take a long time," Elijah says, unfolding his napkin and placing it in his lap. "How about I start with the day I met Sasha online?"

"Even better," Mrs. Cade says, touching his arm.

"There's a popular website for adopted kids to search out their family members," he begins. Everyone at the table watches him. "I signed up under the Texas forum and made a post for my little sister. After a million dead ends, I kind of forgot about it until one day a few weeks later, when Sasha replied to my message. She was mad because she'd messaged me several times over a week but I hadn't checked my email so I didn't get them. But when I did reply, and we started talking, it was like an instant connection. She made me send her a picture of myself, but she didn't send me one right away, saying she had to make sure I wasn't a murderer first."

The Cades chuckle and wait with anticipation for him to continue telling these stories of his life. And he does. He tells us about Sasha's emails, the long stories she'd tell him about her childhood. The kind things she had to say about her adoptive parents, and how she'd wished he could meet them. Mrs. Cade is so engrossed with his stories that she doesn't even touch her salad.

Elijah hasn't had a chance to check his email yet, but I can't wait for him to watch Sasha's final video. He'll probably want to show it to everyone else, but I want him to watch it by himself the first time.

Our food is outstandingly delicious — like seriously, seafood this good should be illegal — and after a few moments, we're talking and laughing and sharing stories about the beautiful girl who brought us all together. And though she isn't here, there's an empty chair at our round table that's set for seven, and I keep staring at it, imagining Sasha's spirit hanging out there just beyond the realm of what I can see.

I think she'd be happy, thrilled even, to see this reunion. And it hits me, as I'm dipping a forkful of salmon into garlic butter, that I'll never get to tell her about this day. She will never again be the girl sitting across from me on my bed, eyes wide, the air smelling like wet nail polish, listening to my stories and telling me exactly what she thinks about them. For the rest of my life, I will only have moments like these. Moments I will treasure, but moments I can't share with her.

The pain of her death hits me all over again, and suddenly I am back in the Cades' library, waking up to find my best friend dead. With a deep, shaking breath, I take the cloth napkin from my lap and dab at my eyes.

Elijah stops talking, looks over and takes my hand. "Are you okay?"

I shake my head, sniffling. My ears burn with the knowledge that our entire table is watching me. I gaze at that empty chair. "I just miss her."

"Oh, honey," Mrs. Cade says loudly, scooting her chair back. She comes and leans over me, wrapping me in a motherly hug that smells like perfume and baby powder. "We all miss her. But we're going to be okay."

The other adults at the table say encouraging things, but I don't really hear them all. I breathe in and out, watching that empty chair across from me, wondering why the hell life is so hard. Sasha is the one who died, after all. All I have to do is pick up the pieces and carry on without her. After my unexpected breakdown, Mr. Cade asks Elijah about his interests for the future.

"Have you looked into colleges?"

Elijah stares at his fork. "Kind of. I have this dream career that I'm pretty sure is impossible to attain, but Sasha was pretty insistent that I try to get into college. She mailed me all these brochures and stuff."

The Cades exchange an impressed look that makes me want to cringe. Is it so hard to think he's capable of rising through poverty and dreaming big dreams? Sasha believed in him, and I do, too.

Elijah continues, "Before I worry about college, I need to find a new job as soon as possible. Mr. Reinhart's been helping me with that."

Mr. Reinhart nods. "Economy has gone down the tubes, Walter. I used to have contacts around here, but I can't find the boy a job anywhere." He adjusts his glasses, frown lines appearing around his lips. "I told him he doesn't have to pay me rent or anything, but we simply don't have the money to help out much with things he may need. College would be a dream, but a job is the first step."

Mrs. Cade clears her throat. "Honey, you seem like a smart boy. You should really look into school instead of another job.

With a degree, your job opportunities will be much better."

She's using that voice she used to use on Sasha when she refused to pick a college our freshman year. Only, Elijah isn't a grumpy fourteen-year-old whose rich parents are trying to get a head start. He's twenty, and grown, and able to make his own decisions.

"I understand, totally —" Elijah begins, but Mr. Cade cuts him off with a wave of his hand. He and his wife exchange another cryptic look and she nods.

"Sasha has a college fund. She won't be using it now."

Mrs. Cade continues where her husband left off. "Walter and I have talked about turning it into a scholarship in her memory. I don't see why you can't be the only applicant for it."

Mrs. Reinhart puts a hand to her heart. Sasha's parents are watching Elijah, their expressions hopeful.

Mr. Cade straightens his back. "I know you already have a home with the Reinharts, but there's a great university near Peyton Colony, and we have plenty of space."

Mrs. Cade cuts in, leaning forward and grabbing his arm. "I know you're too old to be adopted, but we have a spare bedroom and you're Sasha's brother. You're *family*."

Elijah's mouth hangs open. Even his hand that's holding mine under the table goes limp. I'm pretty sure Mrs. Reinhart is crying, and Sasha's dad frowns in this weirdly happy way.

He's no longer the tough Texas lawyer; now he's just a dad. "Will you think it over, Elijah?"

Elijah turns to look at me. I squeeze his hand. "Say yes, you dork."

His eyes sparkle, and he seems to wake up, his hand tightening on mine. "Yes, sir," he says, running a hand through his hair. "I'd love that. Thank you."

"Then it's settled," Mrs. Cade says. "Welcome to the family, at last."

I raise my glass, nodding to the Reinharts, the Cades and the one Delgado. We may all have different last names, but we've chosen to be together. "To family."

"To family!"

As our glasses clink together, I glance over and see a single tear rolling down Elijah's cheek. His hand squeezes mine so hard my fingers hurt. "Thank you," he whispers.

Chapter Thirty-Three

The final letter will arrive any minute now. Mrs. Cade will probably check the mail the moment it's delivered, just like she always does. She'll see the letter addressed to the newest member of the household, Elijah Delgado. Maybe she'll recognize the handwriting. But she probably won't.

Mr. Cade is arranging an internship for Elijah at his law firm, but for now, Elijah is adjusting to his new life, one that now has a cell phone and Sasha's old computer. He's been spending all of his time getting to know his new parents and letting Mrs. Cade take him on the occasional shopping spree. In the evenings, he hangs out with me.

Elijah might be in his new bedroom when Mrs. Cade brings him the letter. Or maybe he's on the back porch, which is his favorite part of the Cades' house. He loves that you can see the lake from every angle of their backyard. He loves the sunset dancing on the water and the deer who hang around waiting for food. Most of all, he loves that he finally feels free.

I am in school as the letter is being delivered. I don't know exactly when it happens, but I feign attention in class while holding my phone under the desk, waiting for a message. Will he call me the second he gets it? Or will he wait a while?

Unlike the others, this letter is from me.

Dear Elijah,

I am sending you on an adventure. It is part business, part date, but dress like it's all business. I'm thinking slacks and that black button-up shirt you have. Drive to the address below, and walk into Building A. Tell the person at the front desk your name and that you have a 3:00 p.m. appointment. (Don't be late!)

After your business adventure, the fun part begins. Meet me at the marina, behind the Starbucks. See you soon.

Raquel

I check the time as I stab two green straws into the mocha Frappuccinos I just purchased. It's almost four, and Dean Marshall told me the meeting would last about half an hour. My phone has been silent all day, and I'm a little nervous that Elijah might be pissed at me. But when I step outside, drinks in hand, I see him leaning against my car in the parking lot, arms crossed over his chest, a carefree smile on his face that sets my mind at ease. The sleeves of his black button-up shirt are pushed up to his elbows, and his pants are crisply ironed, no doubt thanks to Mrs. Cade.

"Hey." I feel like the luckiest girl alive.

He takes a step forward, peeling himself off my car. "I got some mail today."

"Oh yeah?"

He pulls a folded stack of papers from his back pocket, peering at me through his lashes as he opens the pages I'd carefully folded myself the day before. "Step one," he says, "apply for admission. Step two, complete pre-assessment activity. Step three, complete placement testing."

He lowers the papers. "Step four, get a bacterial meningitis vaccination? I have to get a freaking shot?"

I bite my lip and he continues, glancing back at the paper. "Step five, complete new-student orientation. Step six, register and pay for classes. Step seven, collect class essentials and a campus ID card and parking permit. Step eight." He pauses, pressing his lips together before looking at me. "Step eight. Go to class."

I gnaw on my lip.

Elijah leans his head back and gazes at the cloudy sky. I'm standing on edge, wondering if my bold move will pay off or land me in hot water. "You made me have a meeting with the dean."

I nod meekly. "How did it go?"

A few terrifying heartbeats later, Elijah's lips quirk into a grin. "It was ... educating. Did Sasha tell you to do this?"

I shake my head, taking a step closer. "Not exactly. But I know it's what she wanted for you. I also know she'd never have given up on you. So I'm not, either."

He chuckles softly, staring at the papers in his hand. "I have no idea how to do this."

"I'll help you," I say, reaching for his other hand. His eyes peer into mine, a mirror image of my best friend's, but these are all Elijah. "Dean Marshall will point you in the right direction and the Cades will pay for it. You're not going to fall through the cracks, Elijah."

He blinks quickly, then brushes the hair from my eyes. "Thank you."

I touch the silver chain around his neck, then peer up at him. A ray of sun breaks through the clouds and warms my face. This is the moment I've been waiting for since I woke up in the Cades' library that fateful morning. I can feel her all by myself, without her help. I know she's here.

I smile and press a key with a foam keychain into his palm. "Ready for the fun part of this adventure?"

Recognition flashes across his face as he holds up the key. "You rented another boat?"

I shake my head. "I got permission to hang out on *Sue's Paradise*. Since Sasha's not bankrolling our fun adventures anymore, I had to be frugal to set up something romantic."

Elijah's thumb slides across my cheek. "Let's go."

Mr. Cade wrote up boating instructions for us, and Elijah has no problems driving out of the marina and into the middle of the lake. We drop the anchor once we're in a secluded area away from other boaters, and I unpack the picnic-style dinner I prepared for us. There are sandwiches, chips and some of Mrs. Cade's homemade cherry pie.

"You know, Sasha really lucked out that you're so cute," I say, poking him playfully in the arm. It's nearly nine o'clock and we've been talking for hours. Making plans for the future. Making plans for us.

Elijah stands next to me on the balcony that overlooks the back of the boat. "Why's that?"

I shrug. "If you were butt ugly, her plan to set us up wouldn't have worked." I snap my fingers together. "The whole thing would have fallen apart."

He chuckles, his breath warm on my cheek. "You mean my outstanding personality wouldn't have been enough to win you over?"

I gaze up at him, his eyes bright from the moonlight. "Afraid not," I say, holding back a smirk. I suck in air through my teeth. "I'm kind of super shallow."

His eyes narrow, a feisty look crossing his face. In one quick movement, he pulls me away from the railing, turning me around. His arms slide around mine, holding me safe and warm. Closing my eyes, I sink against his chest, letting the sound of his heartbeat and the gentle swish of the lake lull me into a peace I haven't felt in ages.

Chills flutter across my neck when he leans in close, his lips grazing my skin. He smells like Mrs. Cade's cherry pie. "I love you, Raquel Clearwater," he whispers into my ear.

My hand laced into his, I bring my hand up and kiss his knuckles. "I love you, too."

Epilogue

Five years later

It seems like only yesterday that I sat in this stadium, sandwiched between Sasha's parents and mine, cheering my head off when Elijah walked across the stage, graduating with a bachelor's degree in social work.

Now all the same people are in the stands, gathered here to see me walk across this terrifying stage. My toes curl up in my black flats. I ditched my heels in Elijah's jeep, planning to change into them when we go to dinner after graduation. The thought of tripping over my own feet and falling on my face in front of the dean and several hundred parents is enough to make me question *any* type of shoe choice. To make matters worse, walking across the stage today is only the first of two more graduations it'll take for me to be a veterinarian.

Taking a deep breath, I glance around at my peers, a sea of burgundy gowns with gold collars. There's an excited buzz in the air, and I twist my engagement ring around my finger, letting the familiar curves calm my nerves.

When it's time for our row to walk up to the front, I'm so freaking nervous my face feels like it's going to melt off. And here I'd thought getting a degree in biology was hard. Standing on a stage in front of so many people is much worse.

I glance back at the audience, knowing Elijah is there somewhere, watching me. I can't pick him out in the crowd, but I know he's there, those blue eyes crinkling with pride.

"Raquel Clearwater," the speaker says.

My feet move, taking me across the stage to where I shake someone's hand, and then I'm given a fake diploma and I move forward, shaking someone else's hand. I guess it's the dean, but things move so quickly my head is spinning. At the top of the stairs, I pause, smiling — I've been smiling this whole time — while a photographer snaps my picture.

As I walk down the stairs, following the graduates in front of me as we head back to our seats, I realize I've been handed more than just a diploma. Wrapped around the cardboard tube with a rubber band is an envelope.

My name is written on it in pink Sharpie.

Hands trembling, I somehow make it back to my folding chair in the middle of the floor, in the sea of burgundy and gold graduation gowns.

I rip open the envelope. My heart shoots up to my throat when I see a fat cat dressed like a professor, a shiny red apple on a desk and books stacked up next to it.

I glance around. Everyone is on their phones, heads pressed together to snap a selfie, some turning around and waving at their parents. On the stage, the rest of my graduating class continue getting their diplomas.

I open the card.

Hey there Miss Graduate,

Did you miss me? I bet you're wondering how I pulled this one off, huh? Well, it was easy. You've had your heart set on being a vet since you were eight. I knew you'd choose Texas State University because it has a great science program and I knew you'd never leave Texas because, well, I just know you.

The rest was easy. I contacted Dean Marshall and told her my story. She said it was the sweetest thing she'd ever heard, and promised to deliver this card to you on your graduation day.

This is a big day, Raquel. It's only one of the big days that will happen in your life, and although I'm not actually there, hollering your name like a crazy person from the stands, know that I am still with you. I'm in your heart, and all that sappy BS, right? And I'll be there when you graduate as a fully legit animal doctor and I'll watch you from the clouds when you go on to save puppy lives and cut dried poop off Persian cat butts. (Hey, no one ever said the honorable field of animal doctoring was a glamorous job, Rocki.)

I hope you are living an awesome life, now that you are no doubt a super sexy twenty-something ready to conquer the world. How's my brother? Did the two of you fall in love even though I told you not to? Are you two married? How are Mom and Dad? I realize by now that you've probably had to introduce them to Elijah, and they've probably put two and two together. I guess that's okay. I just want you all to be happy.

I better see some gorgeous Rocki babies in the future. You tell them Auntie Sasha is watching them from heaven if they ever try to pull some teenage rebellion crap on you, okay?

Thank you for being the kind of friend who makes me want to go through these extraordinary efforts in my final days. It's been a blast leaving notes for you. I can't imagine a better way to slowly drop dead than to spend all my time making these adventures. So how about one more?

(Check the back of this card.)

Love you and miss you always,
Sasha

Acknowledgments

Here we are. The acknowledgments. This part is almost harder than writing the book. This is the part where I realize all the pages before this point started out as an idea, which was then edited and revised, cut apart and pieced back together, and polished into something that's wonderfully better than what I originally wrote. This book started as my idea, but then it became ours, and these are the people I'd like to thank:

My agent, Kim Lionetti. I am honored to have you in my corner. Thank you for pushing me to write better books, and for being generally awesome. As far as agents go, I won the lottery.

Thank you to my editor, Kate Egan, for loving my characters and giving my book a home. It has been a dream working with you and shaping this book into something even better than I could have imagined.

To Lisa Lyons and the whole publishing team, thank you for welcoming me to the KCP Loft family. I am so squishy excited to be a part of this imprint, and to have my book in the ranks of such inspiring talent.

No one understands the mind of a writer quite like another

writer. To Deirdre Riordan Hall, thank you for being the one who gets me. Thanks to Becky Wallace for the brainstorming lunches and cupcake celebrations. Major thanks to Cassie Giovanni and Lynn Painter for being my writerly sounding boards as I prepared for this book to enter the world.

Tons of thanks to my social media friends, writers, aspiring writers and supporters, who have been there to chat about books, writing and everything else.

To the readers who take books home and invite the characters into their lives, thank you for choosing my story. To the bloggers, reviewers and bookstagrammers, you are the soul of the book community. Thank you for sharing your passion with the world.

There are dozens of friendship Easter eggs hidden in this novel and only Felicia Morgan will find them. Because of twenty-four years of friendship that started with my ugly pair of dollar-store shoes, I am equipped to write a book about two best friends. Felicia, you poetic, noble land mermaid, thanks for everything.

Thank you, Susan Connally, for being my rock as I pursue a passion that often feels like quicksand.

Thanks, love and gratitude to my family in blue. For keeping my husband safe, for the friendship and family, and mostly for thinking it is really cool that I wrote a book.

I promised Matt Howard I would put his name in my book. I trust he will be buying several copies now.

All the thanks in the world go to my family, who is constantly subjected to my writer neuroses, and yet still loves me. Hallee, you are the greatest kid on earth. Chris, thanks for the unfailing support and belief in me. When I am down, you guys are up, and when I am full of doubt, you bring the hope back. I love you both to pieces.

Finally, my love and thanks to Nova, who was never more than a few feet away while I wrote and edited this book. Since you can't read this, I will express my gratitude in handfuls of doggie treats.

About the Author

CHEYANNE YOUNG is a native Texan who has a fear of cold weather and a coffee addiction that probably needs an intervention. She loves books, sarcasm and collecting nail polish. After nearly a decade of working in engineering, she now writes books for young adults. (She doesn't miss the cubicle one bit.) Cheyanne lives near the beach with her husband and daughter, one spoiled-rotten dog and a cat that is most likely plotting to take over the world.

WHAT ARE YOU READING NEXT?

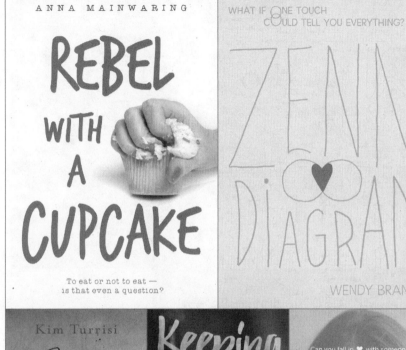

MORE GREAT BOOKS

NEW FROM KCP LOFT